Drugs, Sex & HIV
Courage To Forgive Your Perpetrator

J. Carrington

ISBN: 0-6155-4252-2
ISBN-13: 9780615542522

Contents

Introduction

For the individual who is new to substance abuse recovery and/or living with HIV, who struggles daily with lack of self esteem and determination. This book will inspire, encourage and comfort you, as you face the many challenges ahead for you. Yet, like the main character, you can face each challenge with boldness.

For the family member who genuinely care and is concerned about their love one substance abuse issues, it will help you to learn about the emotional struggles one face in substance abuse recovery.

For the friend, that has gone the extra mile with the substance abuser, and you're tired of being supportive. It will encourage your heart not to give up. Whether you are buying this book for yourself, or someone else, the investment you make in getting the book into some woman's hand that desperately need hope, will give you satisfaction in knowing—second chances are not impossible.

Foreword and Prayer

To women & girls everywhere that suffer from low self-esteem, and who don't have anyone to believe in them; their abilities, talents, and overall well-being, after being beaten up by life circumstances and the harmful choices made out of desperation. My prayer is that you find healing and peace throughout the remaining part of your life.

Chapter 1

THE AMBULANCE RACES down a neighborhood street in Lynwood, CA, its sirens, loud and piercing. Onlookers wondered whose house it was going to. Then it stops at a small yellowish colored house on the corner of Shirley Ave. When the ambulance arrived at Tammy's house, there was no answer to the paramedics' knock. They literally had to push the door open. On the other side of the door there appeared to be something blocking the door. Tammy was laid up against it passed out.

When opened, there was a horrible smell of burnt plastic and of a scorched pot that filled the air. Cocaine pipes, syringes, beer bottles, and ash trays filled with cigarette butts laid on top of the dirty coffee table. The paramedics knew they had walked into a drug scene. Tammy had crawled to the front door and unlocked it, after calling 911, before going into unconciousness. The paramedics moved her body and performed a quick assessment on her airway and breathing to make sure that the trachea, the passage to the lungs was not blocked. They inserted a tube through the mouth into the trachea to help her breath. The paramedics did an assessment of her heart rate, blood pressure, body temperature, and other physical signs. Then she was loaded into the ambulance and taken to the emergency room. A few hours later, Tammy was lying back on the hospital bed, waiting until they move her into her room. The emergency room was busy; there were people coming in on stretchers, and some had walked in on foot.

Nurses and doctors were walking from one partition to the other, checking on their patients. Most patients were assessed and then passed to another area of the department, or another area of the hospital, with their waiting time determined by their clinical need. She laid there thinking about what the doctor has said to her. "How could I have been so stupid?" she said, grabbing the top of her blanket, while clutching it with her hand. "What am I going to do?" she belts out a loud cry. "I'll never forgive him for this!" she tosses and turns in her bed. Restless, afraid, and angry her mind wasn't allowing her to process the bad news.

Late that afternoon, she is moved to her room and monitored by the attending nurse. As she lies in bed, she thinks about what her grandmother had said to her months before...

She told her grandmother what she would do to her boyfriend if he had ever infected her with the HIV disease that she would hunt him down. Madea had told her to stop talkin' crazy.... she would just need to keep living and take better care of herself. It would be a challenge that she wasn't sure that she could handle. She was in a place where she didn't want to be...all because of Harry. Just a few hours before, the ambulance had brought her in for an overdose of drugs.

Right away, the emergency room nurse ordered a blood and urine sample collection. The nurse was looking for the presence of the suspected overdose drug and any other drugs or alcohol that might be present. Later, the doctor put her on Narcan to reverse the effects of the drugs she had taken and he wanted her to stay in the hospital for several days. He comes in and talks with her. "Ms. Brown, my name is Doctor Garza and there are a couple of things I need to talk with you about," he walks over to her bed and gives her his undivided attention. "How are you feeling?" She looks up at him and moans. "I have some good and bad news for you. The good news is you are four weeks pregnant."

"You have got to be kidding me, I'm not friggin pregnant."

He pulls up a chair and sits down next to her. "I have been a doctor for a long time, and I don't want us to play games with each other. I want you to tell me the truth. Are you using drugs?" She looks at him and cries. "Okay does that mean yes?" She nods her head. "What type of drugs are you taking?" he moves closer in toward her. "I want you to be honest with me, is it cocaine?" She nods her head, looks him in the eyes, and says…

"Along with heroin."

"Oh boy!" he whispers, looking disappointed. "Ms. Brown, are you sharing unclean needles?"

She looks down and nods her head. The doctor places his hand on her shoulder. "I know this is not what you want to hear, but we need to test you for the HIV disease," he opens her chart and looks over it. "And, Ms. Brown, you need to get off of drugs!" he scribbles something down, closes her chart and talks directly to her. "Here's why. During the early months of your pregnancy cocaine exposure may increase the risk of miscarriage. Women who use cocaine during their pregnancy have a twenty-five percent increased chance of premature labor. Babies born to mothers who use cocaine throughout their pregnancy may also have a smaller head and have their growth hindered."

"Ms. Brown did you know that babies who are exposed to cocaine later in pregnancy may be born dependent and suffer from withdrawal symptoms such as tremors, sleeplessness, muscle spasms, and feeding difficulties?"

She closes her eyes. "Likewise, Ms. Brown, heroin usage during pregnancy increases the chance of premature birth, low birth weight, breathing difficulties, low blood sugar (hypoglycemia), bleeding within the brain, and infant death. Now…you can see why it's so important for you to stop using drugs…right?" She doesn't say anything. "Ms. Brown, something else you need to know," he touches her hand again. "Are you listening?"

"Yes," she yells back.

"Babies can also be born addicted to heroin and can suffer from withdrawal symptoms, including irritability, convulsions, diarrhea, fever, sleep abnormalities, and joint stiffness.

Now Ms. Brown, treating an addiction to heroin can be complicated, especially when you are pregnant. Your health care provider may prescribe methadone as a form of treatment. It is best that you communicate with him or her so that you can receive the best treatment for you and your baby." He asks the nurse to come in, tells her to test Tammy for the HIV virus, then he writes something in her chart and steps out for a moment.

"No! I don't believe this!...I don't believe this," she places her hands upon her face. "That $#@*# Harry, how could he do this to me?"

The nurse looks at her and asks, "Do you know how maybe you contracted the disease?"

She pushes the nurse hand away. "Don't say that," she hollers. "I'm sorry; I'm only trying to help...Tammy. I'm concerned, and I care." Tammy reaches up and puts her arms around the nurse, she's crying hard. "I'm sorry. I didn't mean to yell at you. I'm just upset and I can't believe Harry did this to me," she burst out crying again. The nurse rubs her hand, as if to say...its okay.

"Tammy I need for you to listen to me. I know you're upset, and you have every right to be. But here are your options. You can take the test and wait one or two weeks for the results, or you can take the rapid test, which you will receive the results in less than 30 minutes. Which do you prefer?"

"The rapid test," she mutters while wiping her eyes.

"Okay! This might hurt but not too bad."

She pricks her finger with a needle and takes a few drops of blood, for testing of the antibodies rather than the virus itself. Then she rubs Tammy's forehead, and steps out. In a fetal position, Tammy lays back into the bed weeping uncontrollably. Thirty minutes seems like eternity to her. Then the doctor steps in with the nurse. Tammy sits up, and lets out a loud cry, piercing into the hallways.

"Ms. Brown, I want you to stop crying for a moment and listen to me," he walks over to her bed. "You have the HIV virus but the good news is we have caught it at its early stages. I'm going to give you a prescription to fight the disease and protect your unborn baby. But I want to get you into treatment so that we can get you off these drugs.

Also, you need to see a health care provider experienced in managing HIV during pregnancy." The nurse walks up to her bed and hands her some tissues.

"You will now have a regimen of taking Anti-HIV medications used at different times to prevent mother-to-child transmission of HIV during your pregnancy, a combination of at least three different Anti-HIV medications," he makes eye contact with her and moves his body toward the bed. "If possible, AZT is included as one of the Anti-HIV medications in the regimen. And, during your labor and delivery you should receive intravenous (IV) AZT. Similarly, you will also continue to take the other Anti-HIV medications by mouth. And, after your baby's birth, your baby will receive liquid AZT for 6 weeks." Tammy stares into space, hearing him, but not acknowledging what he is saying. He stops for a moment.

"Ms. Brown, I really need for you to pay attention to me. I promise you can learn to cope with the disease."

He starts again, "You will have to take Anti-HIV medications for your own health, do you understand me?" She nods and wipes her nose. "Your family care provider will provide prenatal care for you including a review of the anti-HIV medications you have just begun taking. During pregnancy certain Anti-HIV medications may not be safe or may be absorbed differently by the body, so your medications could change… so keep that in mind."

"Do you have a doctor Ms. Brown?"

"No Sir."

"Well I'm going to give you a free community clinic referral." The nurse steps out to get a listing of free clinics. "I want you to call them and make an appointment. But most importantly, please get into drug-treatment." The nurse comes back in and hands Tammy the free clinic list.

After five days, of constant monitoring by Doctor Garza, she is able to go home. With heroin withdrawals, fever, chills and night sweats from the HIV virus, she found herself surviving it. *How did I come out alive?* she thought. As she sat on the edge of her bed, she looks around the stark cold, empty feeling and lonely room. An old chair was in the corner, and there were no plants on the window ledge. Glad to be going home, tears rolled down her face as she pushed each number on the phone pad to call her grandparents for a ride home. Her dreams had been shattered within an instance. Remembering back to when she had high hopes for her life, the day she was released from prison. *How could this have happened to me?* she thought.

Summer is over, and the holidays are right around the corner. The September nights are crisp and the days are a lot cooler. California highways are laced with trees whose leaves are changing to brilliant golden colors. Tammy's grandmother is driving to the California Institution for Women, in Corona, CA, in hopes of picking up her granddaughter. Tammy is waiting impatiently for her.

"I'm finally getting out of this God forsaken place. My new life starts now!" she pauses.

"I can't believe it's been three years since my arrival."

"Yep, Tammy," the prison guard said. "You're right, everyone's going to miss you," he walks back inside. "I know what I want out of life. And, it sure ain't selling drugs. I want to have my own catering business making good money," she whispers to herself. Tammy has always loved to eat and experiment with food, which ultimately lead toward her interest and passion for cooking. Yet, she has no education. "Man, freedom feels so good," she walks down the walkway to see if her grandmother was close by. Her grandmother drives up, parks the car, and heads toward her. Her grandmother's short, small frame body walks in a fast pace to greet her. Tammy runs to her, throws her arms around her and squeezes her so hard that her grandmother can hardly breathe. "Madea, I'm so glad to see you!" she weeps. "Look ah' here, you have gained a little bit of weight, it looks good on you," Madea says. Tammy laughs as she wipes away her tears. They both get into the car and leave.

"Today, Madea…I'm a free woman."

"That's right baby, this time don't do anything to land yourself back in there."

"I won't Madea, I can't go back. It was hell up in there."

Madea laughs. "You see what drugs and its association will get you?" Tammy moves Madea's purse to the back seat. "Yeah, and I'll tell you something else, I met so many women in there that was HIV infected." Madea glances at her.

"HIV infected, what's that? Are you, talking about Aids?"

"Yes, Madea, they have AIDS, some their boyfriends gave it to them, others got it from intravenous drug use and so on."

"Oh! Baby, I'm sorry to hear that," Madea said.

"If that had been me, I would hunt him down when I got out!"

"Hush! Don't talk like that, you would just keep living and take better care of yourself."

"Yeah! Right!...I would never forgive him for that. Madea, you don't know me, I'm not that scary timid little girl I used to be. I would seriously do something to him." Madea focuses on the traffic—while changing lanes. "Tammy you don't know the whole story behind those girls' relationships."

"Uh! I know enough to know what I would do."

"Girl, you're talkin' crazy!"

"Anyway, I can't wait to start looking for work and getting enrolled in culinary classes."

"That's good baby."

"Oh! Did I tell you, I got my GED while in there?"

"Tammy, that is wonderful!"

"Yeah, Ms. Howard, one of the prison guards tells me it will be a challenge finding work though." Tammy pauses, looking up from turning the radio on. "I don't believe her, someone's going to give me a good job with benefits," smiling she looks out the window. "Whatever it takes Madea to find work, I'm going to do it. I do not want to go back to prison. Every day, there was some type of drama going on in there. But that's behind me now...how's Papa?"

"Child, he's the same, he walks with a cane now. He is so happy that you are out. He really does love you, Tammy."

Her grandmother changes the radio to a jazz station. "And I love him too," she says softly.

In all, their drive was every bit of fifty minutes and more. As she approaches, the right ramp for E Imperial Hwy toward South Gate-Lynwood, she turns right onto E Imperial Hwy, and then turns onto Pine Ave.

"Tammy, do you know what I did?" Madea interrupts Tammy's gaze, as she looks out the window.

"No, what?"

"I fixed your favorite meal."

"Ah, Madea!"

"Yes, I did, I fixed seasoned southern fried chicken. Just the way you like it with macaroni and cheese, candied yams, green beans and jalapeno cornbread."

"I don't know when the last time I had a meal like that was." Tammy reaches over to hug and kiss her. "Well, it's your welcome home gift." For a moment there is silence between the two. The radio is playing Madea's favorite jazz music. Tammy lets down the window, stares out at the different scenery, neighborhood streets and the commercial buildings.

"This time it will be different," Tammy whispers to herself. As they arrive into Lynwood-Los Angeles Tammy begins to wonder where Madea is going.

"Madea, have you and Papa moved?"

"No, baby, I have a surprise for you."

"Lawd, have mercy...what is it?"

"Just wait and see," she pulls into a driveway of a little house. Tammy sees a mixture of people, Hispanics, African Americans and a few Caucasians walking through the neighborhood. The house exterior was a light yellowish color with a beautiful light blue entry door and a porch on one side of the home.

"Madea, whose house is this?"

"This is your new home. Papa and I own this house. We talked about it and decided to let you stay here for as long as you need to get yourself together." Tammy jumps out of the car screaming, as she runs to the front door.

"Rocking chairs could be put here," Tammy says with excitement pointing to the porch area. The front of the house has iron and concrete fencing, and a well manicured lawn.

"Now, Tammy, there is a condition. You don't have to pay us any rent. But you are responsible for your electric, gas, phone and food. We'll help you with the electric and gas for two months. After that, you're on your own. You will have to pay it, along with finding meaningful work. Then, I want to see you go to college and study culinary arts, like what you've been telling me about…okay?"

"Yes, Ma'am." Madea puts the key in the door.

"Madea, hurry up!"

"Gal, wait!" Madea fumbles with the key, "You know I'm old!"

"Madea let me do it."

"I got it Tammy, just wait!"

The door opens and Tammy runs in, screaming with excitement, "It's mine! It's mine!"

Her grandmother had furnished the house with everything she needed to feel at home. There was slip covered furniture, lamps, a dining room set, bedroom furniture and accessories, dinner plates, towels, plants, and even $100.00 worth of groceries. "Madea, I promise I won't let you down…Thank you!"

"Well, go see the rest of your home." As she walks through the house, she notices the whole house had mahogany color wood floors. And some of the walls were painted light blue. Tammy runs to the kitchen area. "Oh, My God!…It's beautiful." The open L-shaped kitchen had beautiful white cabinets, a combination of open shelves and glass doors. Granite black counter tops graced the cabinets. Immediately, she goes to the master bedroom, leans up against the wall and starts to cry.

"Who knows, maybe one day my kids will come to visit me here?"

"All three of them are adopted out to good homes. Give them the opportunity to be loved and cared for right," Madea said.

"What do you mean? That I didn't love them?"

"Baby at that time, you were not ready to be a mother. Just focus on getting your life together then you can think about having kids again,"…Madea whispers to her while gently rubbing Tammy's face. "Now, come on gal, finish looking so we can go eat."

Tammy heads for the bathroom. It is nice and spacious with an enclosed tub-shower.

Then they both head toward the second bedroom.

"Tammy you can use this room as a study when you start school, or keep it as it is, a guest bedroom."

Even though her new home was located in a crime area, she didn't care. Most of the houses on the street had burglar bars on their doors and windows. But this was her first home and she didn't have to worry about paying rent.

"That's all that matters,"…she mutters to herself.

Tammy turns off all the lights. In the doorway she stands, looking at her new home.

Madea gives her the house key; she closes and locks the door. When they arrived at Madea's house, Tammy's sister Evelyn and her two daughters were waiting for her at the front door. She runs to them, and her sister hugs her while her two daughters scream, "Aunt Tammy!" At that moment, Tammy feels loved, an emotion she hasn't felt in a long time. Once inside, Papa her grandfather was seated in his big recliner near the TV. He starts to get up, to greet her as she walks in.

"No, Papa, don't get up," she makes her way over to him and hugs him. Tears are welling up in both their eyes. He grabs her hand, placing his hand on top of hers.

"Tammy, I'm glad to see you before I die."

"Papa don't be talking like that," she moves forward to kiss his forehead.

"Tammy how are you?"

"Papa, I'm doing well. I didn't know that drug offense would take so long to serve."

"Just be glad that it wasn't longer," he said. "Sit down next to me on the sofa."

They laugh and talk until Madea yells for everyone to wash their hands and come to the dinner table. Tammy helps him to get up from his chair. He slowly walks toward the kitchen with his cane. She, Evelyn and her two daughters, Keisha and Ebony, sit down at the table.

"Is there anything else, anyone needs before I sit down? Cause I'm not getting up again," Madea said. They all laugh. Papa comes to the table and they grab each other's hands to say grace over their meal, thanking God for bringing Tammy home.

"All right, everyone dig in!" Madea said.

Tammy nods and looks at Madea, "You make the best fried chicken."

"Thank you...baby!"

"Um hum," Evelyn and the kids said. Once everyone had finished eating, Papa begins reminiscing about old times. When he was a young boy, how he enjoyed sitting around the dinner table and talking with his family. He uses his hands to express himself while telling his stories. Tammy laughed about the time he told them his mother whipped him with a switch because he and his brother had set fire to a church.

Then Evelyn talks about the times Uncle Ray would come over to spend the night after his drunken outings. He terrorized everyone, and the women would have to flee the house, going over to a neighbor's house to avoid him until he would calm down and fall asleep. They laughed hysterically. It was a good night for Tammy, being around her family even though she had hurtful memories of her childhood. Her mother's brother, Ray had raped her at the tender age of sixteen. It had left her emotionally crippled and afraid of men. She soon started drinking and smoking marijuana to block the pain. Nevertheless this night, she was filled with excitement about having her very own place and looking for work.

"Well, I need to get home and prepare for tomorrow. I have a lot that needs to be done," she hugs everyone-goodbye, and Evelyn drives her home.

Tammy had spent her adolescences in and out of school. She found herself hanging out with the wrong crowd, students that used drugs and eventually the neighborhood drug dealer. Acceptance and love was needed in her life. She thought she had this with her drug buddies. The root of her pain began when she was sexually abused by her mother's brother. Because of her mother's drug problems, she abandoned Tammy and Evelyn. And their father was deceased, creating even more of an emotional void in her life. This led to her skipping school and hanging out with older guys who would come up to her school to prey on young girls. She ended up being raped again, and this time—pregnant. Overall, in the course of her adolescence years, she was emotionally and physically abused by all her boyfriends.

By nineteen, she had three children by three different men who eventually disowned her and her kids. She had become a functioning alcoholic. Her kids were neglected. Oftentimes, there was no food in the house and she moved every three to six months because she couldn't pay the rent. Each time, to a more degenerated place because she had so many evictions on her record.

Her kids were always dirty and ashy. The oldest child Hannah was found at age five, running around the streets naked with feces all over her. Tammy refused to get any help for her illness. Eventually her kids were taken away and placed in foster care. Her grandmother tried to fight to get them. But it was determined that the children could not be returned to a safe home after support services had been delivered. The kids were eventually taken away and adopted out.

Tammy's first interview was for a kitchen cook position at a children's day care. She gets off the bus and walks a mile to the hidden day care building located in a residential neighborhood. It was a small brown brick building. Nothing is spectacular about its presence. As she walks in and greets the director, small talk is exchanged and she fills out an application. Thirty minutes into the interview, she tries to play-up her cooking and helping skills. But, based on her application, the director knew that she didn't have any child care work experience, even though she had worked in the prison's kitchen.

Moreover, Tammy's personality was a little overwhelming. Tough-talking, opinionated and strong-willed. She could tell the director was trying to be nice, but wasn't interested in her. The director told Tammy that she would let her know one way or another within a couple of days. But she hadn't told her that a background check would be done. The director has a relationship with law enforcement officials, and received information "under the table" about Tammy's record. That afternoon, Tammy got a call from her; she was turned down for the job.

Her second interview required her to take a bus into downtown Los Angeles.

"I hate going downtown," she mumbles to herself. "I bet it's still nasty and cramped with panhandlers, drug addicts, homeless people, and street swindlers."

She gets off the bus and walks to a four story stand alone building on the corner. She is going to apply for a job as a janitor at a healthcare institution. She's greeted by the hospital security desk.

"Hi, I am here to apply for a job!"

The security guard has her to sign in and directs her to human resources. She takes the elevator to the basement and gets off. Not sure where to go, she stops at an office, and the receptionist directs her to the human resources office. Upon opening the door of the human resources office, she notices it is a small area that had several people filling out their application by computer. Not knowing how to use a computer, she's afraid but gives it a try. Nervously, she squirms around in her seat while trying to sit still. It takes her four hours to complete the application. The receptionist tells her that someone would get in touch with her about an interview. "How many people are applying for the janitor position?"

"Well we have had quite a few today," the receptionist said.

"What is the process for me to get hired?"

"The hospital uses an agency to check an applicant's information."

"Such as?" Tammy asked.

"We use a consumer reporting (or 'credit' reporting) agency for information about your criminal record and work histories."

"Thank you!" Tammy smiles and walks out the door.

"I know, I'm not going to get this job," she says to herself. "I gotta keep trying—though.

The next interview, I will leave with a job," she tells herself as she walks toward the bus stop. On the bus, she places her head against the window and stares out. When she arrives at her transfer point, she gets off the bus and commences to cross the street. She is inches away from being hit by a driver that runs the red light. She screams out to the driver, while throwing her hands-up in the air, "What's wrong with you, you idiot? Don't you see me trying to cross this street? With your no driving self," she yells.

This time she has to take three buses to go across town for her last interview for the day with a principal at an elementary school. When she arrives at the second bus terminal, she waits patiently for the bus that's due any minute. Fifteen minutes later and the bus hasn't arrived. While smoking a cigarette, she begins walking and pacing back and forth. At last, the bus shows up but it's thirty minutes late. Tammy jumps on the bus.

"Why are you so late? Don't you know I have to catch another bus, and now, it's going to be gone. You're making me late for my interview," she screams at the bus driver.

"Ma'am, I was caught in traffic. I'm sorry. I'll try to get you there as quickly as I can."

"What time is my next bus coming that I need to transfer to?" she said.

"I'm not sure," the bus driver said. Tammy goes to her seat, and places her head down on the top bar of the seat in front of her. She dozes off and is awaken by the bus driver.

"Ma'am here is your stop."

She jumps up and runs toward the exit, as she gets off, the third bus is pulling off. Running behind the bus she screams, "Stop, stop, wait!"...The bus is moving at a speed that prevents the bus driver from seeing her. Tammy sits on the ground and doesn't say anything.

A young man walks over to her and says, "The next one will be here in forty-five minutes."

"Forty-five minutes," she repeats...sarcastically. "I'm late to this interview, and that doesn't look good." At exactly forty—five minutes later the third bus shows up. Tammy runs and gets on, pushing her way through the passengers. The bus is crowed and she has to stand up. When she arrives at her stop, she's in such a hurry that she almost knocks someone down getting off. She begins walking up the street while looking at her directions.

"Where is this freaking building?" she walks a little to the left and sees the building located caddy-cornered to the street. It is the elementary school.

"Finally!" she yells out loud. Frantically, she runs in the office and asks, "May I use your restroom?"

"Sure," the secretary said. "Make a right around the corner. Who are you here to see?"

"I have an interview with the principal for a janitor position."

"I will let him know you're here. What is your name?"

"Tammy Brown," my name is "Tammy Brown"...she yells out. In the ladies room, she takes out her afro comb from her purse and picks out her black natural afro. She adds lipstick to her beautiful mocha brown square shaped face. Next, she straightens up her peach colored, v-neck, button-up collared shirt while making sure her brown pants looked neat and tidy. Then she goes back to the office. Mr. Robinson is waiting for her.

"Tammy, come into my office."

"Mr. Robinson, I'm sorry, I'm late. I had to catch three buses and the second bus was late. When I arrived at the terminal for the third bus, I missed it, and had to wait forty-five minutes for the other bus."

"That's okay, you're here now," he closes the door behind him. "Have a seat, so Tammy, tell me about you?"

Pausing to catch her breath, Tammy responds, "Well, I love kids. I don't have much work experience because I spent some time in prison. But I can clean and make your school spotless."

Mr. Robinson knew that she was desperate for the job. "What was the offense?" he positions his arms onto the desk and stares directly at her.

"Possession with intent to sell," she looks nervous while wiping the sweat from her face.

"Drugs, huh," he mumbles. He frowns at her and says, "This is a school that doesn't tolerate drug usage." Her hands become fidgety.

"Oh, No sir, I don't sell drugs anymore. As a matter of fact." He interrupts her. "Tammy, this may not work for you. To be honest with you, ex-offenders are a risk to the community due to their high recidivism rates among those released from prison. I'm sorry, but good luck." She drops her arms to her side and looks in disgust at him.

"Oh, I see what this is all about. You think I'm a nobody."

"I didn't say that."

"You didn't have to say it, I can tell by the look on your face that's what you meant. Let me tell you something. Mr. Big Shot, you're not better than me because you have a college education," she gets up from her chair.

"Ms. Brown...I think you should leave!"

"Or what? You'll have me sent back to prison and furthermore," she points her finger at him.

"Ms. Brown, leave now!"

"Yeah that's what you probably want anyway, for all ex-offenders to be gathered together and dropped off the face of the earth. Lookout, here goes the neighborhood right?"

Mr. Robinson stands up and points toward the door. Tammy storms out of his office, slamming the door behind her. She cries all the way to the bus stop. When the bus arrives, she sits down and mumbles to herself, "Who's gonna hire me?"

Isolation and alienation from the world of work is so common among many ex-offenders.

The most challenging situation she faces is that of re-entry into the labor market. Not only is she seeing firsthand the challenges before her, she also has a concern about how much money the employer would be willing to pay someone like her with no experience.

◈

It has been over a month, and she has gone to ninety job interviews. She has applied for every low-skilled job imaginable: shoe sales clerk, home health aide, school bus driver, and many others, but still no work. She has tried to be up front about her past. However, she is judged and given the run-around by most employers. Her food supply is getting low, and she doesn't want to bother her grandparents. But she's determined to make it work. "I've got to get work soon," she tells herself. One late afternoon, she stops by her grandparents home to borrow forty dollars.

Then, she decides to stop by her treatment counselor's office. It will be the first time that she will meet Ms. Williams face-to-face. The treatment program had a linkage to the prison where she was incarcerated, providing her counselor the opportunity to reach in and handle her case. When walking to the bus stop, a young man with a hood over his head walks behind her in a fast pace. She senses he's up to something so she crosses the street. He crosses the street also, and walks faster, as if to catch up to her. Faster she walks. He runs up to her and grabs her purse. Struggling with him, she screams as loud as she can, "Let go! Help!…Somebody help me!" All the while, she's kicking at him. After he sees that she's a fighter, he pushes her down and takes off running. She stands up, places her hand up against her breast and then bends over forward while trying to catch her breath. She composes herself and continues on her journey. When she arrives at her counselor's office, Ms. Williams tells her that she's so sorry for the obstacles she's going through.

"Are you still clean?"

"Am I still clean?" Tammy says.

"Of course, I'm still clean. C'mon, Look!…I'm doing everything I'm supposed to do. But so far, I still don't have a job."

"Tammy, calm down, since you're an ex-felon we have to take a proactive approach toward finding work for you. It may not be what you want but it will be a start while you build up your credibility and work history. We're going to focus on a select number of employers who do not bar ex-offenders, and then help you to develop realistic goals. Also, I will assist you in getting your social security card and driver's license. But I need for you to stay sober and keep trying. Can you do that for me?" she smiles at Tammy while looking up from her glasses.

"Well I guess so, I have no other freaking choice," Tammy yells.

Ms. Williams is trying to be patient with her. She catches her breath, and starts over.

"We will also work on cleaning up any discrepancies if any on your criminal histories.

And, I'm going to talk to you about disclosing this information and give you some examples of what could have happen—negatively on your rap sheet. For example, with an offender a number of violated statutes could be incorrect and a single offense could be entered multiple times by mistake. We need to correct these problems if they exist."

"Are you with me?"

"Yes, I hear you!" she shuffles her feet around on the floor.

"Now, I want you to look at your situation from your potential employers eyes. I have an acknowledgement letter about your substance abuse and criminal history that I want you to read and memorize. It offers crucial explanatory information about your rehabilitation. Here it is. Take it home and learn it well. When you tell an employer the gist of it, I want it to come out of your mouth as believable. Tammy picks up the letter from off her desk, while skimming the paragraphs. Although she had just received a good talking to, regardless, she leaves her office not sure where to begin her next search.

Chapter 2

AT HOME, HER cupboards are practically bare and Tammy has only the forty dollars that her grandmother gave her. Not wanting to spend it unless she has to, she walks up to her neighborhood church soup kitchen, inquiring about dinner. There are about twenty people standing outside waiting to be fed. "Excuse me, excuse me," she said, as she moves toward a man sitting at the entrance.

"What time do they start feeding?"

"In about fifteen minutes."

"Can I go in now?"

"Yeah, you can sit in the dining room but you can't go into the kitchen."

"I wasn't going to go into the kitchen!" she said, sneeringly.

"Well, I'm just telling you, so you'll know," he puts out his cigarette into a large can filled with butts. "Anyway!" she puts her hand up as to block him from saying anything else to her. Once inside she notices, twelve tables lined up in rows of three. The north end had a thrift store and to the east there were bathrooms and showers. Just as she walks over to one of the tables, she gets a whiff of the smell of pee coming from the nearby rest rooms. With her hand over her nose, she wipes off one of the tables and sits down.

A young man walks over to her, and introduces himself.

"Hi. I'm Harry Jones, may I sit down?" he pulls out the old chair before she answers.

"Sure," she said.

Harry was tall, 6'2 with a slender muscular body, an attractive black man with a *Cafe Latté cream complexion* and dark brown eyes. His long highlighted dread locks hung beneath his shoulders. His face is rugged and shows signs of tiredness from the stresses of life.

"Why are you here?" she asked him.

"I'm in-between jobs right now."

"What type of work do you do?" she asked.

"Mostly construction work, day labor jobs."

"Do they hire women?"

"Sure."

"For what type of work?" she asked.

"Industrial, low-skill jobs."

"Hmmm, You think you can get me on there?" she said.

"I don't know, maybe, maybe not, let me talk to my boss."

"What's your name?" he said, while tugging on his wrinkled pant leg, looking up at her.

"Tammy."

"Tammy what?"

"Tammy Brown."

"Why are you here?" he asked.

"I ran out of money and food." He nods as to agree with her.

"Do you have any family in the city?" he asked.

"Yeah, my grandparents, but I hate to keep bothering them. They have already done more than enough for me." He turns his head to watch two people arguing.

"What do you mean?"

She fidgets with the table cloth, "When I got out of prison they gave me a house, so that I wouldn't have to stay at the halfway house."

He whispers, "Okay."

The lady from the kitchen comes out and shouts, "Alright everyone in line!" They both jump up and run to get in line. When they approach the food servers they're given their meal; spaghetti, broccoli, corn, and a dessert.

"They have a good meal today," he said.

"Do you come here often?" she asked.

"Sometimes, especially lately," he grabs their Kool Aid drinks and heads back to their table.

"Where do you stay?" she asked.

"Currently, I've been sleeping in my car and showering here, when I can. They have showers for homeless people to use."

"Why?"

"I lost my apartment. Work has been kind of slow lately."

"Do you have any family?"

"Yeah, but, I'm a thirty-nine-year-old grown man. I can't go back home," he lifts his fork.

"You're thirty-nine and I'm thirty-eight. We're getting old I guess," she said. They talk for a little, and after they finish eating, he gets up and takes their paper plates to the trash bin.

"Well, Tammy, maybe I'll see you tomorrow?"

"Where are you going now?"

"I don't have much gas, so I'm not going too far. I'll hang out here for a minute and maybe go and try to find work."

"Where do you live?" he asks.

"In Lynwood," she walks toward the entrance door into the smoke filled air. Several homeless people were standing around smoking cigarettes.

"Would you like a ride home?" She turns around and looks surprise.

"I need to tell you something. The only thing on my mind at this point is surviving, finding a good job, and hopefully going to college soon. Right now, a relationship would complicate my life. Maybe I'll see you around," she said.

She takes off down the street. Harry gets in his car and follows her.

"Hey, Tammy let me give you a ride," he yells out of the window. He reaches over to the passenger side and pushes the car door open. She gets in.

"Where am I going?" he asked.

"Bullis Rd and Le Sage St. I'm on Shirley Ave. Did you say you were homeless?"

He looks at her, "Pretty much!"

"Are you working?"

"I'm in-between jobs, but yes...Tammy."

"I hate to see people hungry and homeless. We don't know each other but I have a good feeling about you. You can spend the night at my place and we'll take it one day at a time. I have ten dollars. It's my emergency money. We can get some gas in exchange for you taking me on a few interviews...how does that sound?"

He reaches for her hand, "We'll see." Then he stops at the nearest convenience store while she gets out to pay for the gas. On her way back to the car, he asked, "Excuse me for changing the subject but you don't have a boyfriend that I have to worry about do you?"

"No silly," she gets into the car and adjusts her seat belt. "Like I told you before, my focus is on getting into school and finding work... Turn here!"

"Okay, you don't have to holler!"

"I just didn't want you to miss the turn."

"Just like a woman, you're a back seat driver," he pulls into her driveway. Once inside he looks around her place...

"This is a nice place."

"Yeah...I like it," she says. He sits down on the slip covered sofa. "Nice! You've got good taste." Her keys are placed in a basket on the end table.

"I can't take credit for this. My grandmother, bless her heart, fixed it up nice for me."

"What about you? Where are your peoples?" she said.

"I have no peoples, just my grandparents."

"What happen to your mother?"

"She was killed by my step father a couple of years ago."

"Are you serious?"

"Yeah! He made it look like it was a suicide. But I know he did it."

"I'm so sorry."

"Hey, life happens, right? I had to deal with it, and I'm making it."

"Do you miss her?"

"Yeah, I miss her!" he said. His countenance changes to sadness.

"I don't have much to offer. I went through my food pretty quick and with food prices so high, I have not been able to buy any...lately. There are a couple of things left, like peanut butter, can food stuff, and some sweet tea, would you like some sweet tea?"

"Sure...I'll take some." Two glasses are washed and filled with tea.

"Here you go."

"Thank you."

"You're welcome, Harry what kind of music do you like?"

"I like oldies but goodies"

"Like what?"

"Any of the old groups from the 1970's."

"I do too," she said. "My favorite group is the Bar Kays."

He looks around her house. "I like them too," he said. "My favorite group is the Temptations." She turns on the radio to an African American station and sits down on the love seat across from him.

"What are your plans Harry?"

"I don't have anything planned for tomorrow, outside of taking you where you need to go." She smiles, while rearranging a decorative pillow.

"I have an interview tomorrow morning at 9:00am in Culver City, could you take me?"

"Yeah, I'll take you." Then she goes to her bedroom closet and takes down a jigsaw puzzle.

"Do you like to play games?"

"Sure, why not? What is that a jigsaw puzzle?" he asks.

"Yeah," she spreads the puzzle pieces out on the table, face up. He separates the edges and corner pieces while she puts the border together, using the box lid picture. "I'm also working with my treatment counselor on finding work. I've gone to so many interviews since getting out of prison."

"What were you in prison for?" he divides the remaining inner pieces and organizes the pieces of puzzles in groups with similar colors.

"Possession with intent to sell," she said. "You know, it's hard for felons to find work. People look down on you and judge you as being unfit to work," she begins to place the smaller parts together until they fit and form clusters.

"But Ms. Williams has a good plan. I'm not sure where this is going to lead to, but I'll go with it as long as need be. I have no other choice."

He looks at the box lid to find the locations for the groups of pieces. Then, he stops and looks at her.

"Whatever I can do to help you I will. You've met a new friend today. Maybe we can help each other out?" he places his hand on top of hers and smiles.

"Sometimes, we all need someone to talk and vent with. I'm here for you," he said.

Tammy turns up the radio, and goes to the kitchen to get them a refill of tea. They are half way through their puzzle and decide to take a break to watch a movie. By eleven o clock, they both had fallen asleep. She gets up and searches for a blanket, then brings back a pillow, blanket, bath and face towel. Gently she touches his shoulder to wake him up.

"If you don't mine, would you sleep on the sofa?"

"No problem," he stretches.

"You can take your bath or shower tonight or in the morning, your choice." The next morning, she wakes him up.

"I'll be ready to go in thirty minutes."

"Okay!" he pulls on his pants and buttons his shirt from yesterday. "I need to seriously wash these clothes."

"Harry, where are all your clothes?"

"In the trunk of my car."

"When we get back, let's wash all your dirty clothes that way you'll have some clean clothes for work, and you'll feel better about yourself!"

"Yes Ma'am," he said, while laughing.

Tammy's on her way to apply for a telemarketing position, setting appointments for the company's outside insurance agents. She walks into the 2 story glass and brick office building and gives her name. She has been asked to take a seat. A tall dark haired female in her thirties approaches her with a smile and introduces herself.

"Tammy nice to meet you, come on back. Tammy have you done appointment setting before?"

"No ma'am, I haven't."

"Do you like talking to people?"

"Yes, ma'am."

"Read this script for me please."

Nervously Tammy begins to stutter and stumble with her words.

"Mrs. Roberts, I know that I am a good worker and can do this job, if you would just give me a chance," she begs her.

"Okay, tell me about yourself?"

Tammy felt comfortable talking about her past conviction, thinking that her honesty would not affect her decision since there was a rapport between the two. The manager also somewhat led her to believe that if she has changed her life, she would be willing to help her. The manager ended the interview saying that she would be in touch with Tammy about her decision. Tammy is excited and feels confident that she has the entry-level position. As she walks toward the car, Harry opens the car door for her.

"Hey, I think, I've got the job!" He looks surprised…then smiles.

"I'm happy for you, when do you think you'll start?"

She turns to face him, "The manager told me that she will call me tomorrow and let me know. In the interview she acted as if, she would help me... "Oh! I'm so excited," she lets out a scream from the top of her voice.

"Guess what?" he said.

"What?" her hands are almost shaking.

"I went to a couple of food banks and picked up some food for us. I mean...for you." Affectionately, she looks at him, "Ah! Baby, thank you."

She hugs him, and this time kisses him on the lips. Pulling away from her, he said,

"You are going to be stocked up on can foods but there are some other things in the bags as well, seasoned chicken breasts, spaghetti, spam, veggies things like that."

Tammy thinks about how things were beginning to look up for her and how she had someone in her corner.

"Well it's a start. Thank you baby," she hugs him again. "Let's stop by the store and get a liter of Coke."

They stop at a nearby convenience store and Tammy puts more gas in Harry's car.

"I know taking me to Culver City and you driving around for food has put a dent in your gas," she winks at him and gets back in the car.

That evening she fixes a stew dinner for the two of them. They talk for hours, watch television and call it a night. The next morning, Tammy doesn't go interviewing. She feels certain she has got the telemarketing job. However, Harry gets up early and goes to the labor pool. While she's washing clothes, she gets a phone call from the insurance manager, regretting to tell her that she had hired someone else for the position. What came to her mind in talking with Ms. Roberts, she accidently let slip out that she was getting depressed looking for work, and that so far, no one had been willing to take a chance on her.

The manger also added, their expectations. The worker would need to show up every day on time and would need to work hard, be responsible and be generally trustworthy. And, because Tammy battles with depression, she's less likely to be job-ready and will likely face few job offers or will experience high discharge rates upon being hired because of her depression. Ms. Roberts was trying to be kind, but truthful.

Tammy thanks her for calling, hangs up the phone and breaks down crying. She heads for the front door. Mad and angry, she couldn't speak; all she could do at that moment was cry.

"God! Why won't you help me?"

She walks down the side walk in a fast pace, kicking over a neighbor's recycle bin and takes off running. After about five blocks, she stops to catch her breath. She kneels down onto the sidewalk pavement and screams out as loud as she could. An hour later, she calls her treatment counselor for encouragement. Ms.Williams, tells her that periodically she attends the 12 step meetings and that she knew of a cook position at a 24 hour restaurant that was available. The owner/general manager of the restaurant is a recovering addict and attends the meetings. He is willing to talk with her and is known for hiring ex-offenders. Tammy is given the restaurant name, address, owner's name, and phone number.

"He will be expecting you before 10:30am tomorrow, so make sure you're on time," she tells Tammy. Tammy thanks her and hangs up.

At the interview, she decides she's not taking "no" for an answer and has a heart to heart talk with the restaurant owner.

"Mr. Schmidt, I know this job carries a lot of responsibility and that you are probably concerned about whether I can handle it or whether I will start using drugs again. Yes, I have been convicted of drug possession. I will not try to excuse it nor profess innocence or claim I was unjustly convicted," she pauses, while looking at a customer that had just walked in. "But my conviction happened a couple of years ago. I'm not proud about it. I was hanging out with the wrong people at that time and I learned some things about myself since then. I want a better life for myself and to get an education. That's my goal."

She watches his facial expression change from concerned to contentment. He looks at an order ticket a waitress brings him.

"Once I entered treatment, I stopped getting into trouble. My attitude and actions changed when I became sober, which opened doors for me to volunteer in the prison's kitchen."

She looks at him with a stern expression. "Mr. Schmidt please don't judge me by my mistakes, if it would help you to make a decision today, I could provide a reference letter from the lady running the kitchen that I was a stellar worker." Mr. Schmidt was impressed.

"Tammy, I tell you what, I am willing to give you a chance. But you have got to promise me that you will not use drugs. It could be very dangerous. As a cook, you will need the ability to cook good food in a speedy and organized manner. You're also subject to burns and accidents. I don't want that to happen to you, so stay clean. The pay is $7.25 an hour starting out. If you're dependable and a good worker, we'll see about helping you move up, if not here, possibly within the industry. Your training is for a week, working side by side with our head cook, on the morning shift. Then I'll move you to the late evening shift. That's the best I can do." Shocked, and excited, she throws her arms around him,

"Oh! Mr. Schmidt, I promise...I won't let you down."

He walks her toward the front door and opens it for a customer.

"Okay, when can you start your paperwork and training?"

She moves to the side to allow the customer in.

"I can be here first thing in the morning."

"Okay. I want you here at 9:00am."

"Thank you! I won't let you down."

It's now the month of November. Two months after getting out of prison, she lands her first meaningful job. Ecstatic, she runs to the bus stop. When she arrives home, she calls her grandmother and Ms. Williams to tell them the good news and then she cleans up the place. Harry has started back working, she has a job and they both are working in Downey. He could take her to work in the evenings when she starts her 11pm to 7am shift, and hopefully pick her up in the mornings. Her life was beginning to have some type of meaning. It is a far cry from a few years ago when she struggled to keep a roof over her head. Going to prison had changed her, never before had she realized how precious freedom was until she had gone. Within no time, she thinks to herself, she will be able to accomplish her heart-felt goal, to attend culinary training.

Winter has brought some of LA's best weather- brisk, cool, foggy mornings with cold nights. It's a month later at the job, so far so good, Tammy has completed her job training and lately, work has been very busy. Harry comes in that evening, around six o clock. Two weeks prior she made his move in official, hence him being there so often. Tonight he has some extra money and wants to take her out for dinner. They end up going to TGI Fridays. The last two weeks, they both had extra money, and she has managed to open a savings account and save a little. On their way home he stops by an old friend. His friend lights a marijuana joint and passes it to Harry. He takes a couple of tokes and passes it to Tammy.

"No, that's okay," she smiles.

"Are you sure?" he said.

"Yeah, I don't want any!"

Harry's friend, signals for him to follow him into the bedroom. He hands Harry a bag of marijuana. He places it in his pants and tells Tammy, he's ready to go. In the car, she confronts him… "Harry, I didn't know you smoked?"

"Sometimes, there is no harm in it."

"Yeah, but I don't want to get started on that again."

"Look, Tammy, no problem. You don't have to."

He pulls up into her driveway. She gets out in a hurry. In the kitchen she tries to pour a glass of soda, her hands are shaking. Harry walks in, "What movie are we watching tonight?" he asks. She rolls hers eyes with exasperation.

"Whatever you want to watch!" she slams the cabinet door.

"How about an action movie?" he said.

"That sounds good, Harry."

In the living room, he sets up the movie and sits next to her.

"Did I offend you?" She moves over as though she doesn't want to be bothered.

"No Harry!"

He begins to roll a joint, and then licks the seal end of the joint paper. "Tammy, I'm just trying to make you feel better."

She groans, "What would make me feel better is getting into culinary school."

"What kind of job are you going to move up to, once you finish your training?"

"Hopefully, I can become a caterer."

"A caterer! You think they're going to let you into those fancy restaurants?"

"Yeah, I do," she said with a high pitch shout.

"Girl, you're tripping."

"Harry, if you don't want anything for your life, that's on you. But, I have to do this!"

She looks at the TV screen with a penetrating gaze.

"For whom?" he asked.

"To prove to myself, I'm somebody!" she said.

He doesn't say anything.

"I thought you were for my dreams Harry? Now, that's changed since I let you move in."

He laughs at her, "No, I want what you want. Taking a hit from this joint is not going to stop you from reaching your goals."

Then he looks at her, lights the joint and passes it to her. She pushes it back. He grabs her from the back of her head and he begins to kiss her neck.

"No Harry!" Initially she shakes her head in disagreement and then she puts her arms around his neck.

"Just try it baby. It will make you feel better," he whispers softly.

Tammy reaches for it, and inhales the marijuana joint.

"Take another one, it's good stuff!"

This time she inhales longer and coughs.

"Are you okay?" he hits her on the back.

The corners of her lips are pulled back into a sneer, exposing her teeth. "Yeah!" she gets up and runs to the bathroom. He goes and stands near the bathroom door. He hears her coughing non-stop, the water facet is turned on to drown out her coughing and then she opens the door and walks out.

"I'm fine. I have not done this in a while."

"Hey, you don't have to smoke anymore," he said.

That night they are intimate for the first time. While making love to her, he didn't seem to be into it. His body is in a tense posture leaning away from her.

"What's wrong?" she asked him.

"Nothing it's been a long time, that's all."

Harry has some tough emotional issues that he's struggling with. He was molested by his stepfather when he was a young boy. It was his stepfather's (an alcoholic) way of subconsciously feeling in control and powerful. The abuse started at age five and went on well into his teenage years.

With her head laid back unto the white pillows, she gives him her best "come get me" look. He rubs her legs gently, but seems distracted into heavy thought. While kissing him on his shoulders, he moves her head away. She gets into another position. His lower lip begins to shake, his eyebrows are squashed together, and his forehead has a frown, he's having a hard time following.

"Baby what's wrong?"

"Nothing, Tammy, give me a minute," he goes into the living room and lights a joint. For a moment, she lies in bed then gets up.

"Hey, is everything okay with you?"

"Yes and no," he said.

"I mean, what's the problem?"

"Just some issues, I'm dealing with," he says.

"You want to talk about it?"

With a sigh, he leans back into the sofa. "Now, listen good. I was sexually abused when I was a kid for many years. Sometimes when I'm making love with a woman—I have these flash backs of those experiences. I always seem to get stuck right about here. This happens every time I try to be sexual with a woman I really like," he looks up at her and starts to cry.

"Baby, I'm really full of guilt and shame," he hits the coffee table, so hard, it almost shatters. "Why didn't my mother protect me from him?"

"Hey, Baby, Baby, it's okay,"...she moves him forward into her arms.

"It's okay. We'll get through this," she says.

He weeps insanely.

"Hey, we'll just stay here on the sofa tonight if you want," she tells him.

"No, you go to bed. You have to get up in a few hours for work," he says. Leaning forward into him, she gazes directly into his eyes.

"Are you forgetting, it's Wednesday, and I'm off tonight."

He holds onto her, as if to say, don't leave me.

The next morning, she awakens and finds Harry gone. In the middle of the night, she had gotten up to get into her bed, thinking he would follow. Concerned not knowing what he would do, or where he had gone. She sits down on the sofa, and thinks about where he might have gone to. Her coasters are stacked together into one place. The remote control is moved to its proper place as she picks up the haphazardly scattered newspapers, there, she finds his letter underneath, written to her...*Was it a suicide letter?* she thought.

Tammy, you are the best thing that has happen to me. I don't want to screw up your life, or become a burden to you. This pain I'm feeling is more than I can handle. Keep reaching for your goals; I do believe you can make it.... Harry.

She could tell from the tear stained letter that he had cried while writing it. Hysterical she picks up the yellow pages and starts calling all of the labor places she could find. No one knows of Harry Jones. The police missing persons department is called, no luck. At the shelter where they had met, no one has seen him. She is now worried. Not knowing if he is going to kill himself or what? She breaks down and cries. Over the years, just like Tammy, Harry had turned to drugs to block his pain of abuse.

Deep down inside he believed it was his fault. That somehow he caused the abuse for whatever reason. As he got older he grew more and more angry about life. No longer could he protect himself by blocking/repressing his experience. Harry had lost his apartment when he couldn't pay his rent after two months. This was after he went on a drug binge for several weeks. Living on the edge of uncertainty, he works a little to get by, just enough to supply his drug habit. He has no ambition. No dreams. He floats from pillar to post.

Now having to catch the bus to work, she dressed appropriately for the weather in layers, with a fleece jacket on. The temperatures have dropped, it seemed to her, to almost freezing. When the bus does arrive, she's five minutes from being late for work. Meanwhile, she thinks about how she misses Harry taking her to work and picking her up when he could. As she walks up to the entry door, as it were, it is difficult to get into the New Year spirit. No Christmas celebrations or New Year's parties spent together as a couple. He had missed both holidays with her. Since he had entered her life, she was looking forward to spending those times with him at home. There was something about feeling like she belonged to someone, and having someone to share in her ups and downs of life. This is what she has always wanted, to be genuinely loved.

It is the month of January and Mr. Schmidt is optimistic about the New Year.

"Well, Tammy, you've been with us almost three months, how do you like it so far?" Mr. Schmidt asked.

"I love it. It's the best job I ever had."

He pats her on the back and smiles as he walks away. Her coworkers had turned out to be like family. That made the job all the more easier. But there wasn't a day that she didn't think about Harry. The holiday season had brought in a slew of customers. She was busy nonstop all night and this morning. On her way out, she cleans up her work station and rushes to leave.

"Hey Tammy, why the rush?" one of the cooks asked.

"I'm going to enroll today at the culinary arts school. Then attend a party that's being thrown for me tonight." The young man gives her a thumbs up-congratulations'.

"Hey, I hope it works out for you!"

"Hey, thanks," she rushes out the door.

While walking to the bus stop, she tells herself—*nine months isn't a long time, I...can do this.* The application process was simple. Once the paper work was done, the school required her to pay a $25 dollar nonrefundable fee and provide proof of her GED equivalency. Then they notified her of her acceptance and had her to pick up her enrollment package. Her dream was coming true. For all those people that didn't believe she could ever amount to something, she has proved them wrong. Tonight, Madea has made arrangements to celebrate her successes. She has come a long ways since her release from prison. Though this is only a start for her, she knows that she can make it on her own.

After leaving the culinary school, Tammy steps off the bus and opens her umbrella into the wintery rainy season. "Boy, I'll be glad when the Santa Ana winds kick in and warm up the place." When taking the bus, she hated the idea of being placed in close proximity to someone who is already infected with a cold or flu virus. Germs and public transportation. Her gut reaction is that their illnesses would somehow seep into her own body. When the bus driver reaches her stop, she gets off and stops for a moment. She has a funny feeling about something.

Not knowing what it meant or what it was. Upon entering her home nothing seems to be out of sorts as she walks around her house. The alarm clock is set for 6:00pm as she watches television for a moment before dozing off. An hour later, the alarm goes off...starling her. In the bathroom, she washes her face and runs her bath water. With her favorite radio station blaring in the background, she slips into the tub. "Oh! This feels nice," she says as she's sinking further into her lavender scented bubble bath. Submerging her aching and tired limbs into a hot bath helped to wash away the stresses of the day. Her heart is filled with pleasure and of harmony from the relaxed ambiance of scented candles.

Easily startled, not only by people but by noises, it sounded like she heard something. The music is turned down to see if she could hear anything. There was complete silence.

She turns the radio up again and lathers herself from shoulder to feet, then rinses off.

The phone rings, she's scuffling trying to put her house shoes on.

"Wait, wait a minute," as if the caller could hear her. "Wait, I'm coming," she rushes to pick up the phone.

"Madea, it's you!"

"Who did you think I was baby?"

"Never mind...I damn near broke my neck trying to get to this phone."

"I'm sorry baby, look, granny has everything ready to go, what time will you be here?"

"Madea what time did you tell me before?"

"Huh?" Madea said.

"What time did you tell me before?"

"Well, baby, I thought it was 7:00 pm. Baby, you know granny is getting old."

Tammy changes the phone to her other ear, while drying off.

"Okay, it's 7:00 pm right?" Tammy laughs... "Then I'll see you at 7:00 pm," she said.

"How you gonna get here, take the bus?"

Tammy puts the phone down for a second and rolls her eyes.

"No! Evelyn's picking me up," opening her closet door she searches for something to wear.

"Ok baby, I'll see you then, bye!"

Tammy slams down the phone.

"Gee's, I almost fell trying to get to the phone and it's her!"

At Madea house, her street was lined with cars. Family, Madea's church friends and neighbors had come to celebrate Tammy's victories. There sitting on the dining room table, a large rectangle, specialty gourmet cake. It has white icing on all sides, and inside filled with chocolate, strawberry and white filling. Chocolate whip

cream and cherries garnish "congratulations" written on top. Everyone is laughing, talking and having a good time. Tammy makes it a
point to give each guest a few minutes of personal attention. Then
she goes to the kitchen, where her grandmother was filling glasses
with tea.

"Madea, when do you know you're in love?"

"Baby, you got a man in your life now?"

"I met someone. We hit it off pretty good. But I have not seen
him in a couple of weeks."

"Does he have a job? Can he provide for you?" Madea asks.

"What gets me is these guys want a girl to lay up with them. But
he can't take care of her. You can do badly by yourself."

Tammy's countenance changes to sadness.

"Is he nice to you? What are his plans for life?"

Tammy looks down, face turned away.

"You need to find these things out before you give your heart to
him baby!" Tammy's body language shifts to putting her hands on both
hips.

"You're right, I need to know more about him," Tammy pauses,
"I"...

Madea stops and looks at her. "I, what?"

"I miss him so much."

"Well, if he really likes you, nothing will stop him from seeing
you again. You can believe that!"

Tammy goes back to the party. Not wanting to be there, her
mind is on Harry.

"Sis, can you take me home, I'm not feeling well?" she tells Evelyn.

Evelyn screams out, "Madea, Tammy's not feeling well!"

"Not feeling well? Child, what's wrong with you?"

"Madea, I need to go home. I appreciate everything and I've had
a good time, but I need to go home. I'll call you later."

"Ok, say good bye to everyone."

On the way home, Tammy was quiet.

"Sis, you…ok?" Evelyn says.

Tammy fumbles around in her purse.

"Yeah, just tired," she opens the door to get out.

"Hey," Evelyn pulls her blouse, "Come here"…she gives her a hug… "I love you, and I'm proud of you."

"Thank you, Sis,"

Tammy gets out and goes inside of her home, locking the door behind her. Once inside her bedroom, she turns on the radio. "Where is he?" she whispers softly, as she sits on the edge of the bed, legs apart. She gets up, takes off her necklace and changes into her night gown. Then she makes her way to the bathroom to brush her teeth. There is a knock on the door. She can't hear it because the water is running. Now dressed and ready for bed, she goes back to her bedroom, turning off the lights. There is a flicking motion of lights outside.

"What is that?"

She jumps up and goes to the front door, there is a faint knock.

"Who is it?"

"It's me, Tammy, open up," Harry says.

Excited she tries to open the door. But she is having a hard time with the brass chain latch. After going back and forth with it, the door opens. Harry had been on another drug binge, for weeks. He looks and smells terrible. His pupils are dilated, and his skin is clammy and bumpy looking. He stands there looking like a puppy that had deserted his owner.

"Hey baby, are you going to let me in?"

"Oh! Harry," she pulls him inside, holds him for a long time and cries.

"Where have you been?" she said.

"Taking care of my business. Is that okay with you?" he laughs, while shutting the door.

She pushes him away then starts hitting him, while yelling and screaming, "Man, I have been worried sick about you. Where have you been?"

"Ouch, stop girl," he yells back. "Girl, stop!"

Then she screams, "Get out of my house."

She opens the door. He closes the door.

"Tammy...I thought you would be glad to see me?" She looks up at him.

"Baby I am." She hesitates, "I'm just so mad at you right now!"

"Can I sit down?"

"No! Not on my sofa. You look like you have not had a bath in a year, and your behind smells. You seriously need to get in the shower."

In the bathroom, she cleans out the tub and runs the shower for him.

"Don't come out until you're clean!"

From her bedroom closet, she pulls out a t shirt and shorts for him. Clothes that he had left behind weeks ago. While taking his shower, she closes the bathroom door, sits down on the sofa and sobs, rocking back and forth. "God! Oh, God!" she screams softly. "Oh God! Help him."

Chapter 3

ON THE SOFA, she lays his clothes out, then goes to the kitchen to warm up something in the microwave for him to eat.

"He should like this meatloaf and mashed potatoes. I'll even add a salad with it."

He turns off the water and steps out with his towel wrapped around him.

"What kind of dressing do you want?"

"Thousand Island."

"Okay!" she fixes his plate and takes it to the living room area.

"Did you see your clothes?"

"Yes mother," he laughs as he dries himself off.

"Don't you feel better, now?"

"What's with all these questions?"

"Hey!...Don't you get smart with me black man."

They both laugh. He changes into his fresh clothes. Underneath the coffee table, he scoots his body around-positioning it under the table. Tammy turns on the television. Not saying anything. She watches him as he eats.

"Boy, you sure can throw down girl."

"I told you I was a good cook."

"You ain't lying!" he's trying to guide his food into his mouth but misses.

"Uh! Do I need to get you a bib?"

He laughs, "Yeah, and maybe a diaper afterwards," he says.

"Negro, you make me sick!"

She jumps up and goes to the bathroom to clean up after him, placing his dirty clothes into the washer and comes back to sit down.

"You want seconds?"

He belches, "Please!"

He finishes eating and tries to get up to take his plate in the kitchen.

"I'll do it," she said.

His plate is washed and she cleans up the kitchen. Then she brings him a glass of water.

"Aren't you supposed to be working tonight?" he asked.

"I'm on the day shift now, from 7:00 am to 3:00 pm."

"Well, you better get some rest. Morning will be here before you know it."

"Harry, I don't need you to tell me anything, I got this…okay?"

"Yeah, whatever," he smiles.

"What are you going to do tomorrow?" she asks.

"I would like to sleep. No good sleep in a while. Why don't you take the car in tomorrow?" he said.

"You'll let me drive your car?"

"Yeah, why not?"

"Okay, I'll drive myself to work, and you can get some rest."

A few minutes later, Madea calls.

"Baby, I'm just calling to check on you, "You feel better?"

"Yeah, Madea, a lot better."

"Oh, that's good, did you have a good time this evening?"

"I did and thank you!"

"Hey, are you talking to some man?" Harry blares out in the background.

"Man, shut up!…This is my grandmother. She threw me a party tonight."

"Madea, I'll call you tomorrow," she hangs up.

He reaches over to her, "Hey baby, I'm so proud of you. Come here," he kisses her.

"Babe, I need to lie down, are you coming with me?" he said.

The living room television is turned off. In the bedroom, he crawls into bed. Tammy lies on the comforter near him. He dozes off. She sits up and kneels over on her side of the bed. Sadness fills her heart for him. On the night stand, she reaches for her favorite book. Two chapters are read before putting it down. Her alarm clock is set for 5:30 am, and the lights are turned off. Underneath the covers, she turns her back to him. She grabs the tissue box and wipes her tears with a tissue. Harry reaches over and begins to kiss her. Gradually, turning over to face him, she passionately kisses him. Soon after, she gently caresses his back. He moves on top of her. He has no problem in performing this night. Afterward, teasing her, he tells her, "Girl, I didn't know there were that many different positions, whew! Where did you learn that from?" She pulls the cover over both of them,

"Hush, and go to sleep."

The next day, Friday morning—she's rushing to get dressed, trying not to wake up Harry.

At work, all she thought about was Harry. He was different from the men in her past.

He really cared about her. Yet, he had his own demons that he was dealing with. Badly, she wanted their relationship to work.

"Tammy, I need an order of…scrambled eggs and French toast," the waitress yells out to her. They were busy this morning and she loved it. It made the day go by faster. Her team was helpful and quick, they were her second family. Their days were filled with fun and laughter. And her surroundings boosted her confidence to be the best she could be. Once a month, Mr. Schmidt would take photos of the employees in unusual funny faces while working, and post the pictures on the wall with funny captions below the photo. This place was her home away from home.

"Tammy, I need an order of waffles," another waitress yells out.

"Blueberry pancakes. I need an order of blueberry pancakes!"

"Coming up!" she yells back.

At last, it was three o'clock. Her feet were aching from running around so much. She felt good, nevertheless, knowing she could handle the job. She calls home and there's no answer.

"Maybe he's still asleep," she mumbles. Then she tries again... still no answer.

"Hey guys, I'm out of here, see you on Sunday!"

Waving to her crew as she walks out the door. When she arrives home, she finds Harry sitting up watching television.

"Baby, I tried to call, didn't you hear the phone?"

"No Tammy, I must have been in the bathroom. How was your day?"

"It was a good busy day, no complaints. What about you, did you rest up?"

"Yeah, and I feel better."

"That's good to know," she reaches to kiss him. "It's Friday. Yea! What are we going to do?" she stares at him.

"What about we go out to Venice beach. I love that place? We can take a blanket, snacks, some sodas, and for you-water, and watch the sun go down."

"Tammy!"

"Harry come-on, it'll be a lot of fun. We'll go when it gets closer to dusk."

He doesn't say anything for a moment.

"Then, what?"

"We can rent some comedy movies, to watch before going to bed."

He's glued to the TV and isn't listening to her, but then he gets up.

"Let's go," he says.

At Venice beach, he holds her hand while strolling down the west side of the boardwalk.

There are hundreds of street vendors and performers. Tammy smiles while observing the break-dancing to broken glass. The mimes, musicians and jugglers held her fascination.

"See, baby, I told you this would be fun."

Harry smiles… "Yeah, I needed this."

As they continued walking, Tammy notices that people were giving performers $1.00 dollar bills. She reaches into her purse and pulls out a dollar bill, dropping it into the performers' cup.

They make their way through the large crowd of people to the beach area at the end of Brooks Ave. Tammy had brought along with them a picnic basket, blankets, a Frisbee and their jackets, in case the weather turned colder.

"What's all that noise I hear?" she said.

He is trying to keep his balance, as they walk on the sand.

"Performers playing their drums, shakers, congas, and their percussions," he said.

She holds onto him while taking off her shoes.

"Let's take off our shoes, and walk…like they do in the movies."

Harry slips off his flip flops, and carry's his and hers during the course of their walk.

"This is nice Tammy!"

"Baby, I'm worried about you. I want us to make it. And I need you to fight!" she said.

He looks at her and squeezes her hand.

"If anything happens to you…I don't know what I would do."

"Nothing's going to happen to me, I'll be fine," he reaches down to pick her up.

"Put me down, I'm too heavy for you to be picking up," they both laugh. "I thought you were romantic? Where's the romance?" he puts her down onto the sand. "Do you know how far the beach goes? she asked."Oh, it's about a three mile stretch. They do a good job of keeping it maintained." She eyes a spot where she wants to sit down. "Are you getting tired?" she asked.

"Yeah, let's find somewhere to camp down."

"Right there!" she points… "That's perfect."

A few feet from the ocean, she runs and spreads out their blankets.

"Here baby, sit here."

She motions for him to sit down. Inside their carry bag, she takes out sandwiches, chips, napkins and their can drinks. He unravels the plastic wraps on their sandwiches.

She had made a huge turkey club with bacon sandwich for him, and a turkey, roast beef and cheese sandwich for her. He pops open their cans of soda, and open the big bag of multi grain chips. He takes a bite, "Hmmm!" he motions with his hand. "Just right, baby."

Tammy smiles, as she takes a bite of her sandwich while having to hold the roast beef from falling out.

"Darn, I may have put too much on here. You want some of this roast beef?"

She hands him a few pieces. He looks out into the ocean.

"Beautiful. Just beautiful," he said.

While during the winter, the sun sets over the ocean with breathtaking glimpses of it.

"Are you glad you came?" she bites down into her sandwich.

"Girl I would go anywhere with you," he smiles and wipes the mayonnaise from his mouth.

"I wonder if we will see any rich and famous people out here?" she said.

"Hey don't worry about rich and famous people, we are rich and famous right now," he jokes around. They both finished their meal, and he begins to cleanup. Afterward, he lies back on the blanket and looks into the stars. Dusk had begun to fall, and the waves were forcefully moving back and forth among the shore.

"What are you thinking about?" she asks.

"I'm just breathing and relaxing baby girl."

Tammy takes out her second blanket, positions it on both of them and lays her head on his chest, by night fall, neither wanted to leave.

"Baby, we better be going, it's around 11:00pm," he said.

She picks up the orange Frisbee, looks at it.

"And we didn't even get a chance to play," she said. He helps her to get up.

"There'll be other times that we can play," he said.

At home, she puts up everything and begins setting the mood for intimacy, by lighting a few aromatherapy candles and placing jazz music into the portable stereo. They both undress. He turns on the shower, and motions for her to join him. He gets in and begins to lather her body with soap. There are no words spoken. She gestures for him to turn around so that she can do the same for him. Once their bodies were fully lathered he increases the hot water. He holds the shower head, directing its flow up and down her body, and his. Once out of the shower, he leads her to the bedroom where the lights are low and the music is playing softly. They dry each other off, and embrace for a second. Tammy steps back from him and pulls back the sheets.

"Baby, I have something really special for you tonight and this weekend."

He looks at her with a puzzled look.

"Get into bed, and I'll be right back."

She slips away into the kitchen and brings back a bowl of strawberries and hot fudge.

"This is my first surprise!"

On his side of the bed, she sits down and hand feeds him.

"Umm"…he groans with each bite. Now he feeds her a fudge dipped strawberry.

Into his eyes, she looks, focusing on him alone.

"Harry…this weekend, I just want to talk, relax and enjoy each other's company. How does that sound?"

He looks at her with a mouthful of strawberries and smiles. Once they finished eating the strawberries and fudge, he tells her…

"I want you to relax and unwind."

He touches her shoulders and arms. While she looks at his full lips with a smile in her eyes and gestures she wants to be kissed. Her body language is open and approachable, with a little girl innocence. Again, she looks into his eyes, and then his mouth and back to his eyes—she smiles at him in innocence. Then moves closer to him and whispers...

"Are you ready for your next surprise?"

He nods his head. Slowly she moves in a little more and kisses him, then looks once again into his eyes.

She compliments him on his silent inner strength as she reaches for her scented body oil.

"Why don't we give each other a massage?" he responds.

"Oh, I would like that!"...she says.

The eating bowl is placed on a nearby table. He has her to lie on her stomach. He takes the oil and rubs it in his hands. Room temperature, slightly heated, he wanted it to be. When he touches her, she purrs like a kitten. He rubs it onto her shoulders, then she begins to tell him what she likes about him. Every now and then she looks up at him to keep the conversation light and encouraging.

"I'm ready to give you a massage now," she said. However, he turns her over and pulls her forward. With his lips pressed hard against hers, the blood rushes in her veins. She feels dizzy and in love at the same time. She gazes up at him adoringly—watching the expressions on his face. He leans forward to whisper and to kiss her, and then he makes love to her...

Between Friday night and Saturday afternoon, frequently they make love, only stopping to shower, rest, fix something to eat, and to curl up together to watch movies. *It was a much needed weekend of relaxing and unwinding for them both*, she thought. Harry was in a good spot. He felt that this was his true love but he still struggled within his mind about his sexuality. Late that Saturday afternoon, he takes her to meet his grandfather, who lives in South Central-Los Angeles. He knocks on the door, a stout older man with a beard answers the door.

"Oh my word, I can't believe it's you. Mama, Harry is here... Son, come on in."

"Boy I thought you were dead!"

"No, I'm still hanging around," he embraces his grandfather.

"Who is this young lady?"

"This is my girlfriend, Tammy."

"Tammy, well it's nice to meet you...Y'all come on in," he guides them to the family room. "Boy, I was telling your grandmother the other day, that I hope you were okay. Are you?" Harry's sitting with his legs splayed.

"Yes Sir, I'm working and doing fine."

His grandfather hits the arm of his arm chair, "Young lady, are you taking care of him?"

Laughing she says, "Yes sir, I'm trying to, he can be a little stubborn at times."

They sit around for about an hour. Then Harry tells them he needs to go. His grandfather pulls Harry to the side, while Tammy talks to his grandmother.

"Boy, are you off of that stuff?" his grandfather strokes his own face.

"What stuff?"

"Boy, don't play dumb with me—that heroin...are you off of it?"

"Grandpa, I'm working and everything is okay. Hey, we'll come by next week and have dinner, is that okay?" Harry said.

"Sure son that will be fine."

Harry hugs him and his grandmother and leaves. On their way home, Tammy asks him...

"So those are your infamous grandparents...huh?" Smiling, he nods... "Yep."

She looks at him with tender eyes, "They seem to be some nice people."

He stops at a stop sign and looks both ways. "Yeah, I'm almost forty years old, and he still calls me boy!" She crosses her legs and stares straight ahead.

"Oh, he's from the old school. Madea does me the same way. What is his name?"

Harry checks the sight distance ahead and mirrors for rear traffic.

"Robert and Doris Wilkerson." She leans back into her seat.

"Okay...well I loved meeting them," she then places her arm into his.

"Hey baby, I need to drop you off at home, but I'll be back shortly?"

"Where are you going?"

"I going to see some of my friends, get out for a bit."

"Can I go?"

"Hey, Tammy, I know you don't want to be hanging out with a bunch of knuckle heads right?"

"Yeah, you're right. I'll wait for you." He kisses her and drops her off at the driveway.

It's going on 10:00 pm, and no Harry. "Where is he?" pacing the floor, she picks up their clothes along the way. Finally from exhaustion, she sits down to watch something on television. The clock on the wall, ticks away pass 10:15pm. Suddenly there is a sound of someone driving up into the driveway. Harry gets out and taps on the door.

"Do you think I'll get a key sometime soon?" he asks her as she opens the door. With a penetrating stare she asked, "Have you been drinking?"

He runs to the bathroom and yells out, "Yes, I have had two beers." She walks toward the bathroom door, to listen in on him. "You didn't bring one back for me?" He opens the door.

"Baby, I'm sorry, but I have something else for you," he goes to the bedroom and changes into his night clothes.

"What does he mean, he has something for me?" she mumbles.

A few minutes later, he sits next to her.

"I'm falling in love with you Tammy," he looks into her eyes.

"Why do your eyes look so funny?" she asked.

With his hand, palms up, he stretches out his hand to her.

"Funny? What do you mean?"

"Like you are about to take off running." He squirms around in his seat.

"There you go, tripping again!"

Wondering what he's getting ready to do, she looks at him with anticipation.

"I'm not trying to be funny," she's laughs.

He pulls out a homemade pipe and $100 worth of crack cocaine.

"Oh no!" she puts up her hand to him.

"Hey, if you don't want any, the more for me," he puts a piece of a rocked icy looking substance onto his pipe and inhales. He holds it, and then blows it out.

" @#$*#@ that's powerful," he said.

Tammy gets up and goes to the bathroom. While brushing her teeth, she stops for a moment.

"This Negro has brought this mess into my house!"

She slams the medicine cabinet door so hard the hinges almost come off. Then, makes her way to the kitchen for some orange juice. Not wanting to go back to the living room, she glares into the refrigerator to bypass time.

"What are you doing," he asked.

Holding up a pitcher of orange juice, she peeps around the refrigerator door with a disgusted look on her face.

"Want some?" she asks.

"Yeah, I'll take some."

Trying not to look at him, she sets their glasses down. The volume on the television is turned up.

"Baby why so loud? Turn it down!" When she turns to look at him, he hands her the pipe. "C' mon…take a hit," she puts her hand up defensively.

"No!"

"Hey, one hit," he puts the pipe in her mouth.

"Suck in," he coaches her as she draws the substance in.

"Now hold it!"…he yells.

She blows it out. "Man!" she said. Her head freezes for a moment and she gets quiet.

"Uh huh, told you it was powerful."

He takes another hit, and then gives the pipe to her. This time she holds it on her own, taking another hit and then blows it out.

"Whew!…This is some bad stuff!" she said.

"I told you," he said.

This went on for several hours until they ran out of crack cocaine. Both are wired and she's on the floor looking for crack cocaine crumbs.

"Hey baby…let's chill," he said, and then he reaches in his pocket and takes out a valium to give to her.

"This will help you to calm down."

Tammy couldn't sit still, one minute she's up walking, another time she's looking out the window, thinking someone was outside their home.

"Hey, sit down next to me," he tells her.

After grabbing a large glass of orange juice, she begins to look up and around her home every few minutes.

"Hey! I'm going to put you to bed if you don't settle down," he said. Her mind begins to settle down and they spend the rest of the evening talking.

"My uncle Ray is a trip!"

"Where did that come from?" he asks. He looks at her with a surprise look.

"You know, he was the one that raped me at sixteen—he's a loser."

She begins shifting her weight from side to side. He watches her. Not saying much, he puts his head down.

"All my life I felt abandoned by my parents," she said.

"Why?" he mumbles.

"Because my father died, and my mother deserted us. By twenty nine, I found myself in a lesbian relationship that lasted six years. I tried to show courage in spite of my many hardships," she begins to cry.

"Hey Tammy…C'mon, don't do this. You're spoiling the moment."

"I'm sorry."

She stares down at the floor, looking for small white crack cocaine crumbs. Her heart is racing fast, and she doesn't know what to do with herself. This is the first time she has used cocaine. Not able to sit still, she gets up and gets a tissue.

"My then lover asked me to make a drug drop. I had no idea that I would be busted for delivering a kilo of marijuana, possession with intent to sell is what the officer called it. This would be the start of my life being changed forever."

Harry goes to the kitchen and opens the refrigerator, and decides that they should eat something. He places an order for a takeout pizza. On their way back from picking up the pizza, he accidently makes a wrong turn into ongoing traffic. Tammy screams, almost dropping the large pizza.

"Harry, we're going the wrong way!" Quickly, he maneuvers the car into the right direction.

On their way back home, he takes her to the ATM machine and they stop by a drug dealer's house to pick up more crack cocaine. That night they stay up all night talking about her deepest issues, in between getting high. The next morning she calls into work and tells Mr. Schmidt she has a family emergency and that she would need a couple of days off for a funeral-out of town.

Once again, she goes to the ATM machine to draw out $100.00 dollars. But instead, pulls out an insufficient funds receipt. The little savings she did have was gone, and she was beginning to turn into a full blown drug abuser. So, Harry calls his drug dealer over and makes a deal with him so that they could get their drugs for free. It was nothing for the drug dealer to give him an eight ball for allowing him to deal to a few customers out of Tammy's home. Because the dealers place, was usually running hot from selling.

Within a couple of days, the house was disheveled and smelled of drugs. When Tammy did decide to go back to work, she told herself everything was under control.

"Hey Tammy, I need a side order of sausage!" One waitress yelled out.

"Toast!…Where is my toast?" another one yelled.

Tammy spills grease on the floor and almost falls.

"No, doll…this is the next order that should go out," the other cook tells her.

"Hey man, I need to take a break," she yells.

Today she can't get her orders right and she's irritable. Mr. Schmidt walks over and asks if she was okay.

"I'm okay, I'm still down about my Aunt that passed away," she said.

"Tammy why don't you take off for the rest of the day. You're off anyway on Saturday and come back on Sunday refreshed." That was all she needed to hear.

"Thank you, Mr. Schmidt."

That evening, Harry introduces her to "Speedballing" inject-ing heroin in combination with cocaine, a drug that lasts six or more hours. He began using heroin in an inhaled form when he first became homeless at eighteen, after his mother's death. Someone at the homeless shelter had turned him on to it one afternoon. He liked how it helped him to block his emotional issues that had dominated his life for years. Later, he switched to injecting the drug. By this time, he had become a hard core heroin addict, with no problem resorting to petty crimes. Just to get his fix.

His body has become accustomed to the drug. But this was a new experience for Tammy.

Immediately after trying it, she felt super good, like she was on top of the world. She didn't want to live without it. Soon she found her-self, doing anything to get it, even if that meant allowing drug dealers to sell out of her house. Their drug parties grew to all night partying. It wasn't uncommon for them to consume alcohol, marijuana, cocaine, heroin, and tobacco all in one night.

Now, she was missing more and more days from work. Yet, call-ing in every chance she got with excuses. When she would go in, she would always make some type of mistake and have an excuse for it. Her co-workers also noticed she was having a hard time keeping track of the multiple orders and making sure the customers who ordered first were served first. Several customers had begun to complain. Customers with special requests, such as changes to the regular order; substituting scrambled eggs for over easy eggs was a hassle for her. Work wasn't joyful, but now tedious for her. Mr. Schmidt thought she was back on drugs, but was trying to keep from firing her since she had been with the company for a couple of months. And he truly liked her.

One night, she, Harry and two of his drug buddies had gotten so stoned, that she and Harry ended up in a heated verbal confrontation over drugs. In front of his drug buddies, she asked him to leave. He was barely working and when he did, it was only to buy more drugs for him. He wasn't contributing around the house anymore. Their utilities were turned off, and there was barely any food in the house.

She goes into the dark bathroom and looks at the mirror, "Where are those candles?" she tries to straighten up her appearance but was looking slouchy and tired. Stumbling from room to room in the dark, one candle is found. The glimmer from the candle provided some warmth for her cold body. She goes back to the bathroom and turns the water on. "Man this is cold," she turns it off quickly while shivering. Her pajama pants were hanging off of her. She looks down and notices that she had lost weight but not a significant amount. Because of her drug usage she had been feeling ill often, and was looking more and more disarrayed, something that hadn't happen before in the past. She only cared about getting high. It took no time for speedballing to become her drug of choice.

❧

Today was a brisk Saturday morning for the month of March. When Tammy awoke, she sat up in the bed for a moment before dragging herself to the bathroom. On her way back she started to feel lightheaded, nauseated, sweaty and weak. As she held her head, the room appeared to be spinning. She had begun to have respiratory depression—hypoventilation, along with going in and out of unconsciousness. The cocaine had worn off and the full effects of heroin were felt. On her way back to the bathroom, she throws up in the sink. "Ah"... "Ah"...

"Ah"… "God, help me!"…she musters out. Her body was quivering with chills, from her throwing up everything inside herself. Scared and thinking she was dying, not knowing what was happening to her body, she picked up the phone and called 911 for the emergency ambulance. The paramedics arrive and take her to the emergency room. Later that day, she is moved to her own room. Five days later, her doctor has given her permission to leave. Her grandparents are called to make arrangements for them to pick her up.

"Madea."

"Tammy, I have not heard from you in a while, are you ok?"

"No ma'am."

"Baby what's wrong?"

"Madea…I need for you to pick me up."

"Where are you?"

"I'm at the hospital."

"Well, baby which one?"

"Madea, please…come pick me up," she starts to cry all over again.

"Tammy where are you, what hospital?"

Tammy sighs and rubs her head.

"Will you listen to me. I'm at the Los Angeles County Hospital on State St."

There is a second of quietness.

"Baby, can you give me about 30-45 minutes? Papa and I are on our way."

Tammy hangs up.

Tammy's grandparents make it to the hospital. Her mind was filled with mixed feelings about seeing them. She needed a ride home but was dreading them finding out she's back on drugs. Her grandfather opens her hospital room door.

"Hey Toot" (her childhood nickname) "How are you doing?"

Her grandmother walks in behind him.

"Tammy, why haven't we heard from you all this time?"

The nurse knocks on the door and comes in to check on Tammy.

"Oh, we'll step out until you're done," her grandfather said.

He catches hold of his wife's hand. Her grandmother whispered to him, "Oh, my Lord... Papa, she's on drugs again."

Her grandfather looks disappointed. The grandmother rubs his shoulder.

"I figured that when we hadn't heard from her in a while," he said.

After her discharge, she tells her grandparents about the prescription. But not what it is for. Her grandfather doesn't ask any questions until they all get home. Tammy gets into the backseat of the car. Madea puts in her gospel CD. While Tammy listens to every word that conveyed what she was feeling on the inside. No one but God could help her. She breaks down crying.

"It's alright baby! It's alright!" Madea said softly.

"No Madea, it's not alright," she mutters out the words from the song as she sheds bitter tears. She could barely get the words out. Frantically, she cries out, *"God help me sing this song!"*

They pull up to her grandparents' house.

"Papa please help Tammy get out of the car," Madea said. He opens the door.

"Come on baby, can you make it?" he said.

Tammy nods her head. When they enter into their home, Tammy runs to the bathroom and throws up. Madea goes in behind her and starts praying.

"Baby, are you pregnant?"

Tammy gag's again and throws up. Madea opens the linen closet and takes out a face towel, and soaks it in cool water. When Tammy finishes, she wipes her face and guides her to the sofa in the family room. Her body is limb and motionless. Papa turns the television down in hopes of hearing what she has to say. Madea goes to the kitchen and gets her a glass of Sprite.

"Here, baby, drink this."

Tammy takes a sip and pushes the glass away.

"Madea and Papa, I'm pregnant again."

Her grandfather looks at his wife.

"Is it by that man you like so much?" Madea asks.

"Yes ma'am."

"Where is he now?"

"I kicked him out."

"You mean he has been staying with you all this time?" her grandmother looks disgusted.

"Yes ma'am."

Her grandmother gets up to find her hair rolling curlers.

"Well are you going to tell him?"

There's a pause…

"No ma'am."

Madea spreads out her curlers into her lap and takes one to roll her hair.

"Why not, it's his baby, too?" Tammy looks up at the ceiling.

"Madea he's on drugs."

With a flustering tone, Madea asked, "Baby do you still have your job?"

"Yes ma'am, Mr. Schmidt has really been kind to me."

"Does he know?"

"No."

"Well you're going to have to tell him…right?"

"Yes ma'am."

"Tammy you were doing so well. Now, you have another unnecessary challenge. Why didn't you use protection if you were going to be sleeping with him?"

Tammy doesn't say anything.

"Madea, (Tammy pauses)…all my utilities are cut off."

"What!…What did you say?" her grandmother's voice elevates higher.

"The utilities are off," Tammy said angrily.

Her grandmother drops her curler into her lap and stops with disbelief. "Tammy, you mean to tell me, he's been laying up with you, and he can't even keep the lights and gas on?"

"Girl...this is pitiful. What about your education? You went down there and signed up for school, whacha gonna do now?" Tammy sits up and takes a sip from her glass of Sprite.

"Baby I don't mean to be fussing but we put you in that house so that you would not have to worry about anything. All you needed to do was work, focus on school and get your life together. And here comes this devil and distracts you!" By this time, Madea is rocking back and forth in her recliner.

"Tammy what are you going to do about your job now?" her grandfather asked.

"I really don't know. I'm going to have to talk with my boss and see if he will work with me."

"Well, how far behind are you on your utilities?" he asked.

"Two months...Papa."

Madea doesn't say anything. Papa looks at her and asks, "Tammy, are you on drugs again, smoking that marijuana?"

She looks into his eyes, "Yes sir." He slams his paper down.

"Tammy you're going to have to go into treatment, that's that. We're old, and we can't take care of you. We will do what we can. But you're 39 years old. It's time for you to get your life together!" She tries to get up, but falls back onto the sofa.

"Papa...don't you think...I know this?"...she snaps at him. "I've been trying," she starts crying again. Tammy puts her head into her lap and cries nonstop.

"Ain't no need in crying Tammy. You've been pregnant before. We will take care of the utilities. But this time I want you to work something out with your boss man and get into treatment."

Her financial award letter had come in for her to attend Culinary Arts School. Madea wasn't about to tell her this, figuring she would use the money to buy drugs. Madea looks at her. "Tammy, Tammy Jean, what's really wrong with you? I know there's something else that you're not telling us. What is it?"

"He gave me HIV!" Tammy slowly lifts her head.

Madea thrusts her finger toward Tammy with wide-opened eyes and mouth, "That low down dirty dog. He probably knew he had it when he gave it to you."

She stands up, curlers falling to the floor and shouts, "Oh Lord"... walking back and forth, hitting one hand into the other.

"Oh Lord, have mercy. Lord, you said in your word...you were pierced for our rebellion, crushed for our sins...Lord, help, help this child!"

Madea kept pacing the floor, hitting one hand into the other.

"Well, I tell you what we're going to do," her grandfather said.

"God said call on the name of the Lord in your time of trouble and that's what we're going to do."

He reaches for both of their hands. Madea begins to hum an old gospel spiritual while he prays...for about twenty minutes.

"Tammy, it's in God's hand now. But you have to do your part," he said. "You have to get into treatment and focus on staying clean. Once you get out of treatment, your focus needs to be on God, your baby and your education. He'll work it out. But you've got to obey. If that boyfriend of yours come around again, be nice to him. But if he's not going to marry you and take care of you and the baby, you have to do it yourself. So stop sleeping with him. And for heaven's sake don't let him back, in there. He's a man. He should be able to take care of himself. You're not his mother. As far as the baby's concern, this time, you will be able to focus on raising your child. You need to make sure that when you get on your feet, that you also get your child some 'life insurance' in case something happens to you, he/or she would be taken care of. We'll help you the best way we can until you can get on your feet."

Tammy gets up, makes her way to both of them and hugs them. "As a matter of fact, why don't you stay here for the rest of the weekend? But Monday morning, you need to make two phone calls, to your boss and your treatment counselor," her grandfather tells her.

Still angry, but relieved that her grandparents are behind her. Though still, she was hoping someone from the hospital would call her and say a mistake had been made on her HIV test. She knows this won't happen. Her situation is very present and real. Her mind keeps going back to her conversation with Madea months ago. *You would just keep living and take better care of yourself. This is where the rubber meets the road*, she thought. Indeed, she would have to learn how.

All night long, as she laid in bed, tossing and turning, she couldn't seem to rest. Her mind was filled with anxiety about her condition. Mentally and physically tired, she kept getting up going back and forth to the bathroom. Each time, she seemed to be sicker or at least she thought so. "What am I going to do...I've really messed up?" she slams her pillow into the bed, and hits it repeatedly. Early Sunday morning, she gets up to take a bath and dresses into an old dress her grandmother had given her. Papa was an early bird. Every morning he would get up and make breakfast. He had an habit of making hot oatmeal and sitting it in the window for a second to cool.

"Good morning young lady," he says as she makes her way to the dining room table. "Good morning," she mumbles.

"You were up, off and on all last night."

She nods her head. He turns the stereo on to a gospel music station. It's music softly blaring in the background. Madea comes to the dining room, hugs Tammy and sits down.

"After church today, would you like to go to that fancy buffet restaurant?" Madea asks.

Madea looks at Tammy, waiting for an answer. Feeling ornery, Tammy doesn't say anything.

"Tammy...baby you hear me?"

Angrily she snaps at her, "Yes, Yes, Madea that's fine." She had an attitude and wanted to be left alone.

After church, they drive to the restaurant. Everyone's quiet. Tammy eats with her head down the entire time. Her grandparents try to engage her in conversation but her mind was on her problems. When they had finished eating, Papa decided he would take them on a drive, nowhere in particular. He thought it would do Tammy some good to get out. They stopped by her home, allowing her to gather a few clothes to change into in case she wanted to stay longer. Harry had come by and left a note on the door-saying he was trying to reach her. She tears up his note and walks inside. The house has a bad odor. Quickly she looks around for something to wear so that she could get out in a hurry.

While stuffing her carry bag with clothes and toiletries, she has an urge to do drugs. On her way out, she stops in the kitchen, digs into the garbage bag and shuffles around the cigarette butts and ashes looking for the homemade pipe they used. She takes it out and dusts it off, while looking for any crack residue that might be still left. The whiff of the residue brought back those feelings of getting high. Then she takes the crack pipe and places it up to her mouth. *One more hit won't hurt*, she thought to herself.

Her grandfather blows the horn. Jumpy, she tries to stay focused, while flicking her broken lighter over the stained pipe. "What am I doing?" she looks at the pipe again and throws it back into the trash. He blows the car horn, again.

"Coming,"…she yells out. Grabbing her bag and heading for the door.

"Who was that note from?" Madea asked. "Don't tell me…Harry!"

Tammy scoots her bag over unto the next seat.

"Yeah, he's trying to reach me."

Papa barges into the conversation, "Tammy! Leave him alone. You've already seen that he doesn't care about you. What more do you need?"

Tammy thought about how much she hated Harry. She could never forgive him for what he has done to her life. He proved himself to be no different from the other men that had been in her life before. Her life is now screwed up, all because of him and she wanted to kill him.

It had been a long afternoon. Her grandparents' usual Sunday routine was to lie down and take a nap. Nonetheless, she stays up and watches a movie. Mr. Schmidt crossed her mind, but she was too afraid to call him. Fretful and unable to sleep, she decides to take a walk around the corner and come back. In haste, she walks down S. Keene Ave toward the elementary school. Her grandparents' home is located in an upscale part of Compton, borderline Carson, next to the 91 freeway.

In all, the neighborhood still looks good. Their neighborhood yards were for the most part, maintained and clean. Into an hour of walking, she thinks about her disease. What would become of her life now and how would she raise a child that could be a drug baby and/or HIV infected? Fear, that was the biggie. Not like the other events in her life that she had recovered from. Prison was a piece of cake compared to this. Honestly, she didn't know how to cope with it. Now broke, with no savings, possibly no job, a drug problem, no transportation and a baby to care for. Bottom line, she was right back where she started several months ago. All of her hard work had been in vain because of her life choices. At the door, Madea is waiting for her.

"Baby were you out walking?" Tammy removes her jacket hood from her head.

"Yeah, the neighborhood hasn't changed much," Tammy said.

Her grandmother helps her take off her jacket.

"We've been here for a long time and probably will be until the Lord calls us home. Well, do you feel better?" she hugs Tammy.

"Yes!"

"Baby, it will all work out. Papa and I are praying for you. You need to start praying too."

"Madea, please!"

She goes to her room and slams the door. Not knowing what to believe about God. She couldn't understand, how God would allow her to be abused at sixteen by a man she knew. Or why her mother would abandon her and her sister. Her heart had been crushed for many years. And now, an illness she didn't want to have. *Why did he allow this?* she thought. God was just like any other man. She knew he existed but she doesn't know him personally.

Chapter 4

MONDAY MORNING, TAMMY had to take an honest look at her situation, knowing that spending useless time thinking about making her two important calls wouldn't do any good. She needed to look at the good side of things and make her calls even though she's terrified about the possible outcome. Her voice tremors with varying speech tones while talking to her case manager. "Ms. Williams, this is Tammy...How are you?" she clears her throat.

"I'm fine, how's the job coming along?" Ms. Williams asks.

"That's what I needed to talk with you about...Do you have a minute?"

"Sure, are you no longer there?"

"I don't know-yet. I made some bad decisions the last couple of weeks.

"Like what?"

"Well, for starters I relapsed."

"Tammy...No! Have you used today?"

"No, but I have been feeling sick."

"We need to get you into treatment as quickly as possible. What caused you to relapse?"

"It's a long story and I don't want to go into it. But I really need some help and a friend right now." Ms. Williams listens without interrupting.

"This weekend I had to go to the emergency room at the county hospital," she licks her lips and takes a sip of water.

"Who was your attending physician over there?" Gasping and holding her breath, "I believe it was Doctor Garza." Tammy pauses.

"Okay, go on," Ms. Williams said. Tammy's speech becomes flat. "I almost overdosed from a mixture of cocaine and heroin," Tammy clenches her fists.

"Um, Um, Um. My Lord. Tammy, you're very fortunate to be alive. Do you know that?" Tammy's face turns pale.

"Yes ma'am. Well, the doctor ran a series of test and I'm four weeks pregnant and have HIV."

"Oh, My God! Tammy. I'm so sorry. We really need to get some help for you. What is that organizations name?" Ms. Williams shuffles papers around. "There is a women's facility—Oh, I can't think of the name of it. But the residential treatment program that comes to my mind offers several programs that you are going to need within a live in setting. It will be an abstinence-based medical structure with a 12-step program orientation. They provide substance abuse counseling, education regarding HIV/AIDS, mental health counseling, vocational rehabilitation and support groups.

Here it is. I found the information I was looking for. Now Tammy, these programs tend to be focused on helping an individual make the transition from active use to living without substances. It does enforce rules against substance abuse, and a client's substance abuse may result in her dismissal from the program. Do you understand this?"

"Yes."

"Are you willing to go?"

"Yes!" she sighs.

"Your treatment may last from one week for detoxification to twenty eight days or even more. When it is completed, I highly recommend you going to a strong intensive outpatient treatment facility for a few hours evenings and on weekends. It should allow you to continue working while participating in treatment. The program could last six to twelve weeks or longer. Could this be worked out with your employer?" Tammy breaks out in a cold sweat. "I'll call him, after I hang up from you to see if, I still have a job," she takes another sip of water. "You didn't call in?"

"No,"…she whispers.

"Either way, if you still have a job or not, I will call and get everything set up for you. Hopefully, I can get everything done before tomorrow," she said softly.

"Tammy, I…know that mentally, you're dealing with three overwhelming circumstances here, and the stress may be too much. But keep in mind, the best time to treat HIV is as early as possible. The sooner an HIV-infected person receives treatment, the more likely his/her survival will be prolonged and the symptoms less dire. Do you believe that?" Tammy's quiet for a moment, thinking about what she just said.

"Ms. Williams I don't know what to believe anymore," she said-angrily.

"Well I understand, but don't lose hope. A couple of other pointers, I need to touch on that will help, number one—breast milk transmits HIV, make it a point to use formulas only…ok?" Tammy's countenance changes to sadness, "Yes ma'am." "Secondly, please consider having a cesarean delivery—it reduces the risk of vertical transmission of HIV from mother to child.

And thirdly, usually after a client has managed to obtain medical care, the next challenge is to find the means to pay for the drug therapy. People with HIV can have multiple prescriptions and drug costs may exceed $1,000 per month."

"Did you say $1,000 dollars? Where am I going to get that kinda money?"

"Well, some public programs are moving toward a copayment system to reduce costs.

However, the AIDS Drug Assistance Programs (ADAPs) have helped many persons with AIDS."

Tammy sighs, "Are they going to be able to help me?"

"They should, because they're federally funded programs administered by the States.

That has allowed persons with AIDS who are underinsured or have no insurance to obtain funding for AIDS—related drugs, including some prophylactic treatments. I want you to call your employer and I'll get started on working out the details for you. It will get better, just don't give up."

"Thank you. I love you, Ms. Williams."

"I'll talk with you soon," Ms. Williams said.

Tammy takes a deep breath, "Oh I don't feel like calling this man!" she cries out loud.

Her throat clears, as she dials the restaurant phone number. "Mr. Schmidt, please." Then she's placed on hold.

"Hello, this is John." Her hands are nervously shaking. Fear is penetrating throughout her body.

"Mr. Schmidt," she whispers.

"Tammy?"

"Yes sir!" There's silence.

"Mr. Schmidt, I know, you're disappointed in me but I'm on my way to treatment and need to know if you'll give me another chance." Frustrated about his efforts to help her, "Tammy, you didn't call in."

Interrupting him. "I was in the emergency room for a week," she's loud and emotional.

"I almost OD'd, Mr. Schmidt," she hollers.

"Well, darling, you're making the right decision. Remember what I told you when I hired you?" Mr. Schmidt gets quiet.

"Yes," she begins to weep.

"I can't have you working here and you're on drugs. The environment is fast pace and could be dangerous for you." She ponders about what he said.

"I know, I know, but can I ask you something?"

"Go ahead."

"Remember when you used and how you felt? You just wanted someone to give you a chance."

"But see…Tammy…that's it, I have given you a chance."

"Mr. Schmidt, I need this job. I've enrolled in culinary school and I'm just waiting on my financial award letter. Isn't there something I can do? I mean, I don't have to be a cook." He opens his spreadsheet program to work on his monthly budget and then pauses.

"I'll tell you what I'll do. Make sure you get into treatment? How long is it for?"

"My case manager said twenty eight days at a live-in facility, and after that, I can go to intensive outpatient treatment, nights and weekends. Please, Mr. Schmidt don't fire me," she yells. "Tammy, what I was about to say was…finish your treatment and call me. We'll see at that time, if you're serious about staying clean. More than likely, I'll move you to prep work instead of cooking and maybe have you make sure the food is delivered quickly. We have to see, when we touch bases again… ok?"

"Yes Sir. I'll call you in a month."

"Take care Tammy," he hangs up.

She goes back to bed, and thinks about how pregnancy and having a baby will impact her work. Lately there has been some cramping in her lower abdomen, and emotionally, she's feeling emptiness and despair. It has been tough to function. Exhausted all the time and just getting through the day is overwhelming. Her hopelessness ranges from moderate to severe, although the early symptoms of pregnancy like morning sickness, off and on food cravings, mood swings and frequent urination are common. This time, she's not sure if the symptoms are from morning sickness or her HIV disease.

Late that afternoon, Tammy gets a phone call from Ms. Williams. The live-in facility she had talked about had an opening. They offered a specialized treatment program for her specific needs in Arkansas. If she wanted to get clean, she would have to leave the next day. Her grandparents paid for her round trip bus ticket and she leaves the next morning. Upon arriving in Arkansas, she is greeted by a slender older white man. "Are you Tammy?"

"Yes…I am."

"Hello Tammy, my name is Sam. Let me take that suit case for you." She follows him to an old truck. He opens the door for her. She's quiet the entire ride.

"You sure don't talk much, do you?"

"When I'm in a better mood…I do." He helps her to get out of the truck and shows her where to go. At the center's first meeting, she's surrounded by sixteen people, sitting among two long tables. The drug counselor talks to them about the program and their disease, getting each one involved in a question and answer session. Then she tells them that their program will consist of: 12 step meetings, counseling, house chores, working in the kitchen, and attending group outings.

Late that afternoon, the group takes a break. Tammy stands at the window looking out at the heavy rainfall. It was April, thunderstorm season. But earlier she could see that the pine trees were tossing out their yellow pollen dust all over everything. Now, she was homesick, and wanted to leave.

Week one: Two months pregnant and she feels crappy. She has one on one with her counselor.

"I hate this place," she tells her counselor. "I want my freedom to do what I want to do."

The first few days are filled with arguments, disputes and conflicts. Irritable, stressed, disorientated, vulnerable and loneliness are her gripping emotions. Not wanting to be there. Her counselor has scheduled for her to see a doctor in order to assess how effective her HIV treatment regimen is. Her CD4 cell count testing is done, and she learns she has to see a doctor regularly, plus stick to the antiretroviral medication plan that the doctor prescribed. At the drug treatment facility, her bedroom is shared with three other females that she doesn't like.

From the start, she knew they were trouble makers, gossipers and back biters, who were miserable. They seem to thrive on conflicts, going to the staff and reporting little petty incidents. There have been several times where she had to control herself from cursing someone out. In one of the meetings, one of the clients had told everyone that Tammy and another girl had stolen her ring. Tammy and the other girl had come in after her and taken a shower. The accusing female had left her ring on a stand, and it fell back against the wall. Tammy and the other female searched for the ring and found where it had fallen— against the wall. In their meeting, Tammy holds the ring up.

"See this is what I'm talking about...little petty stuff like this. Here is your ring. You accused us of having it, but it fell behind the stand in the bathroom." Tammy gets up and walks out. That night she calls home.

"Madea, I don't want to be here. Can't you and Papa come get me?"

"Baby, you have to stay until you get that stuff out of your system. Why don't you like the place?"

"The staff is rude and these girls here are trifling."

"Well baby, that's anywhere you go. There're always going to be rude people."

"I know, Madea!"...she snaps at her. "But these people's rules are so strict. There are rules about the music, television, phone calls, and we're not allowed to consume food brought onto the premises. Madea...it's hard."

"I know, Tammy, but you have got to do it."

"Okay I'll talk with you later," Tammy slams the phone down.

"Madea"...Tammy calls back again. "I don't want to be here."

"Tammy Jean, don't call me anymore tonight. You got yourself in this fix by sleeping with that no good boyfriend of yours. The choices you have made are going to affect you for the rest of your life. I'm not being mean. I just want you to see how serious this is. You're in the real world now. That treatment facility will help you get your life back together. So you stay there until you get your problem worked out."

"It's okay, Madea don't worry about me," she slams the phone down.

Week two: Tammy makes up her mind that she's determine to get through her treatment program. Alone sometimes, she would try to encourage herself, amidst her tears—"I did this to myself. But I can make it. I can be clean again. I have to for the sake of my baby." Self talk kept her from losing her mind. But one evening, she gets into a shouting match with one of her roommates at a meeting. Tammy had to refrain herself from jumping on the girl. She runs to the bathroom and breaks down and cries. The counselor meets her in the hallway and talks to her. Then takes her back to her office to counselor her, and work with her on her medical and nutritional needs, since she's pregnant and has HIV.

The next couple of nights, she awakens to a taste of cocaine in her mouth. In the bathroom she throws up repeatedly. The next morning because of her morning sickness, her body doesn't have the strength to attend the meetings for the day. At her last meeting, she had met two new friends, a female from Texas and another female from Arkansas. Their friendship will help her get through this tough period in her life.

When she missed her meeting, they came to see her.

"If only I can get pass this morning sickness, I could feel better," she said.

"Well you're pregnant, and you know how your body goes through changes...anyway," one of the girls said.

"Yeah...I just feel really crappy."

"Did you want to talk about it?" Veronica asked her. Tammy plumps up her pillow.

"Veronica, I feel very angry, sad and anxious about my situation," she didn't want anyone to know that she had HIV fearing that they would look down on her.

"My life is overwhelming right now, and I fear losing my job and not being able to care for myself or my new born child. I guess, it will all work itself out." Not sure how to respond to her problems, Veronica sits on Tammy's bed and listens to her until lunch time.

Often when not feeling good, she found herself having to retire early to bed. There always seemed to be an ongoing fight about it with one of the staff persons since no one was allowed to go back to their room. But she always tries to make her group therapy sessions when possible. She found that it helped her to face why she has used drugs more realistically, and to come to terms with its harmful consequences. The meetings provided a boost in motivation to stay drug free. There, she talked about her personal issues, got feedback and listened to others who have experienced similar situations, even though learning effective ways to solve her emotional problems without resorting to drugs was still hard.

Week three: Her counselor has begun to establish a positive, therapeutic relationship with her, to discuss her goals. Tammy knows the plan has to be followed in order for her to make her dream come true. One day after coming back from an afternoon outing, the front desk person hands her a letter. Quickly, she opens it and sees it's from her grandfather. He had gone to the trouble to write it and she couldn't wait to hear what he had to say. In the bathroom, she reads it slowly and smiles. He tells her how proud he is of her and that he knows she has what it takes to reach her goals. He's pulling for her and wants to see her make it. Reading the letter out loud helped her to express his words with his appropriate emotion, at the time of its writing. *Heartwarming and encouraging*, she thought.

"Maybe he really understood that I'm hurting with strong, pent-up emotions," she mutters. On days when she was down and depressed or didn't feel well physically, she would take out his letter and read his words of encouragement.

Week four: The end of April and she has been clean for a total of five weeks.

"Hey Tammy, when are you leaving?" one of the resident clients asked her. Several of the center clients had finished their program.

"I leave tomorrow, and I'm ready to go home. I will finish my intensive outpatient program in Los Angeles," she tells her. That afternoon, she and four other women, sit around, talking about their experiences. They were a different group of women that came in a week after she did. The former group of women, who had made her treatment experience very miserable, had left the week before.

But with this new group, she found new friends that she could talk to. Similar to back in the day when she enjoyed hanging around her drug buddies. Yet this time, the camaraderie was built on sobriety. That evening they sat and talked about men, life and their experiences. She had begun to find comfort. Their sharing was uplifting, fun, and filled with laughter. The old Tammy, optimistic and determined was beginning to emerge again. Each day, her goal became more and more reachable. As she had decided, nothing would stand in her way of staying clean, not even Harry. They all exchange phone numbers and vow to keep in contact. Ms. Graham, her counselor, sits down with her and compliments her on her strength and determination to focus on what is most important in her life and her world. The next morning, she is taken to the Greyhound bus station to return home.

Today, California's weather is around 70 degrees F with dry and pleasant temperatures inland of the city. Commonly, wildflowers in a range of eye popping beautiful colors add touches of spring with each colorful bloom. Now, three months pregnant, Tammy thinks about the responsibilities of parenthood. Her grandparents, made sure the utilities were turned back on and sent Evelyn over to clean the place for her arrival back home. They didn't want her to come home to any reminders of drug abuse. Harry had come by numerous times; each time leaving a note on the doorway. Her sister Evelyn laid the notes on the coffee table. Evelyn picks Tammy up from the bus station. On their way to her house, Evelyn stops at a burger place, grabs a salad for Tammy and a burger combo for herself. Not saying much to Tammy on their drive home.

"What's this?" Tammy looks at the notes on the coffee table.

"You know what it is. He has come here looking for you." Tammy takes out an old shoe box and stuffs them in there.

"Girl this place was a mess...I had to let up the windows and air it out. I could barely stand it!...I cleaned those nasty slip covers and I cleaned up the place. You like it?" Tammy walks around the house.

"Yeah, looks and smells good." They sat down to eat.

"Sis, I don't want to get in your business. I'm not even going to ask you what happened. All I know, is...you're better than this." Tammy takes a bite out of her salad.

"I know, Sis."

"Any man, that gets you strung out on drugs and won't take care of his business is not worth fooling with." Tammy listens to her. "He's got no future, Sis!...If I can make it as a single parent...so can you."

"You know about the baby?"

"Yeah, I know everything." Evelyn says.

"I can't believe he did this to me."

"Hey, you're right. You have every right to be upset. But you have got to go on with your life, stay on your medications, eat right, and try to not be so stressed out." Tammy sloshes her drink around in her cup.

"I know...I've got to do whatever it takes to take care of me and the baby." Evelyn tilts her head sideways.

"Do you think going to school is wise...now?" Evelyn asks. Tammy lifts her head up quickly. "Yeah! Evelyn I have to. I can't stop because of this. There are plenty of people dead that had dreams and didn't act on them. Well guess what? I'm not one of them."

"I know, Tammy—but?"

"But what?...It's all good. I can do this. I just need your support." Evelyn looks at her and smiles.

"Are you going to allow Harry to be in your baby's life?"

"No! I don't want to see Harry. If I had seen him a couple of weeks ago, I probably would have killed him."

"Girl I know what you mean. I don't know what I would have done."

"Well the doctor told me that people are living longer with the medications. As long as I take them and eat right, me and my baby will be fine."

"See, that's what I'm talking about...Tammy. Is school going to be too much for you?"

"Hey Sis,"...she slams down her fork. "Who's going to take care of me and my baby? I lost three babies already, and I can't lose this one. I can manage. Black women are strong. Look what they came through back in the day." Evelyn whips her head with attitude.

"Yeah...but." Tammy covers her ears with her hands.

"No butt's, I have to make my dream of becoming a caterer come true. Besides, they make good money. Me and my child can make it off of that kind of salary. Now, I may need you to baby sit sometimes. Could you help me with that?" Evelyn looks steady into her eyes.

"Girl you know I will. What about your job?" Tammy's eyes get wide.

"I need to call Mr. Schmidt. He said for me to call him after treatment and he will let me know if I still have a job. He said he would put me on prep work for the kitchen."

"Well, that would be easier but you would still have to stand a lot. What about when you get closer to delivery?"

"I just have to work up until that time. I have no other choices."

There's silence, while Tammy gazes into her almost finished salad.

"I hate him?"

"Who?" Evelyn asks.

"Harry!"

"Yeah...well he has jacked up your life. Although he has been a negative influence on you, you're going to have to forgive him."

"I can't forgive him. He has jeopardized not only my life but possibly our baby's life."

"Have you thought about asking God to help you?"

"Help me do what?"

"Forgive him."

"Hey, I can handle this. Do you think God likes what he did to me?"

"Tammy you're going to have to work your 12 steps. If not, you may end up right back using."

"No I won't!" Tammy gets up and gets a glass of water.

"Okay…Ms. know it all, I'm serious."

"From now on, I'm going to focus on doing what's best for me, case closed." Evelyn gets up and throws her burger sack into the trash.

"Okay, if you need anything call me," she walks over and hugs Tammy. "Oh, by the way"…she opens up the refrigerator. "Madea and Papa gave me some money to buy you some groceries. And here's $5.00 for bus fare, you're set," she lays the money on the table.

"I love you…bye!" Evelyn closes the door. Tammy gets up and turns on the television, then goes back to the table to finish her salad. There's a faint knock at the door.

"Who is it?" she says.

With her eyes wide and staring at the door, she doesn't say anything.

"Tammy, C'mon, it's me … Harry!" She sighs.

"Open the door!"

She throws her napkin unto the table and storms to the front door, opening it, she stands there with her hand on her hip.

"What do you want?"

"Hey baby!"

"Don't 'hey, baby' me!" she pushes him and they get into a scuffle. He tries to push her off of him. Then there's a cry… "Ump"…she catches her stomach and bends over.

"Girl…what's wrong with you?"

"Just leave me alone," she screams.

Harry had gone on another drug binge. He has lost a lot of weight and didn't look like himself. Tammy manages to catch her balance. "Look at you!" she sneers at him. "You look awful. No better for you, you @##&%$$."

"Hey, hey, hey…what's this about?"

"I tell you what this is about!…You gave me HIV and I'm three months pregnant."

"Woman you are lying!"

"Would I lie about something like that Harry?" In shock, he leans up against her sofa.

"I want you to get off of my sofa!" she tries to grab him. "Ain't no telling what you have picked up," angrily, she says.

"Hey would you please stop tripping?"

"It's bad enough you are a junkie but you just had to infect me."

"Well, maybe you gave it to me," he yells back.

"Man, you know what? I'm not going to have this discussion with you. That's %#@$*$# and you know it. I have not slept with anyone in three years…but you. You #@&&%%##, you are a loser! Just get out of my house, I don't ever want to $#@$&%%$* see you again. I hate you!"

"What about the baby?"

"The baby doesn't have a father!…Now get out of my house!" she pushes him outside, slamming the door behind him. She plops down on the sofa and tries to refrain from crying. Then she turns the television up loud. Later that evening, she falls asleep on the sofa. The next morning, she takes the bus to see Ms. Williams and spends an hour with her, discussing her goals before she leaves Ms. Williams' office to enroll in intensive outpatient treatment on weekends. Ms. Williams gives her a bus pass. By the end of the day, she had met her first goal, along with signing up for social service assistance.

When she arrived in, she calls Mr. Schmidt and askd if he had made his decision. He told her that since she had kept her word and completed treatment he would give her one more chance. She would help the cooks by doing prep work and making sure the orders were delivered on time. He would also allow her to sit down and work, only when she needed to. However, he cut her hours to part-time, twenty five hours per week. *How would she pay for her HIV medications?* she thought to herself. *Hopefully she could get approved for some assistance,* she thinks too herself. She would talk more with Ms. Williams about this. That evening she calls Madea to let her know she was okay.

"Hey baby, how are you?"

"I feel okay. I had to runs some errands today. I enrolled in out-patient treatment and applied for (SSI) Supplemental Security Income, Medicaid, and food stamps. With my short hours I should qualify for it."

"Short hours, what do you mean?"

"Mr. Schmidt gave me my job back, but cut my hours."

"Well, I guess we can be grateful that he didn't fire you."

"I know. Maybe since I don't have insurance, I can qualify for the Aids Drug Assistance Program? It's a grant that provides assistance with payments and co-payments on my anti-retroviral medicines."

"Baby, all that sounds good. You've been taking care of your business today. I'm glad to hear that. How long have you been clean for now?"

"About five weeks"

"That's good, Papa will be happy to hear that. Did you get his letter?"

"Yes ma'am, it made me feel so good when he sent it."

"Well, we're behind you."

"Thank you! Madea."

"When do you go back to work?"

"He wants me to come back on Friday."

"Do you think you'll be up to it?"

"Honestly, I really don't know, but I have no other choice."

"Well baby, why don't you give your body more time to rest before you go back? I'm sure he'll understand."

"Madea, with so many people out of work, I don't want to lose this job. You know how hard a time I had finding work. All those interviews I went on and everyone turned me down, because I'm an ex offender."

"Yeah, baby, I know. Well, don't over stress yourself."

"I won't, I promise."

She then calls the culinary school to let them know she will be attending classes in the the spring semester of next year and to find out whatever else information she needed to know.

The next morning she goes to see her prenatal care doctor, a referral from Ms. Williams.

Her daily regimen requires taking 300mg of AZT two times a day for her HIV, a multi-care approach is needed for her to have a healthy pregnancy and delivery. It will address her medical, psychological, social and pregnancy challenges with the disease. Her pregnancy is managed by an experienced obstetrician-gynecologist and an HIV specialist. It is this team effort that will provide the best prenatal care plan for her lifestyle.

Tammy goes back to work and is greeted by Mr. Schmidt who was on his way out. He calls her back into his office to speak with her privately. "Tammy, are you sure that you will be able to work?"

"Yes Sir."

"What are your plans?"

"I don't understand," she said.

"Are you planning to work up until you have the baby?"

"Yes!"

"I need to get something off my chest with no offense to you. I believed in you and trusted you. That trust has been severely damaged. I want you to know that."

"Yes sir," her facial expression changes to sadness. "I"…he interrupts her… "I'm not finished. I only allowed you to come back because I know it's hard right now for you and you were a good worker. But this cannot and will not happen again. If I even suspect that you are using, I will fire you and you will not be allowed to come back. Am I clear?"

"Yes!"

"As I informed you last month, you no longer will be cooking but will be helping with the prep work and at times making sure the orders are delivered on time. Your shift starts at 9:00am and ends at 2:00pm. You're part time and will cover the lunch shift. If you need to sit down, I don't have a problem with that. But I do expect you do a good job. I had to hire a replacement head cook/manager because Peter found another position."

"Where did he go?"

"He went to an upscale trendy restaurant. So, I expect you to work well with your new manager." Even though he was congenial, she knew he had become detached and their once, easy going relationship has been damaged beyond repair. He walks her to the kitchen area to meet the new head cook.

"Dustin this is Tammy."

"Hello Tammy, nice to meet you!" he extends out his hand to her. "I understand you will be helping us out with the prep work?"

"Yes sir."

"Well, as long as you do what you're supposed to do, everything will be fine," he says.

Already she felt a dislike for him. He appeared not to be as friendly as Peter, and to top it off, a couple of her co-workers had left or had been fired. There were new people that she would be working with. Mr. Schmidt walks toward the front entrance and leaves.

While chopping vegetables, she notices Dustin going into a rage with a co-worker. *Boy, I hope he doesn't start messing with me,* she mumbles to herself. One of the new employees had dropped a crate of oranges and Dustin goes off on him. An hour later, Dustin comes over to her station, "Tammy is there anything you need?" Not looking at him, with a trembling lip—she said, "No I'm fine, but thank you for asking." Later that afternoon, he chews her out, for being three minutes late from her break. Not only was he rude and too direct, she suspected he was bipolar.

Tammy couldn't wait for 2:00 o'clock to get there. Tired, and ready to go home as she walked out the front door, she noticed Harry sitting in the car waiting for her. She walks pass him in a hurry.

"Hey, Tammy, C'mon, please talk to me!" She doesn't say anything, nor does she look back. She walks faster. He gets into his car and pulls up near the bus stop. When she arrives at the bus stop, she throws up her hand.

"Hey Harry, let me tell you something. You have messed up my life and I can't forgive you for that. I don't need you. I can't stand the sight of you. As far as I'm concern, I never knew you. I let you come into my home and life and this is how you repay me." He moves closer toward her, "Tammy, I didn't know I had it! Do you think I would have done this to you on purpose?"

"Yeah, I believe it! Just get out of my face," she yells while pushing him away from her. Her facial expression turns into a full snarl and she gazes at him for a long time. He steps back and walks away.

"You need to go and get yourself checked out," she yells out to him as he walks away.

Two weeks later, at work, while on her break, she had begun to have fainting spells and was feeling weak. Not wanting to say anything, she kept quiet about it, fearing she would lose her job. The following week, she was tested for anemia at her very first prenatal visit. Anemia is an iron deficiency in your body. She had been unable to eat well because of constant nausea and vomiting. Her health care provider advised her to take an iron supplement and to try and bring her iron levels up to what they should be by eating healthier and taking iron supplements daily. Likewise, she's now having to have regular evaluations and appropriate prophylaxis for opportunistic infections (OIs) as well as vaccinations for people with the HIV infection (e.g., pneumococcal vaccination) and other evaluations and support measures through-out her pregnancy.

That afternoon, she catches the bus to another intensive outpatient treatment session.

Every weekend, different activities are done to engage the group; one-on-one counseling, group therapy and educational activities that include films, reading, speakers and homework assignments. In addition, she has to get a signature from the group leader to prove her attendance at every session.

This particular session, she's having problems identifying and discussing her feelings of shame and guilt, associated with her drug use. Everything she learned in Arkansas, she was having a hard time applying to her circumstances. Depressed all the time, her mornings were filled with dread for her life, her job, her health and for her baby. In her 12-step meeting group, she just couldn't seem to apply the steps.

It was as if—she had been going through the motions to appease her counselor. But within her heart, she wasn't living out her steps. It was a long night physically and emotionally for her. At the end of each meeting, occasionally, someone from the group would take her home. If not, then she would catch the bus and pray that she makes it home safely. Sometimes, on her way home, she thinks about her baby and how she will support him or her.

That night she gets a phone call from Harry.

"Tammy, can I come by and see you?" She hangs up the phone. He calls back. She lets the phone ring. He calls her thirty times and she doesn't answer. The next day, after work, she goes for her HIV monitoring. Her doctor tells her that she needs to continue to come in for doctor's visits, to be on the safe side of things.

Several days later, when she arrives at work, she walks into the usually crowded and overheated kitchen. Her day starts off by chopping, slicing and cutting ingredients. The shift is fast-paced and hectic, so she assembles her salads in advance for the lunch shift. It is brought to her attention, she made a mistake on an inventory order, a miscalculation on the amount of food they needed. Dustin confronts her about it.

"Tammy, I am giving you more responsibilities to see how you can handle them. I noticed you've made a mistake on this order. I have enough responsibilities that I have to deal with, without having to back tract and check your work. Either you can do the job or not. And if you can't, then maybe you need to find another job." Nervously she continues to work...

"Dustin, I'm sorry! This won't happen again I promise."

His body was erect, and thrust forward.

"It better not!"...he storms off.

The next day, Tammy had a doctor's appointment. Her doctor detected something unusual about her ultrasound. She was referred to a screening test for diagnostic testing and will be referred to genetic counseling. This will provide insight about potential hereditary birth defects. Her stress level is so high at work that it is affecting her physical and mental health. Her doctor makes an appointment for her to see a specialty doctor.

Back at work, throughout the day she is nervous that Dustin will bring something else to her attention. He ran the kitchen with his emotions on his sleeve. So his decisions weren't always the best. He has a problem with other people's faults and she tries to avoid him as much as possible. As she preps the food, she thinks to herself...*God I really need this little job.* Her lower back is bothering her, she constantly complains about it. It's a pain that can be associated with sciatic nerve pain, when there is pressure from the growing baby on the nerves in the back, characterized by pain in the lower back and down the leg, often making sitting or even standing very difficult. Temporarily for now, she has to take a specific pain medication prescribed by her doctor. She stops for a moment to rest. Dustin yells out to her,

"C' mon, Tammy let's go!" he then walks over to her and screams at her for not monitoring the soups.

Chapter 5

A BREAK IS needed, so she steps out to the ladies bathroom and sees Harry sitting in one of the booths. He looked as if he had a runny nose, and he was sweaty looking. One look at him, and she knew he had been using. He signaled for her to come to him. But she pretended not to see him. She closes the bathroom door.

"What is he doing here? He's going to get me fired!" In one of the bathroom stalls, she sits there for five minutes with her head in between her knees. Then stands up and rubs the side of her stomach and walks out. She washes and dries her hands before heading back to her station. Harry calls out her name, and then gets up to meet her. He grabs her by the arm and tries to pull her back into the restroom area.

"Harry, let me go!" she scuffles with him. "What are you doing?" she said.

"Tammy, I just want to talk with you. Would you please listen?" She snatches her arm away.

"I don't have anything to say to you, and if you don't leave, I will have someone to call the police!" she looks at him with hatred in her eyes.

"Okay, fine…if that's the way you want it—fine," he goes back to his table and takes a sip from his glass of water and leaves. One of the new waitresses saw what had happened and later tells Dustin about it.

At the end of the day, Tammy stores her shift leftover food ingredients and begins cleaning up her area to leave. Dustin yells out to her.

"Tammy, come see me before you go." She walks over to him while he was talking to two other staff workers.

He stops and says to her, "I don't know where you're going when you disappear. But we need you at your station at all times."

With her elbows drawn into her side, she tells him, "Dustin, sometimes I have to go to the ladies room." His face turns red.

"Well, I can understand that, but it shouldn't take you that long." She's trying to hold her temper.

"Frankly to be honest…Tammy, I think you're lazy and inconsiderate." He looks at her, waiting for her to say something.

"Jana told me that you were out in the restaurant area with your boyfriend…that's unacceptable, especially while you're working." Her mouth gasps open from shock, angry that the waitress told on her.

"Dustin, he's not my boyfriend any longer, and I didn't know he was out there, until I went to the ladies room."

Not paying any attention to what she just said, he says, " Jana also tells me that he looked as if he was on something."

"What? What does she know? She's all up in my business!"

"Well, I'm just telling you, this won't happen again," he walks away.

Tammy runs out of the restaurant and runs to the bus stop. When she arrives home she calls her grandmother.

"Madea it's me," her eyes tears up.

"Yes baby! What's wrong?" The emotional pain was intense; she starts wailing and couldn't talk for a minute.

"My new boss is making it so hard for me to work there."

"Well baby, you should have known that. Right now you're walking on egg shells. He's probably trying to find any little thing against you to fire you. Those jobs are a dime a dozen. He can get someone to replace you easily."

Tammy blows her nose.

"Madea, I'm so tired. It feels like a truck has run over me. My lower back is bothering me, and I have to stand and walk constantly. My morning sickness makes me sick all the time and Harry is showing up at my job and at the bus stop."

"What?" Madea is surprised. "What does he want?"

"I don't know. I told him it was over, but he keeps coming around. I can't stand him. Then this old witch on the job, one of the new waitresses, went back and told my new manager that I was out in the dining room with Harry and wasn't working."

"Well, baby, you have one of two choices. You can stay and put up with it, or you can look for another job. That's a long time to be dealing with pettiness. Your schooling is for nine months...right?"

Tammy groans.

"Yes ma'am. Madea...who's going to hire me? Especially since this man has knocked me up."

"I'm pretty sure there is something out there for you. But, can you handle all that job searching on the bus in your condition?"

Tammy lifts her voice, "I don't know—I'm so depressed right now."

"Well, baby, don't be depressed. Things are not what you expected but hang in there."

"Okay...I love you," Tammy says.

"I love you too."

Afterwards, she takes a hot bath and relaxes on the sofa. The phone rings.

It's Harry, "Tammy before you hang up, I need to say, I'm sorry." She slams the phone down. It rings again. This time, she lets it ring. He calls again; she answers.

"Tammy I'm in really big trouble, can you help me?" She hangs up. *Was her 12 step meeting doing her any good?* she thought. Her negative emotions: anger, resentment and bitterness, toward him and even now her supervisor, was starting to get to her. With the remote control in hand, she turns the television up and falls asleep.

The next morning, she goes to see her doctor about her baby's health. On her last visit she learned her baby may have Down's syndrome. Her doctor informed her of a new, safer method of testing that has been developed to allow mothers to screen their baby for Down's syndrome, as well as Trisomy 18, in the first trimester. It is known as the "Combined First-Trimester Screening" (CFTS), a prenatal assessment test involving examining a sample of the maternal blood for specific proteins and hormones. Also, the ultrasound or sonogram images of the fetus are analyzed to determine the thickness of skin on the back of the baby's neck, thereby eliminating almost all risk to mother and child. The assessment confirms her fears.

Not only does she have HIV but her child is now subject to Down's syndrome. On her way to work she is silent. Thoughts are racing through her mind. It was devastating to hear that her baby has potential for Down syndrome. *Her world really was turned upside down*, she thought as she ponders her feelings of embarrassment and shame.

At work, her pelvic pains are happening suddenly. Tammy had noticed that she is experiencing episodes of bleeding and spotting during her pregnancy, especially common in the first trimester. However, she's worried and concerned about the baby's health. The manual work at her job is too much. Sometimes, she has to unpack and stock ingredients when they arrive, besides her normal prep work. The bending and the hectic pace of the job is getting to her. She doesn't know how much longer she can stand it.

Several weeks later, she and another employee disagree on the way a customer situation should have been handled. The employee tells Dustin about it, and he reprimands Tammy in front of other employees. The employees had witnessed Dustin throwing tantrums with wide eyes and gapping mouths over the last couple of weeks. Yet today, she's so upset she leaves early from work in fear of going off on him. When she arrives home, she finds Harry had left six red heart-shaped helium-filled Mylar balloons. Each one had a message of "I love you" written on them. The balloons are taken and released into the air. "I don't want anything from him," she opens her front door and slams it.

Now in the second half of her pregnancy, she developed what's called pregnancy induced hypertension characterized by high blood pressure, fluid retention and protein in her urine. Her doctor is trying to keep it from developing into HELLP syndrome (the breakdown of her red blood cells in the body). A serious case could restrict blood flow to the placenta. Should the blood flow to the placenta be restricted it could seriously harm her baby. Her body had begun to experience severe swelling in her hands, face, and unexplained headaches, fever, stomach pain and itching were becoming a problem. The doctor suggested to her to reduce her blood pressure by getting plenty of rest (on her days off), eating a proper diet, exercising, and work on getting the stress out of her life. *Should I keep my job? If, I quit the job how would I take care of myself*, she thought. The thought of applying for and getting housing assistance was appealing but she dreaded going through the red tape and the waiting period.

When she goes into work, Jana always finds something about her work to report to Dustin. It was always about Tammy's work, never anything good, always bad—any and every slight mistake. It got so bad that he would come and stand over her while she worked. Humiliated and angry, still—she didn't want to give him an opportunity to fire her. He loved to fly off the handle and berate her and others for any minor offense. At times, he was immature. He gossiped about customers and employees, and here he was supposedly in a management position. She was stuck. Every day, it seemed clearer that her job was on the line and she didn't know what to do about it. But she had to stay because she hasn't been offered a position elsewhere and can't afford to not have an income. Mr. Schmidt only came in on paydays to distribute the pay checks, and she couldn't talk to him. If nothing else, he liked the freedom of not being there and Dustin made that possible.

That night, she decides to eat something light and go right to bed. Thirty minutes later she could hear the engine of a car pulling up in front of her home. She sits up in the bed and leans forward to listen. The car engine cuts off. Curiously, she gets up and goes to the window. The curtains are slowly pushed back, trying not to be seen. It is Harry's car parked out front. Immediately, she makes her way to the phone on the night stand and calls the police. Within twenty minutes they show up but Harry's gone. They knock on her door, and she tells them that someone was parked outside of her home. Fearing that maybe he had a warrant out for his arrest, she wouldn't specifically identify him or give his name. She just wanted to scare him away from her home. He was popping up all over the place. He watched her at home, at work or when she would get out walking to the store. He always seemed to turn up unexpectedly.

At her meetings, she feels she's losing the battle in her anger toward Harry. Resentment and bitterness has ensnared her. She tells her group that she doesn't know how to break free of it, knowing her resentment is not good for her or the baby. On the other hand, she had developed deep-seated hatred for Harry. That couldn't be denied. All men in her age group were whores, and dogs, with no respect for themselves. Not capable of being a man or wanting to take responsibility for being one, they were simply bent on using women and taking everything they could get from them with no considerations for women's feelings. They would sleep with anyone, and were capable of doing anything—scrupulous and low down. Her 12 step group leader tells her he will work extensively with her to offer support and guidance for her anger management issues. A few days later, she gets a call from Harry's grandfather, Mr. Wilkerson.

"Tammy"

"Yes sir"

"Harry asked me to call you. He wanted to know how you and the baby were doing."

"We're okay," she says..

"Harry was severely stabbed this past weekend with multiple stab wounds. He was rushed into surgery where his condition was stabilized. That boy got into an altercation with one of those drug dealers.

Luckily, someone found him. He was walking alone down the street barely making it. His car was impounded, and I had to go get it out." Tammy doesn't say anything.

"Has he gotten treatment for his HIV virus?" she asks.

"He's on some type of medication for it. I think that's what sent him over the edge. I told that boy years ago that he needed to leave those drugs alone. I'm going to, try to talk him into treatment again, this will be his fifth time going…you know."

"I didn't know that."

"Well, he needs to go. I'm not going to hold you long. But he wants you to come down to the hospital to see him. He wants to talk with you."

"Mr. Wilkerson, I'm sorry. But I can't do that."

"Okay, I'll let him know." When she hangs up, she thinks about how her baby will have two parents that are HIV infected and how their lives would be different.

Mr. Wilkerson goes to see him at the hospital. He talks to Harry about his drug issues, and Harry tells him a secret that has plagued him for years, the molestation by his step father. Mr. Wilkerson was shocked and couldn't believe it. Harry tells him about the flashbacks and how he has used drugs to block the pain. *Mr. Wilkerson sits down next to him and tells him that just because it happen, this doesn't make him gay.* "Son, until you come to terms with this personally yourself, you will continue down the same destructive road you have lived. You need to make the decision to change your life. There is a baby on the way, and it's no longer about you and Tammy. You have to be everything that you didn't have. What you missed from your parents, you can learn to give to your child. Therefore, you need to get mental counseling and drug treatment, and this time, try to make it work."

His grandfather talks to his doctor and learns that healthcare regulations require that intravenous drug users on a waiting list for drug treatment, receive interim services within forty eight hours of requesting them. Interim services must include referrals to HIV healthcare services as well as HIV counseling, and in treatment he will be offered a pneumococcal polysaccharide vaccine. Harry and his grandfather make arrangements for his treatment.

The next day at work, Tammy monitors the temperature of food at regular intervals. For a moment she thinks about her life situation. No benefits, and her low part time salary will not support her needs. She needs to buy a car soon. But doesn't know how she's going to do it even though the public transit system has helped her to get around. *"What if there is an emergency? I can't depend on the bus or anyone else for that matter,"* she thought to herself. And of course, she's too tired to look for something else, especially while dealing with a complicated pregnancy.

Dustin shouts out at her, "Tammy help out with chopping food for the other cooks."

Slowly, she walks back to her area and begins chopping up the chickens. She didn't want to argue with him or anyone. There was a lot on her mind.

Jana comes into the kitchen area and makes a remark about the salads that Tammy had made earlier. She said a customer wasn't happy with his salad. Jana would not call out the specific name of the person, but hinted it was Tammy. Tammy overheard her conversation with the cook, and trying not say anything, she ignored her. In essence, she had become the object of Jana's unhealthy interest. Days and weeks have passed by, and she came to the conclusion that Jana was a person with dysfunctional behavior. Tammy started doubting herself and her work, wondering whether if she had done something wrong or could at least be partially to blame for Jana's hatred toward her. Most of the time, Jana didn't need anything to get her going, always in everyone's business, most knew she was a busybody. They all knew that Jana brown nosed Dustin. After all, he was the one that hired her. It had been rumored that Jana was sleeping with him because he showed more favoritism for her than any of the employees.

This time, Tammy was determined to be firm and to fight for her dignity. She is going to be aggressive in confronting the bully, by being assertive and making it clear that Jana needs to focus on her job and stay out of everyone else's business. Tammy confronts her,

"Jana, I overheard you talking with Steve about the salads I made this morning."

"Oh you made the salads, well there was a customer who complained that the quality of the lettuce wasn't good, and that it didn't have the usual amount of condiments on it."

"Jana, every day you have something to say about someone. You're always in my business and everyone else around here, and I'm sick of it."

Jana tries to bully her physically by standing too close in a threatening manner. Tammy pushes her off of her.

"Who cares about what you feel," Jana said.

"Girl, you're messing with the wrong person. I'll mop this floor with you," Tammy says. One of the cooks run over to separate them. The cook tells Jana to leave from the kitchen and for Tammy to take a walk to cool off. That afternoon, Dustin wants to terminate her before her six month probation period. He has reprimanded her before, he claims, for her not doing her job right. She wished she had been more alert and kept a diary of events the small incidents that had built up to bigger ones. Instead of going for a walk, Tammy calls Mr. Schmidt and informs him. He said he would take care of it. She didn't know if he was on her side or if he too wanted her fired.

That evening at home, she tries to unwind from the day stresses. Harry has gone into a one year residential treatment program where he receives around-the-clock care in a distraction and temptation-free environment. His focus is solely recovery. He calls Tammy and gets her answering machine. He leaves a message that he was in treatment. In short, he is disappointed that she didn't come to see about him when he was in the hospital. Then he goes on to say, a letter was sent to her apologizing for the hurt he has caused her and how he wanted to be a part of her and the baby's life.

He had begun to send her letters occasionally, expressing his struggles with his inner demons and his thoughts about his progress. But Tammy didn't care. She had washed her hands with him. *The further he stays away from me the better*, she thought.

The next morning at work, Mr. Schmidt shows up and has a meeting with the entire staff.

He starts the meeting off with the incident that happen with Tammy and Jana. He explains how the staff needs to cultivate an atmosphere of teamwork. "Instead of focusing too much on individual achievements, give emphasis on team achievements. This way you'll realize that you need each other to be successful," he said. He developed a policy that does not tolerate office bickering, quarreling, and disrespect to one's co-workers. He takes both Tammy and Jana into his office and says… "If this happens again I will let you both go." He knew Tammy was a good worker and that she really was trying to do what was right. Therefore, he wouldn't fire her.

But even after implementing Mr. Schmidt new policy, and his talking with the staff, when he wasn't there, nothing had changed, partly, because Dustin didn't care. About the six month of her pregnancy, she realizes the place was going downhill. She no longer felt comfortable in her workplace culture. She joined the company when it was fun, laid back, and when she could be herself. The environment has changed to an uncaring and sloppy work place. A war zone between co-workers, everyone was afraid of losing their jobs. And would do or say whatever it took to promote themselves at anyone's expense.

Each morning, when she gets up, she's filled with dread and emotional distress. As she turns off the alarm clock, she sits on the bed, staring onto the floor. Often, she lies back down and sleeps for an extra ten minutes and then forces herself to get up and get dressed. Her boss curses, yells, and threatens everyone. Some of her co-workers are just as worst. The behaviors are draining her emotionally. There is no one whom she can talk to, that would understand the intensity of her depression. She has gone to intensive outpatient treatment meetings faithfully. Yet—still, she struggles with her emotions.

Several weeks later, around the eight month of her pregnancy, she has a talk with Mr. Schmidt. He agrees to give her some time off to have the baby. The last couple of days she has had false labor pains and no longer could take the bus back and forth to work. She has been clean seven months, and he was impressed with her. He gives her ten weeks off, with the option of returning, one month after the baby is born. Even though she enjoys not having to get up, she will have no money coming in for those ten weeks. And at home, after one week, her days are filled with boredom. She tries to read baby books and eat healthy to pass the time. She goes for walks in her neighborhood for exercise but not too far from home. Madea and Evelyn make frequent stopovers to check on her and to see how she's doing.

This weekend Evelyn takes Tammy and her girls to Tanaka Farms in Orange County for a strawberry tour and to pick up a pound of organically grown strawberries. They spent half the day out there in hopes of getting Tammy out of the house. Tammy stops by the produce stand to buy other fruits and vegetables that the farm produces. No longer could she think about herself, as she and the baby needed to have a healthy lifestyle, which meant healthy foods in the house. By her ninth month of pregnancy, she was tired of carrying the baby, and she wanted to get it over with. Her baby wasn't due until the end of November. Still, she knew from her other pregnancies that anything could happen. Upon her return home late that evening she felt what seemed like labor pains back to back-again. She doesn't eat any food, or have any liquids, instead takes a long bath. It will be a while before she can bathe again. As she tries to get out of the tub, she thinks about her long hospital stay because of the C-section delivery.

It's the fall season with its glorious sunny wintery days. A time when the rainy seasons can make Los Angeles look more like a rain forest, but after it rains, the skies are sometimes exceptionally clear. Now, the middle of November her labor pains are getting sharper and sharper. Tammy is sitting on the sofa watching TV and had begun to feel labor pains mostly in her lower abdominal area, manifesting as low back pain, as her uterus began to contract more intensely. She turns the television off and listens to the sounds of raindrops.

Tonight, there was something about the pureness of the pitter-patter of rain. It was soothing, aesthetic, and pleasantly distinctive. It helped somewhat to soothe her pain. But then her labor pains had begun to progress. She calls her sister, who takes her to the hospital. In order to be awake for the baby, she wanted an epidural. It has been many years since her last pregnancy. Nothing had changed with the delivery method of having a baby; the intense pain that accompanies labor was all too familiar. Though, after all these years, it was still painful.

The upper part of her uterus muscles started to contract. Her contractions are every five minutes, then every three minute, and then every 2 minutes. Pressure and pain are coming more frequently now. Tammy's taken to the operating room and given an epidural to numb the lower half of her body. A catheter is inserted into her bladder so that it can drain, and an IV is also put in her arm to keep her energized.

Ten minutes after the surgery begins her baby boy is born. But there is something wrong. The nurse takes the baby. Tammy is faced with her own dire situation; first her due date was not accurately calculated, the baby was delivered too early. Her blood loss was twice as much with the cesarean birth as with a traditional birth, and then she had a reaction to the anesthesia. Her health was endangered by an unexpected response, her blood pressure. It dropped quickly from respiratory complications. When it dropped to 80/25 the doctors and anesthesiologists were concerned.

In the same way, she has also developed an infection. Her kidney and bladder became infected during the c-section. Her doctor was trying to keep the infection from spreading to her bloodstream and becoming life-threatening. He had a kidney function test done and it revealed she had developed "Sepsis" she's taken immediately to the intensive care unit (ICU).

Antibiotics were administered through a vein for the infection and medications were used to increase her blood pressure. He wanted her monitored up close until her temperature returned to normal and she no longer had any symptoms. Not only was she fighting for her life, it was learned, that with her cesarean delivery, her baby developed abnormal fast breathing problems after his birth that possibly would continued for the first few days thereafter. The baby was taken to be monitored for a couple of hours and then released to the maternity ward.

The doctor informs Evelyn about Tammy's and the baby's health, and she calls Madea and Mr. Wilkerson. Harry had a pass from the treatment facility and had been at his grandfather's for a couple of hours. Tammy's grandparents drive to the hospital. When Harry and his grandfather arrived at the hospital he was ecstatic. He had been clean for thirty days and looked good. He had picked his weight up, and his face looked healthy for a change. Mr. Wilkerson kept in touch with Tammy regularly and thought it was best for his grandson to see his first child.

Harry goes to see the baby and was told by Evelyn that some problems had occurred with Tammy and that the baby was diagnoised with Down syndrome. "What does that mean," he asks angrily. "I think it means the baby will have some developmental issues, and he may not live to be normal," Evelyn said. He holds the baby and starts to cry while kissing him on its forehead. It's a day he will never forget. His emotions were overwhelming. Evelyn thought he would pass out. The first words that came out of his mouth were, "He's my son. Oh my God I'm a father." He had thought about it, and he wanted him and Tammy to take a newborn care and CPR class together. They both needed to learn the details of what is and is not safe for the baby, how to prevent household accidents, and how to do emergency procedures if necessary. But he knew she would never agree to it.

When Tammy's grandparents arrived, they learned they couldn't see Tammy. They decided they would spend the night at the hospital, each one taking turns staying until she was stabilized. Harry had gone into the chapel to pray for Tammy and the baby. He walked in and stood at the doorway. He slowly made his way down to the front and kneels before God's alter. "Oh God!" He pauses because he feels uncomfortable. "I know I have not been a good person, all this time. But I'm asking you to do me this big favor. Would you please allow Tammy and our baby to make it and have a healthy life?"

He sits there silently. Back in the waiting room while talking to Madea, Evelyn tells her that Harry was there. Madea doesn't say anything. Then she asks, "Where is he?" Evelyn picks up a magazine to read. "I don't know," Evelyn says. Mr. Wilkerson walks by and introduces himself. Evelyn ask him where was Harry. He tells her, he may be in the chapel. "I have a good mind to say something to Harry,"...Madea said. "But the less I say, the less I have to repent for. It's best for me not to see him or speak to him."

Hours pass and Madea decides to go to the ladies room. On her way back, she asks the guard where the chapel was and he points her in its direction. As she entered the Chapel, her eyes were drawn up to the stained glass window, rich smoldering blues, greens and its brilliant touches of reds, oranges, gold's and whites. There she sees Harry, sitting on one of the church pews. She walks out quietly and heads back to the waiting room. An hour later, Harry walks back to the waiting room and sees who he thinks is the woman that Tammy lovingly talks about. He walks over to her and introduces himself. He extends his hand to Madea and she looks at him, but she refuses to shake his hand. In sensing her anger toward him, he sits down next to his grandfather, and they decide to leave. They part with good byes and he is taken back to the treatment facility that morning. Every day he calls to speak with Evelyn to learn the progress of Tammy and the baby.

Four days later, Tammy and the baby are released to go home. She had decided on the name "Ethan" for the baby. The first couple of days she is feeling a bit sad and let down. Weepiness, mood swings and irritability are her emotions. Within the first two weeks, she was on an emotional roller coaster. When she finds herself down, it's sudden and out of the blue, usually attributed to the sudden, quick change in her hormones.

The emotional and physical stress of giving birth along with any general physical discomfort was enough to keep her in bed. However, when awake she looks at baby "Ethan" as he sleeps, placing her finger inside his and gently wiggles it. The first couple of days after spending time with the baby were confusing, frightening, and overwhelming.

She didn't have a clue on how to cope with a special needs baby. Whispering to herself, as she rubs the baby's little head.... *God I don't know what to expect. How would I care for him the right way?* She has conflicting emotions. She loves little Ethan but having a Down syndrome baby was not what she expected. All three of her kids had turned out healthy. But this time, it is an experience that she doesn't know how to handle.

At home, she takes her pain medication to help ease the pain of her c-section delivery, along with periodically taking walks to speed up the healing process. Everything she needs for her and the baby are kept within arm's reach in her bedroom; extra set of diapers, wipes, clothes, paper plates, cups, and nutritional snacks. Evelyn and Madea take turns coming over on certain days and helps with grocery shopping, washing clothes, fixing meals, and visiting the baby, while Tammy takes care of her personal hygiene or when she needs to nap. Most of her days are spent resting when she can after taking care of the baby.

The phone rings and it's Harry. Evelyn answers and lets her know he's on the line. "Tell him I'm asleep." Evelyn relays the message and he hangs up. She goes into Tammy's bedroom and sits on the bed. "Sis, did you feel like talking?" Evelyn asks. Tammy sits up and lays her head against the headboard. "Yeah, what's on your mind?" she pulls the covers up to her waist. "We thought we were going to lose you for a moment." Tammy yanks the comforter up further and looks at her. "Harry was so scared for you."

"So what,"…she yells out. "Harry, Harry, Harry…I'm so sick of hearing that name."

"Sis, when he held his son, he actually cried."

"Evelyn, I could care less about that man."

"He told me he's been clean for weeks, and he looked healthy."

"Hey, is there a reason you're telling me all of this?"

"You are so cold," Evelyn looks out the window.

"I'm your big sister and I want you to listen to me for a moment. He loves his baby, and maybe you too! Just consider allowing him to be a part of the baby's life. You and he now have a bond between the two of you and the baby's going to need his father." Tammy kicks her feet out from the end of the comforter.

"Yeah right, he's a junkie," Tammy says.

"He's clean. Give him a chance. How many men are walking around here, not even wanting to be in their child's life. Look at me! Look at my baby's daddy, that's all I'm saying. I am going to head out and Madea will be here tomorrow....Okay?"

"Okay...love you," Tammy said.

That evening, Madea called to tell her that a friend of hers from her church had sold them a small car for practically nothing. "Baby we couldn't afford to buy you a new car. But I think this one will work. Mrs. Green said that she has a Silver 4 door Subaru Impreza Outback that belonged to her deceased granddaughter, and she would sell the car to us." Tammy begins to cry. "Madea my prayers have been answered, when can I get the car?"

"I guess Evelyn would have to drive it over there and bring me back home."

"Well, I go back to work next week, and I would need it before then."

"Okay baby, Evelyn and I will work out the details. But just know, you have transportation."

"Thank you...Madea," she hangs up and goes back to sleep.

A few days later, on her first day back to work, feeling sad, and crying all the way to work, she wanted to turn back so badly because she felt she was abandoning Ethan. It really made her feel like a bad mother, even though he was safe with her grandmother. But that didn't stop her from thinking about him. Just this morning she observed her baby's first smile. And suddenly she was filled with love and joy for him. She needed to work, to be able to take care of him with no choice in the matter, being the sole provider.

That evening, when she gets in, she checks her mail box and there is another letter from Harry. He wanted her to know that he had been sober for a little over sixty days and that he was feeling better. He went on to say he came to the hospital to see her and the baby. And how he's so proud of her and wanted to express his love for them both. He tells her that he wants to make up for his mistakes and short comings. She reads the letter and puts it into her shoe box.

The next day she begins her day with breakfast; a yogurt-and-fruit smoothie, a bowl of oatmeal and scrambled eggs on whole-wheat toast. She has been working on changing her diet to eating healthier as much as possible; first, by starting with a good breakfast that will give her longer-lasting energy, and help keep her full longer. Her choice of breakfast will take longer to digest and offer her body more nutrition in the form of vitamins and minerals. She eats small meals throughout the day, and drinks lots of water to keep from dehydration when possible.

So much has happen since the last year. Today is her second day back to work, and it's the month of December. It starts with a brief meeting with Mr. Schmidt. He welcomed her back and congratulated her on her baby. She told him that she would be starting culinary school next month in January and she wanted to work the dinner shift so that she could attend daytime classes' fulltime. He agreed to it and decided that she would still work prep. But when there was an available cook position, he would allow her to apply and be considered.

She goes to her work station and begins to prepare the cold foods and shellfish, chopping food for use by other cooks, slicing meat, and constructing salads. Then as the deliveries came in, she had to receive them, store the food correctly, rotate stock to maintain freshness, and write out the orders. By 2:00pm she was tired, sluggish and wasn't up for anything, other than resting.

Dustin shamelessly asked her to stay late to finish writing up the orders with no notice.

When she said that she couldn't because she needed to pick up her baby, he went into a rage, slamming doors, and throwing objects around. On her drive to Madea's to pick up baby "Ethan" she had made up her mind that she was tired of his crap. When possible, she would start to look for work at a catering company.

His fury had no mercy on anyone. That same week, Dustin almost got into a fist-fight with a cook over nearly nothing. The argument happens in front of a customer, with Dustin cursing loudly at the cook. He later sent the cook home without pay. All of the people she had worked with previously were no longer there. The rumor was that Dustin would hire inexperienced new waitresses every week that would exchange sexual favors for their jobs. Even one of the waitresses that had befriended Tammy had let it slip that this was how she was hired. Tammy knew from her very first meeting with him that he was no good.

Today, Tammy takes the baby in to see his pediatrician for his first check up. The doctor checks the baby's weight and measurements to make sure he's growing at a healthy rate and to see if the cord stump has fallen off and the belly button is healing well. She examines his penis, and provides him with a hepatitis B shot. Tammy tells the doctor that the baby is having sucking and feeding problems and constipation. The doctor offers insight into his development, feeding, and sleeping habits. His eyesight and hearing are checked, and there is an evaluation of the red reflex of the eyes (red eye) to look for cataracts, and assess the eyes for strabismus or nystagmus. Then Tammy tells her that the baby has a wandering of one or both eyes at times. The doctor refers her to a pediatric ophthalmologist, experienced in dealing with children disabilities. The doctor wanted his eyes looked at from a specialist and tells her that the baby needs to see this particular doctor before six months of age.

"Regular follow up's every one to two years will be needed." The doctor goes on to say, that getting regular eye exams is very important in children with Down syndrome because eye disorders are so common and are difficult for the pediatrician to diagnose. Glasses will help his vision and possibly the eye alignment in the development of normal vision pathways in the brain. This will help her child with his learning and functioning. The doctor inquires when, how, and how often is her baby eating? She was trying to determine if her baby is getting enough formula to thrive and to see if Tammy has any concerns about feeding. She discusses with Tammy her findings.

As Tammy sits in a chair, while he's being examined, the doctor talks to her about Down syndrome children. "Ms. Brown, I want you to understand that even though your baby was born with an average size, he will grow slowly and remain smaller than other children of the same age, and this is a common case with Down children." Tammy shakes her head in surprise. When checking his hearing, the doctor determines, baby "Ethan" has developed hearing problems, and slow mental development. She referrals her to an "Early Intervention" program that provides a wealth of learning activities; therapy, speech exercises, language and occupational therapy, available up until he turns three years of age. The program addresses issues of Down syndrome children.

After the baby's appointment, Tammy takes him to the early intervention center for an assessment. A caseworker was assigned to coordinate the various services for which the baby and she qualify. Tammy is told that she qualifies for a therapists and early childhood teacher to come to her home, every week, to work on her child's development. Tammy wants to give Ethan the best chance of meeting his developmental milestones. Then, she's invited to attend parent support groups for parents of Down syndrome for emotional support and help in bringing up her child.

She is also informed that Down syndrome children are guaranteed resources under the Individuals with Disabilities Education Act (IDEA). And those professionals who work with the IDEA program will help support her and find additional resources and treatment for her Down syndrome child. That's what she wanted to know. What were the available resources that will help her to successfully raise baby Ethan on her own.

That evening, Tammy checks her mail box and gets another letter from Harry. This time he said he's depressed and miserable without her. He wants her to see how much pain he's in. He tells her that he is trying to process his emotional pain of abuse in counseling, yet it has been hard. He can't let go of the anger he feels toward his step father. Tammy reads the letter again and thinks about her unforgiveness that she carries for him. She folds the letter up and puts it into its envelope, and hides it away in her shoe box. She looks at baby Ethan face, while listening to the different sounds he makes while breathing. Then she touches his little head and feet. There is a soothing sensation from bonding with him. Baby Ethan tries to imitate her facial expressions. She laughs. He loved it when she would talk baby talk to him. *"Does she really need his father in their life?"* she thought. "We can make it without him,"...she whispers to Ethan.

Chapter 6

THE NEXT DAY at work, Tammy and another co-worker talk briefly about a movie that had came on television that both had seen. It was about two imprisoned men that bonded over a number of years as friends. Dustin overheard the conversation as he walked by them both and made a comment regarding people that had gone to prison. Basically; he said, how they didn't even have the right to vote, they were unredemable, and that society viewed them as second class citizens. It offended Tammy. The young man she was talking to couldn't believe that he would stoop so low to make such a comment. Everyone knows he has a racist point of view of the world, along with the power to belittle the staff every chance he gets and in any way he deems appropriate. This day, though, she decides she wants to talk with Mr. Schmidt about it, but she is informed if she does Dustin will automatically fire her, so she doesn't.

All day long, Dustin had been a complete jerk to the food runners and servers. If one little thing went wrong, instead of being helpful and giving them constructive criticism, he would go into a rage. Tammy doesn't know how's she's going to survive the next few months working there-while in school. She wants to look for an entry level catering job, but her doubts and fears of her past history keeps her from searching. On her breaks, she would sit somewhere in a corner and think about how she could make her move to another job. But then, her self-defeating thoughts would win, paralyzing her from doing anything.

A month later on a busy evening, Dustin got into a shouting match with Tammy. While yelling at her in front of the kitchen staff, he accidently spit on her. Tammy looked at him with anger and wiped her face. He looked at her and said, "I guess you expect me to apologize?" She turns and walks away. The place wasn't the same anymore. He was the boss from hell, who constantly changed the rules to accommodate those he liked. Then, there were never enough food supplies in the kitchen. She would have to remind him to stay on top of it. He would sometimes allow her to place orders, when he actually worked (was too busy to do it himself), but most of the time, he would do it. And then there were the odd chores he would come up with for staff members to do. Busy work is what he called it, even though they had enough work to keep them busy beforehand. When she stops at her grandmothers to pick up the baby, she tells her about how Dustin is making everyone's life there miserable.

"Madea, should I start looking for another job?"

"Tammy why even ask me? You see how the man is treating you. He wants you to quit. But how are you going to take care of the baby and yourself if you do? You have a lot on your plate, the baby with his special needs, your health, and your job and soon school. I don't know how you're going to do it. The only thing I can tell you, try to stay there as long as you can. Once you get into school, nine months will have passed before you know it."

"Madea I've been thinking. I want to open my own private catering business. You get to work for yourself; determine how many clients you can comfortably manage, and work as much or as little as you want to."

"Well, if you want to do that, you're going to have to get the training. Sweetie, it takes a great deal of concentration, intelligence, creative artistry, and energy, to oversee a busy catering business. Just take it one day at a time and ask God to help you," Madea says. Tammy picks the baby up and heads home.

The next week, she takes the baby in for his second doctor's appointment. The usual is done, he is weighted and measured to see if he's growing at a healthy steady rate. Today, her baby also gets his first big round of vaccines. The doctor addresses her health concerns like baby acne and diaper rash. She checks to see whether Ethan's head is developing a flat spot. The baby's doctor wanted to know what his posture was like. Did his legs come down when he's lying on his back? Reality hits Tammy as she looks at Ethan. She starts to cry. Not only does her baby have special needs, and is considered retarded. He also has the potential to develop leukemia and Alzheimer's disease after he turns thirty five years of age. "Who would care for my son after I die?"... she cries out loud. Her doctor tries to comfort her. "Tammy, Down syndrome children can live a quality life. But you will need support. That's why it's so important to get into those parent support groups so that you can be among others facing the same challenges. You will meet new friends that will inspire and help you." Tammy wipes her nose with a tissue and smiles. "You're right, I need to stay positive. It's just that I don't know what to expect."

That evening Harry calls to see how she's doing. He tells her that there is a woman at the treatment facility that likes him, and he needed to know where he stood in her life. Pre occupied with Ethan and thinking about what lies ahead for him and her, she breaks down into tears and becomes emotional. "Harry you can do whatever you need to do," she hangs up. He calls back and she turns on the answering machine. She picks up Ethan and holds him, rocking him back and forth. Ethan had begun to look at her as his main interest and fun. Bonding with him is important to her, she tries to give him time to react to her voice by clapping her hands, and calling out his name, while at the same time, fighting back her tears. She plays with his face, whilst speaking babbling sounds to him. He has become fascinated by the sound of her voice, and follows it around the room, wherever she goes. Her greatest joy, though, is his collection of cooing sounds he uses to communicate with her as she rocks him to sleep.

The next morning, she goes into work and starts her normal routine. Then, she takes out the garbage that wasn't taken out last night. Dustin yells at her to combine the cooked ingredients for serving. Their shift is getting busy. The kitchen staff is working, and he's sitting at a table eating and texting one of his girlfriends. This time, she has had it with him and wants to give him a piece of her mind. The kitchen staff gets slammed; everyone is running like chickens with their heads cut off and the hostesses are running back in forth into the kitchen, confused. One of the cooks goes looking for Dustin. After Dustin finishes eating, he's nowhere to be found. Later that afternoon, he sees her prepping food and gives her additional work when she was already busy with prep work. "How long can I deal with this?" she slams her cutting knife down on the hard surface. She does her deep-breathing exercises that her counselor told her about. "Take it easy," she tells herself. She counts to ten and breathes out.

John Schmidt stops by the restaurant. He comes back to the kitchen to see how everything was going. "Tammy, how are you?" he waves at her. With sorrow in her eyes, she looks up at him wanting to tell him about what just happen and the other things...but the words would not come out. "I'm doing good...Mr. Schmidt. I'm doing well."

John Schmidt is a hands off—kind of owner. As long as Dustin is running the restaurant and customers are getting served, he's happy. However, he has no idea about what is going on at his restaurant. He doesn't know about or is kept in the dark about the customers miserable experiences, Dustin's rages and ineptness, lack of service, and his staff attitudes and behaviors. Tammy has decided if it's meant to be known, through the act of God...maybe, one day he will find out.

When she arrives home, there's another letter from Harry. It had an overly nice tone to it.

He starts out saying that he doesn't know when the best time to call her is. He doesn't want to wake the baby. *Tammy is there any way that I can see you and the baby anytime soon?* She starts to fold-up his letter but stops and continues reading it. *He's my son and I don't even know his name. I would like to just hold him again and look into his eyes. A man's first child will always be special to him.* Then he writes, *There is not one day that I don't think about my son or you. I want the opportunity to give him what I didn't have. Would you allow me to? Why don't you write me sometimes?* The letter is folded twice into horizontal thirds and placed into its envelope. "Ah! Man"…she mumbles. "I'm not ready for this, I'm just not ready."

The next morning, on her way to work, she turns on her favorite radio station to help her relax before going in. The work environment was a circus. How she wanted to quit but couldn't. Mentally, she had to prepare herself for whatever came her way for the day. Dustin now had only his friends and women who would sleep with him working there. He has turned out to be shady, and allows anything to happen, as long as it doesn't affect him—directly.

No one says a word about him sexually harassing his female employees. In like manner, he uses his power to talk down to the female employees and reminds them daily, he could fire them at any moment. If that's not worse, he allows a few of the men workers to steal from the place. A new girl that he hired a month ago, who befriend Tammy, got tired of his harassment and unfair treatment and decided to quit. He later told everyone that she couldn't cut the work and that he had to fire her. *If only I can hold out a little longer, until after school*, she thought to herself.

It's the spring semester and culinary school has started. Tammy's excited and can't believe this day has come for her. She wipes the tears from her eyes as she dresses into her culinary uniform; her chef's coat, checkered pants, apron, and neckerchief. For the final touch, she puts on her white cloth hat and stares at herself in the mirror. "I look like a totally different person," she says as she looks at herself from all angles in the mirror. Sixteen months ago, she had gotten out of prison and was trying to start a new life for herself. Today, she has a two month old special needs child and doesn't know how to care for him emotionally and financially. On the other hand, she's about to meet her first major goal, attending culinary school.

She had mapped out her classes ahead of time by finding them a day or two before, wanting to make sure on the first day that she wouldn't end up in the wrong place. As she drove around the school, she stood in awe of the idea that she could get her culinary diploma. "Me, a nobody that had gone to prison," she whispers. Everyone had given up on her; they told her that she was just dreaming. This present day, she stands, doing the unthinkable, she's sober, has a job, and is now in school. A surge of confidence was beginning to build.

It is her first day of class at culinary school. Nine months of class, with studying, and lectures is what she is looking forward to, though, lately she has been feeling physically tired. But she knows that she can do this. Her classes, begin with six weeks dedicated to learning the "basics" baking pastries, cakes and desserts of all kinds. She looks around in her classroom and noticed a diversified number of races, and ages. Forty five percent of her class seemed to be in their late thirties, early forties, and every age in between. She felt comfortable knowing she wasn't the oldest one in the bunch. Later, she would find out that most didn't have any prior food experience at all. Yet in spite of the emotionally abuse at her job, at least she has had the opportunity to work in the restaurant business and learn some things, an advantage over her classmates.

But what most intrigued her was that, after talking with some of her classmates, she found a common thread. Everyone was passionate about food. And were happy to finally be on the track they had wanted to pursue for a long time. *Yeah, she had made the right decision...*she tells herself.

In her first class, the instructor, painted the picture that some student's would not make it through the nine month program. Wondering if he was talking about her, she whispers to herself as the instructor speaks. *No Tammy, you're delusional, he's not talking about you.* She had stayed up late with Ethan the night before, work was hectic and she's mentally exhausted—today. Nevertheless, she had made it there and that was the most important step for her.

Then he goes on to say... "I will tell you that it's the effort, enthusiasm and focus you put into it that will determine your outcome. And if you carry those traits over to the culinary world, you are bound to be successful. It's all about self-motivation and the desire to succeed." *Self motivation and a desire to succeed...* she whispered to herself. *I have to keep going, in spite of these struggles.*

Orientation to the food industry, historical overviews, careers, professionalism, kitchen organization, equipment, and units of measurement are explored. Emphasis is on food-borne illnesses, proper sanitation techniques, and kitchen safety. She would receive her health department food handler's permit after its completion.

Once she went to a few classes, she would begin to feel comfortable meeting new people.

By her second week, she was even able to recognize her instructors and their lecture style. Within a month, she found out that it wasn't as bad as what she thought her first month of class would be.

She made it a point to meet each of her professors at the very beginning, and drop by periodically to just say hello. Her favorite instructor, Chef Dewey, impressed her with his talent and skill. Periodically, she would go to him for questions and to chit chat before she left for work. Her goal was to be the best student that she could be.

He was the only chef that she could really go to with questions. In the following weeks she learned it was hard to get one on one time with the other chef's when there are twenty six students also needing assistance. One chef in particular stood out like a sore thumb-chef Michaels; he would ask the students, "Why do you want to do this?" Then, he basically said he only became an instructor because it got him out of the kitchen.

He wasn't inspiring, she thought to herself when she would go to his classes. Another instructor of hers didn't even have a formal culinary education. She wondered how he was able to teach with authority. There were good and bad points about the school. However, one of her disappointments was that the school did not supply the correct ingredients for lab. "How could I...follow their recipes and make these fantastic dishes if I don't have what I need?" she tells a student. *It's like playing the piano with bandaged fingers*...she thought.

Then there was the time she was ridicule by an instructor. One of her classmates had asked her what the instructor had said. Apparently she missed the instructor's comment. When Tammy tried to fill her in on what was said, her instructor screamed at her...

"Ms. Brown would you like to share your conversation with the class?" he said.

"No sir, I was only telling Misty, what you had said previously. She couldn't hear you and asked me...that's all."

What a jerk! she thought. This was the same chef, when a classmate asked if she could get instructions on using a sharpening stone, she was belittle and flat out-told "no" ask someone next to you.

When she spoke one-on-one with some of her instructors she was amazed at some of their attitudes. Some wanted to keep their jobs so they were very politically correct about school and its courses, fearing if not they would lose their jobs. However, the better chef's were honest about what was going on within the school after she got to know them. Still, this place was nothing like her work. She enjoyed coming to class more so than going to her job.

The following week, baby Ethan is taken to his fourth month examination. The usual general examinations were done: he is weighed and measured and given another set of shot's that he hated. The doctor tells Tammy, the vaccines address any health concerns, constipation, colds, and the flu. Then they talk about childcare and transitions. It is determined that physical therapy is needed to help the baby gain head control and pull up to a sitting position with help, with no head lag, because he has low muscle tone.

He hasn't been able to make his development milestone. Once again the baby's eyesight and hearing is checked. Tammy's doctor suggests ways of setting up a bedtime routine to help her and the baby get more sleep since she's in school. She wanted to know if Ethan could roll over one way or sit with support. Tammy tells her that he's not rolling over at all nor can he sit up without support. "That's okay, this usually occurs in a couple of months," the doctor said. After her doctor visit she drops the baby off at her grandmothers on her way to work.

That night she cuddles with Ethan. She likes to look at him as he laughs out loud, he startles himself until he realizes it's him making his favorite sounds, "Ahhhh" "gooo" "oohs" and "ahhs." His soft spoken babbling has almost a mellifluousness sound too her. She chats back with him as he squeals to let her know he's listening. It has become one of the most pleasurable experiences she has had lately. She takes off his clothes, gives him a gentle infant massage, then changes him into his sleep wear for the night, and puts him to bed.

School is coming along great. Her second class enables her to explore basic cooking techniques, herbs and spices, knife skills, and diary & beverage products. She loved the marinating techniques as she looked through her recipe books; she thought to herself, *a good season-ing is everything to certain foods*. She was trying to take on as much as she could, knowing the pay off would be well worth it.

One of her biggest challenges is having to prepare for research projects using the Internet on such subjects as world cuisines, cheeses, desserts and types of seafood. At first, she is intimated; after all, she doesn't even know how to use a computer. She will have to buddy with another student who will show her how to use the Internet and search within the search engines. On weekends, when she isn't too tired, her free time is spent at the public library, learning how to use the computer. In a way, it provides an escape from the baby, she could be alone, and concentrate.

Weeks later, the instructor talks about the students developing their own business plan.

Excited and scared, she isn't sure how to find the information she needs. After all, this is a task that requires a lot of research and she isn't sure that she can do it by herself. Each student is responsible for writing one for their own restaurant or catering operation. She puts her pride aside and asks the instructor to help her. He gives her tips on resources, information for the plan, and how to format it. On weekends when she has time after her library computer classes, she visits trade association via the Internet to gather information for her plan. "Boy this is a lot of work"…she tells the librarian. "It is, and here are some other resources for you."

The librarian gives her referrals to free community based programs that help disadvantaged women with start-up small businesses. When she contacts one of the outreach programs they help her to gather only the information that she needs; a breakdown of the services she will offer, food suppliers, identification of her best target market, detail marketing plan structure, and financial statements. It was a lot of work but worth it.

In all, at school—the participation in their regular discussions, trends in food service, and learning how to keep on top of new developments in their industry, she enjoyed. The school had its advantages and disadvantages, but at least for now, she just needed to continue to focus.

Back at work, her workplace environment has constantly been spiraling down since Dustin came on board. *Why couldn't Mr. Schmidt, see it?* she moaned. The kitchen was dirty with cockroaches, the staff had poor food handling skills and there was moldy bread at times. It was all in an effort to cut corners, she guessed. *It was a shabby way of doing business*…she thought.

This day, she has a lot that needs to be done. Work that wasn't completed by the other prep person. She needed to store food in its designated containers and storage areas to prevent spoilage. Prepare a variety of foods according to the supervisors' instructions, package take-out foods and/or serve food to customers. In addition, she has to portion and wrap the food or place it directly on plates for service to patrons. That night, she was so tired that she falls asleep laying sideways across her bed.

The next day at work while placing food trays over food warmers for immediate service, she informs Dustin that supplies are getting low and that an order needs to be done. At that point, she measures ingredients and assists the cooks and kitchen staff with various tasks as needed, while providing the cooks with needed items. Just after things finally slowed down, she sees a co-worker taking food off plates and eating it right in front of her. He laughs about it. He doesn't wash his hands thereafter.

She mentions to the co-worker that it is unsanitary. Later, he tells Dustin, and Dustin chews her out for making the suggestion to him. He tells her to mind her own business and not to address the cross contamination with anyone. "Dustin, do you understand how dangerous that is? What he has done?...That's not the first time this has happen!" He yells at her...

"I don't need you to tell me about restaurant sanitation. I've been doing this longer than you have."

"Well okay...I know this Dustin, I'm just saying it's not sanitary."

"What do you think, since you're taking a diploma course, you now have management experience?" Tammy walks off, leaving him to argue with himself. Thirty minutes later, Dustin walks over to her and tells her to help the cooks by placing side dishes alongside the entrée on the dinner plates. As she helps out on the food line, one of the cooks inappropriately touches her from behind, and says to her... "I like the way you bend over," as he walks away. The place was getting to her—from the sexual innuendos, verbal abuse from Dustin, cooks stealing, people half doing their jobs, and the sexual harassments. She had enough. She goes to Dustin after her shift to inform him about the harassment and he tells her he thinks she is making it up and threatens her, calling her a liar in so many words.

"I know a lie when I hear one".... he tells her.

"Dustin, it seems you always have a problem with me, what am I doing wrong? Why is it that other people can say whatever they want to say or do, but somehow, if I have a complaint, or something is done to me that is not professional and I come to you about it...there's a problem. I mean, what have I done to you?" He was always against her, and she couldn't pin point what it was. Sure, he was a bona fide jerk, but still, it was as if he didn't care.

"Young lady, these are serious allegations, and I can fire you for this. Now get back to work." Before she leaves for the night, she sees Dustin and the cook laughing and talking. *Clearly*, she thinks to herself, *he has no respect for himself nor his employees*. "I've got to get out of this place," she screams as she drives out of the parking lot.

The next day at class, chef Dewey walks over to her, "Tammy you seem sad today, what's wrong?"

"Oh nothing."

"Are you sure?" he says.

She looks down at her recipe, "I'm just wanting to hurry up and finish school so that I can start my new career."

He laughs, "You're that excited, huh?"

"Yeah...I am. I just need to learn everything so that I can start my own business. Your classes are helping me to do that."

"Thank you...Tammy," he smiles at her.

"You're the only class that I'm never put to sleep, and the experience is vibrant and alive as well as the food."

He laughs, "Well you're a good student...I want to see you make it."

Even though she was doing well in his class there were days when she was flat right out tired with school, work, caring for Ethan and her own health. Some days were more challenging than others. In all though, she has to learn how to really focus with her reading and test preparations. The hardest part has been getting and staying organized. She wanted to get on top of her studies, making sure she didn't have to rush to turn in her work by keeping her notes for each class together, writing things on her calendar when everything is due, and reading everything when it was supposed to be read. In her next class, she has a hard time hearing the instructor. The bits she could hear she hardly understood due to the instructors accent. Likewise, some of the recipes were riddled with errors, so she and her classmates had to scribble many changes, which was a disappointment for her.

They were just beginning to cover salads, sandwiches, pastas, grains, vegetarian cooking and preparing salad dressing. Moreover, she really wanted to learn about the nutritional subjects, its basics and studies of the human digestive system. Some of the guest speakers would bring industry professionals into the classroom for cooking demonstrations, lectures on kosher and halal cooking, nutrition and the business of running restaurants and institutional food service. Henceforth, there were the field trips that allowed her to visit local restaurants for behind-the-scenes tours, farmer's markets and food retailers.

But what was really annoying, sometimes—getting only 2 hours of real cooking time at school. Plus there were other things that troubled her like she remembers one dish called for deep frying but the equipment had not been set up. And, some of the younger students were so disruptive, as well as a distraction to the other students. It seemed the younger students were so bored, frustrated, constantly checking their watches, getting out of their chairs, which was a distraction for everyone sitting down. *I'm here to learn, not to kid around*, she tells herself. This would be her livelihood, and she took it very seriously. Other disappointments and frustrations included issues with the school not having everything the students needed. *Then there were those few instructors who were lousy*, she thought. They didn't care a hill of beans about the students.

By the third month of school, she has started to feel the full effects of school, working and caring for the baby. Sometimes she would have to catch herself when spending time with her baby. The stress had begun to trigger feelings of resentment toward his illness. At times, he would cry for no reason at all. And when she was tired, she didn't want to be bother with hearing it or having to baby him. In the same way, she had begun to resent not having her life that she had over a year ago. She didn't want any distractions in the way of her finishing school.

At work, it was no better. This particular day, she completes all her work for the day.

And it's nearing the last 30 minutes before she gets off. Things had slowed down and she had run out of things to do. Dustin walks over to her and starts making passive aggressive comments toward her, ignoring him she goes to the ladies room. *He's a trip! He has a nasty attitude and the nerve to not pay me for my overtime last week. I've requested days off, and I haven't gotten them. Man…he's lucky, I really need this job while in school, or else, I probably would curse him down to his shoes ..* she thinks to herself.

Later that week, Tammy needed help with an order that she was doing. She asks Dustin for help, and he snaps at her… "Are you stupid?" or "Are you an idiot?" She walks back to her prep area before stepping out back to get away from it all for a moment. Her shift had been busy, and she needed a quick break. The baby had kept her up all night—again, and when she arrived at work, the place was already packed and busy. Five minutes later, she comes back to her station and Dustin is waiting for her. He tells her to go home since she didn't have anything to do even though she had work that needed to be finished. "Dustin what are you talking about?" she said with raised eyebrows and her mouth opened. "Well you were out back, apparently, you could use a break, just go home"…he yells. She grabs her things and leaves.

On her drive to Madea's to pick up baby Ethan, she worries about her job. When she arrives, she bangs on the door. "I'm coming, hold on," Madea yells out. "Baby, what are you doing here so early?"

"Dustin sent me home early."

"Why Tammy?"

"Because he's a jerk…that's why!" she looks down at the baby and plays with his hand.

"What's wrong with him?"

"Madea I honestly don't know. I've been trying to figure that out since the first day I met him. I have my suspicions. He treats everybody bad. But, I can never do anything right in his eyes. Every co-worker that I use to work with at the beginning have left or he's fired them. Enough about him."

"How's school coming along?"

"Madea…I really like it. There are some things that puzzle me but I'm not complaining."

"Have you heard from Harry?"

"He sends me letters just about every month. He's trying to get back with me."

"Is he still clean?"

"As far as I know, he is. Madea, I have something to ask you."

"Well, I don't have any money."

Tammy sighs. "It's not about money!" she sits down at the dining room table with her grandmother. "Madea…school, work, and the baby have become too much for me, I need some help, can you keep Ethan on a regular basis?"

"Oh No!…Missy. I'm done raising babies. I'm only doing this until you get on your feet. Tammy, he's your baby. Papa and I told you we would help the best we can and that would be too much. He's already a handful…baby." Tammy droops back into her chair, and her face becomes flushed. "Madea…Just until I get out of school?" Her grandmother grabs the newspaper and starts to read it. "Ok, I understand," she said. She grabs the baby and heads for the door.

"I may call you tonight, depending on how I feel, I love you."

"I love you too…baby," Madea said.

At home, she checks the mail box and goes back to the car to take the baby out of his car seat. Once inside she gets the baby settled and goes into the kitchen to fix something to eat. She comes back into the living room and turns on the television. She looks at Harry's letter, and opens it… "Why is he constantly sending me letters?" Harry had invited her to meet him for coffee on Saturday. *Tammy if you're not busy this Saturday, I have a pass for a few hours. I would like to meet you for coffee at McDonalds or some place. How's my son doing? Remember when we use to hang out together? I want to get back to how it use to be. I'll call you Friday night and we can talk more…. Harry*

Tammy hasn't reached a state of forgiveness for Harry. He's hurt her dearly, being near him is tense and stressful for her. She walks around the house contemplating if she should allow him to see her and the baby. He has been cleaned six months, and it has been fourteen months since they were together. *Boy I don't know, I just have to play it by ear…*she mumbles to herself. That night he calls around 9:00pm.

"How are you?" he said. She doesn't say anything.

"Tammy!"

"Yes, I hear you," she says with an attitude.

"Did you get my letter?"

"Yeah!"

"Well what do you think?"

"About what?"

"About us meeting tomorrow for coffee."

"Harry, I don't know. Ethan is a handful, and I'm not sure how he will act in public."

"Ethan"...he repeats back to her. "My son's name is Ethan."

"I thought you knew that."

"Hey Tammy...C'mon, let's not play games, you never told me his name. I've never heard of a man not knowing his own child's name."

"Hey did you call to argue with me?"

"No...I just called to see if you will spend some time with me?"

"What time?"

He's silent ... "Did you say what time?"

"Yeah man," she said.

"Oh okay! Well what about 11:00 am, would that work?" he laughs. "You caught me off guard there for a minute," he said. She walks around while talking.

"Yeah.... Okay," she said... "I'll see you in the morning."

Saturday morning, she gets up, showers and gets Ethan ready, while mimicking his baby cooing and other sounds. The baby laughs. Then she picks him up and holds him in the air. "Hey big boy...you're going to meet your daddy today." The baby smiles back at her. She dresses him and loads him into the car. When she arrives at McDonalds on Long Beach Blvd, immediately she notices Harry's 1997 Eggplant colored Nissan Maxima—Sedan parked. He comes outside to her car and tries to hug her. She pushes him away. He opens her car door and picks up the baby. "Wait a minute!...Let me put his little hat on good!" She tugs at Ethan's hat to make sure it's secure on his head, then throws the blanket around him. Once inside, she sits down at his table and he orders coffee for them both. "You look good," he tells her.

"Thank you!"…Blushing she turns her head away. "So do you, you've gained some weight."

"Yeah. There's nothing else to do at the facility. I can't use any-more…so, I just eat when possible."

"How do you like it?"

"Man…it was rough at the beginning."

"I can imagine so. Your grandfather told me that you had been in and out of treatment five times."

"He told you that?" he glances away for a second. "Yeah, well… it's true." There's silence. "Can I pick up my son?

He looks just like my mother, he has her eyes." Tammy hands Ethan to him. He plays with his feet. "I don't know about that. He looks like me," she said, as she hands him the baby's blanket. "There you go!"…he said, while laughing. Her fingertips taps—drums onto the top of the table, she cocks her head with a raised eyebrow. Meanwhile, as she looks at him, she could only see anger, and he knew it. "Hey, you got anything planned for the rest of the day?" She crosses her arms. "Actually I do."

"Oh!" his countenance changes to sadness.

"I'm in school now."

"You're in school?"

"Yeah, I have been in school for several months."

"How do you like it?"

"It's a lot to learn, but I enjoy it. Soon, I will be starting my own catering business."

"Oh!…So you're not going to work at a fancy place like you had in mind?"

"No, I want to work for myself."

"What's your specialty?"

"You know I want to do children's parties, healthy snacks, sand-wiches, desserts and drinks. It will be fun, and I would have something in common with my clients." Harry looks at Ethan.

"What's wrong with his eyes?"

"Harry, he's a Down's syndrome baby."

"I know that."

"Some of them look this way," she said. Harry kisses Ethan and holds him up.

"Don't drop my baby"...Tammy yells out.

"Woman, stop tripping. I'm not going to drop our baby," he lays Ethan in his lap and gazes into his eyes.

"What are you doing?...Harry!"

"I'm bonding with my baby. Is that alright with you?" She doesn't say anything and takes a sip of her coffee.

"Have you been going to counseling about your problem?"

He looks at her, "You mean the molestation? Yeah. I have had extensive therapy on that and I'm still getting it."

"How do you feel about it today?"

"I know that it wasn't my fault, and that my stepfather was a sick man. I'm coming to terms with some things, but it'll take some time."

"I'm glad to hear that you're working on it," she relaxes and smiles.

"Hey when you're done drinking your coffee, I thought we could go over to Lynwood Park with the baby."

"Harry...it's April!"

"And?" .. he said.

"My baby may get cold."

"Tammy he has a little jacket on!"

"Still...I don't want him to catch a cold."

"Alright, why don't I follow you back to your house? You park your car, and I'll drive us over there, and we'll just seat in the car and talk or we'll walk around. What do you think about that?" She doesn't say anything. "Well?" he stares at her. "Yes"..."No"...or..."Maybe—so?" he says.

Chapter 7

HE PUTS THE blanket around Ethan, and she grabs what's left of their coffees and walks out to her car. She sits their coffees on top of her car hood and opens the passenger side. Hence, he puts the baby in his car seat. He follows her home and waits in the car, while she parks her car in the drive way. Before long, he gets out, grabs the car seat and takes it to his car. Tammy position Ethan into his car seat. "Umm, your car still looks good!" she scoots around trying to get the seatbelt in, while thinking about how luxurious it looked on the inside. The black leather-like buckle seats were clean, immaculate, and looked brand-new. "Yeah, my grandfather has help me take care of it. It's not dirty and filled with trash like before," he said. They head over to Lynwood City Park. On their way, he turns on the radio. Tammy is doing her best to keep an open heart and mind.

She has always cared about him and maybe even loved him. Her struggle has been that he gave her the HIV disease. It was this that she couldn't forgive. Deep down inside the core of her being...she was very angry at him. Yet she wanted to be fair since they have a child together. After all, she never knew her father and barely knew her mother. Likewise, Harry never knew his father, and the one father that was in his life...destroyed him emotionally. *Maybe if he bonded with little Ethan...it would help him toward his emotional healing...*she thought.

He parks near the play grounds. "Did you want to get out?"

"No!"

"Okay," he turns up the music a little. Turns to face Tammy. He touches her hand, then he takes his hand to guide her face in his direction. "Harry, don't do that!" she shifts her feet, and folds her hands unto her lap.

"Okay!" he said, and he backs off. "You know Tammy everyone and anyone can make a mistake."

"Harry, we're talking about our lives," she brushes her hair back and raises her eyebrows. "Tammy, I don't know how many times I have to apologize," he squirms around in his seat.

"You know, have you ever thought about someone had to infect me? You're a victim. I'm a victim, and someone infected them. Hey, if I had known this was going to happen to me, I would have never done it the first time. I can't beat myself up about it nor can you," he touches her face. "We have to move forward if you would allow us to. I will be the best father to my son as possible, you know that alone...says something."

"Oh...why is that?"

"Tammy, you know how a lot of black men are not there for their sons. They grow up without a father and most times, I'm willing to bet their father's, father didn't have a father." She looks at him and puts her finger up to her head, leaning her head next to the window. "You may not want me back...that's understandable but for the sake of Ethan, let's try to make life good for him?"

"I've got to go," she said.

"What?" he looks disappointed. "We just got here."

"I know, but I need to go. I can't handle this right now!"...Harry shakes his head, and starts the car. The drive back, neither one says anything. Then she begins to open her door, as he pulls in front of her house. "Hey Girl, would you wait until I stop the car?" he yells to her, then he turns off the car and gets out. "I can do it," she said, as she opens the backseat back door and grabs the car seat.

"Tammy...please, baby...please...stop for a moment!" She looks at him. "Let me help you," he grabs the car seat with Ethan still inside of it and takes it to her front door. She opens the door, and takes the car seat out of his hands. "I think, this is as far as you should go."

"Tammy! Can I come in?"

"Harry, No!"... "Now, you asked me if you could see your son and I did that. I almost didn't come. My mind told me to turn around as I was driving to McDonalds. Still and all, I kept my word. So please don't rush me," she closes the door. Harry puts his hands into his pockets and walks to his car. She gets Ethan settled in and starts cleaning up the place. It was her way of releasing some of the emotions that she felt. Her emotions the last several months had been like a yo-yo, depending on her circumstances. That afternoon, she and Ethan needed to attend an event for mother's with Down syndrome children. She desperately wanted to be among others who could be a friend to her and help take her mind off of her circumstances.

Sunday morning she lays in bed, reading the paper. She wanted to stay in bed all day, until she had to go into work at 5:00pm. She played with Ethan, fed him, and watched him in between dosing off. That evening, when she arrives at work she learns there is an opening for a line cook. She goes into the office to talk with Dustin, and tells him she's interested in the position. He tells her its already been filled. Disheartened she goes back to her station and begins work. After a couple of hours of work, she leaves early, saying she's not feeling well. When she arrives home, Evelyn had put the baby to sleep. They talked for an hour. Evelyn leaves, and Tammy finishes her homework for school.

Several days pass and she gets another letter from Harry. *Tammy, I need to say I really enjoyed seeing you and my son. It is no secret that I want to be in your life, and we both give Ethan what our parents couldn't give to us. I'm striving everyday to heal from my childhood abuse. It's taking me time and effort to develop a positive sexual self identity. Not only do I have to watch for trigger situations and false beliefs about who I am, resulted from my abuse, I also must replace old ways of thinking. My counselor is working with me on a strategy for change and healing. It will be lengthy and sometimes a difficult journey, I would imagine.*

Who has ever heard of a man keeping a journal....guess what? That's exactly what I'm doing, recording my thoughts and feelings to help me manage my emotions. It does feel funny, writing down what has been bothering me all these years. Yet-the one thing I have been learning is; forgiveness is not denying or excusing the damage caused by your abuser. We forgive because God forgave us. When we forgive, we allow God to heal us. Forgiveness is a choice, not a feeling. I needed to forgive my stepfather, so that I could make room for God, to handle everything else in my life that is wrong. Likewise...I need for you to forgive me....I would like to take our relationship to the next level, give our relationship another shot. I'm willing to take it as slow as you need it to be.... signed Harry.

Tammy looks at baby Ethan as he sleeps and begins to cry. He needs his father, especially now since he is changing and trying to heal from his emotional wounds. *But how could I really forgive him?* she thought. She couldn't go on holding animosity toward him. It was only hurting her. This deep emotional pain had been carried for awhile, and it was draining her emotionally. What he had done had affected every part of her emotional life. No one understood this. Not even her.

The next day at work she makes a mistake and Dustin berates her in front of the other employees and restaurant patrons who happened to be within earshot. His favorite tactic was to scare the employees by making them feel as though they were disposable. Threatening them with the fact that they are "at will" employment. He yells out to her....
"Hey Tammy, when you're done with that, why don't you wash the utensils and dishes cleared from the tables. And while you're at it, take out the garbage!" She walks toward the dishwashing area. "I'm so sick of him and his attitude. If only I can hold on for a little longer," she would mutter to herself. "But when I do finish school and get another job, I'm going to curse him out real—good!"

That night, when she arrived home, she checked her answering machine. Harry had called and said he would call back later. He called again around 10:00pm.
"Tammy how are you and Ethan?"
"We're fine, how about you?"
"Things are still looking up, did you read my last letter?"

"Yes...Harry."

"Well, what do you think?" he's sounding anxious. "I just need to understand what went wrong."

"I can't believe you're asking me this," she says.

"Hey Tammy, relationships are about two people. I know I made some mistakes but what about you?"

"Hey!"...she catches herself. Waits a minute before responding. Then softly says...

"Harry, I remember the last time we used drugs together. You and I both said some pretty terrible things to each other, some things we will never be able to take back. I'm hurt by what you said and I'm still hurting over, having HIV."

"Tammy, I'm hurting too. Can't you see or understand from my point of view?"

"Harry, I can't talk right now!"

"You know what Tammy, every time you have to deal with something emotional, you can't deal with it right now. What have you learned in your treatment sessions?"

"Harry...don't go there!"

"No, I'm just trying to be real...I need to know. That's what treatment is all about right? Getting better and learning how to cope with your circumstances," Harry says.

"Okay, I tell you what. Let's talk about this some other time. I'm tired and need to get ready for tomorrow," she hangs up.

Several weeks later at work, she and another co-worker wanted the same day off, but only one could have it. So, Dustin gave it the other co-worker. Tammy was furious. She had been there longer than the other person. It later ended up causing a conflict between her and the other co-worker. That night she begins journaling to release her pinned up anger. She also has begun to pray after attending a church service that Madea had invited her to. The minister had talked about how life was hard and that everyone has had something at one time or another that they have had to experience, good or bad. But it's how you handle that experience, how you chose to react to it, that's what's important.

She started to reflect on times when she had hurt others, in the course of her life—intentionally and unintentionally and how she had been forgiven. She was learning that forgiveness had the potential to increase her sense of peace and overall well-being. And that's what she really wanted and needed. To feel whole, in every part of her life.

After several months of school she has learned to operate all major types of kitchen equipment, identify and use herbs and spices, prepare salads, hors d'oeuvres, soups, sauces, meats, poultry, breads, pies, cakes and cookies. Heavy emphasis had been placed on proper, yet imaginative use of ingredients, seasoning and plate presentation. The rest of her class time is hands-on cooking projects in the school commercial kitchen. However, sometimes, there were general annoyances, like when she would have to listen to an instructor that was disengaged and disinterested or when there weren't enough ingredients to go around. Then there was one of her instructors, who became sick within the first two weeks of class and wasn't replaced until weeks later. She felt cheated. Her frustration was learning a lot of information at one time—trying to get a full semester worth of lessons into a few classes. She always felt she needed to work extra hard at trying to grasp everything.

Today, she goes in for her and the baby's check up. Tammy watches as the doctor weighted and measured the baby. Another round of vaccines is given. The doctor asks if he is ready for solid food. Tammy answers yes. The doctor helps with how to begin, and then she wanted to know if the baby had started teething. Ethan had gotten his first tooth and he had been suffering from red, swollen, and tender gums. The doctor suggested ways to soothe the baby's gums. Next, she was asked if the baby is able to bear weight on his feet when she holds him up.

"No, he still needs help in this area. But, doctor there's one good thing, I should be grateful for."

"What is that?"

"He is able to grab his little toy and roll over one way."

"Tammy that's wonderful. See there, he is making progress. Just allow him to grow at his own time."

"Yeah, you're right," she said.

She leaves the doctor's office, drops the baby off and heads to work. Today, she is overwhelmed. The other prep person has missed two days of work, and her area is behind. She has to wash, peel and/or cut various foods to prepare for cooking or serving, receive and stock the cupboards and refrigerators, tend the salad bars and buffet meals. She was already exhausted, and her day had just begun. The beverages needed to be prepared and served, coffee, tea, and soft drinks. Plus, she had to carry food supplies, equipment, and utensils to and from storage and work areas. Additionally, make special dressings and sauces as condiments for sandwiches. By the end of the day, she needed to scrape the leftovers from dishes into garbage containers, remove the trash, and clean the kitchen garbage containers. Exhausted, she stopped off at Madea's to pick up the baby. When they arrived home, she was too tired to play but forced herself until he fell asleep.

The next day at school the much eagerly anticipated "cook-off" competitions were getting ready to take place. Each year, she was told teams of students compete for the "Top Chef" dishes. This was the perfect time to show that she could be the best that she could be. Just being around the chefs that had a real passion and love for teaching helped her to go on, day by day. *You get out of it, what you put in*, she tells herself. Her determination was beginning to pay off. When she could, she would practice what she had learned at home.

Six months into her studies; she's now studying principles of "off" premise meal and beverage service, menu development, cost management, food preparation, garnishments, formal place settings, food preparation for staff events, and preparing menus and pricing for clients. This is what she has always strived for. Most Saturdays, Evelyn would come to get the baby so that she could go to the library and take her computer classes, and then research information for her business plan. She was almost half way through her business plan, layering information as she went along. After her library visits she would go home and practice what she learned at school and catch up on her rest. When Evelyn brought back the baby, they would eat and talk for a few hours. It was the only time she had to spend with her.

"Sis, how's school coming along?"

"I'm about to drop dead, but outside of that, it's going good."

"Girl, you are making it. I'm so proud of you. How many more months do you have?"

"Ah, Evelyn…less than three months."

"Well hang in there, you're almost there. If you need anything let me know."

Evelyn leaves and she spends time on her recipes. Every chance she got, when not tired, she focused on cooking at home, work and school. Most of the time lately, her class was spending only two hours a week in an actual kitchen. And the stoves in the kitchens were hard to light. Though all schools vary in equipment, level of instruction, and amenities, she knew the common goal is to put out good cooks who are prepared and ready to get into the culinary world. Chef Dewey was her personal mentor. He went over and above to help her. Oftentimes he would allow her to vent her frustrations, always telling her that nothing comes easy. "You have to work smart and hard for it," he would say.

Even though she attends a no-name institution, not highly well known as other famous cooking schools, she has put a lot of effort into it, knowing that she needs to be in good academic standing to qualify for an internship. She made sure that her grades were kept up, taking any prerequisite courses needed before her internship.

Though she was turned down for the promotion at work, she thought about how the prep worker position had given her more hands on experience that she could use for her own business. She used manual and electric appliances to clean, peel, slice, and trim foods. She stirs and strains soups and sauces. At times, she distributes food to waiters and waitresses to serve to customers, and when allowed, Dustin even let her keep records of the quantities of food used. Now, she was well on her way. If only she could keep going without burn-out. Because the school also operated a full-service catering company, she was able to gain more hands on experience. She would have the opportunity to work in food preparation for their events as well as set-up, take-down and serve during those events, providing invaluable experience working for paying customers under expert supervision. It was the ideal situation, giving her the hands-on experience that she needed for starting her own business.

That night, Harry calls her, and to his surprise for the first time she was ready to talk. She told him about her achievements at school and the problems she has had with Dustin at work. Optimistic about her future, she had begun to let her guard down a little. She wanted to see him without the baby. They make plans to rent two bicycles and go on a bike ride. On their outing at the state park, they cycle the bike trails then stop later for a quick lunch. After their outing he walks her to her door and tells her he will call her later within the week. Not wanting to be overly aggressive with her.

As Ethan develops, she tries to keep up with his milestones. The one's that he makes and those that he doesn't. This time, he is going on his ninth month doctor's visit. He has had problems with tear duct abnormalities. She has notice frequent discharge and tearing from his eyes. It was worsened by colds. The doctor tells her to massage over the space between the eye and the nose-tear sac region 2-3 times a day to attempt to open the tear duct. "If it continues beyond a year of age, the tear ducts may need to be opened by a surgical procedure," she said. Similarly, prescribed glasses that have bifocals would be needed for his far-sightedness. It was also determined that he has what's call "lazy eye." The doctor tells her to make sure she gets a head start on these problems. Then general safety for the baby was discussed such as car seat safety, childproofing her home and poison control. They talk about the baby getting colds and ear infections. After the doctor completes all of her routine checks of the baby's development, she wanted to know if he was crawling. Tammy informed her that he could roll over both ways, and he could sit by himself. "I hope he starts crawling in a couple more months. He's kind of heavy," she laughs. The doctor tells her to not stress out about his development. But to take every milestone as it came.

It's the weekend, and she's meeting Harry at El Chico Restaurant in Los Angeles. They had planned a casual dinner in a more relaxed atmosphere. Recently, Tammy has been looking different. She had gone to the beauty salon to have her hair and makeup done, something that she had never done before in her entire life. He takes one look at her and falls in love. "Baby you look beautiful," he says. She smiles. He asked her if she wanted an appetizer. "No, I know what I want." They both order a soda; she takes a sip while looking into his eyes.

"Have you fully recovered from that bike ride?" she said playfully.

"Yeah, it was fun," he said. "Maybe we can do it again."

"Maybe," she said. Not sure what else to ask him. She was still feeling a little awkward around him. They were now face to face with no distractions. On their bike ride, it wasn't so close and intimate. Nervously, she asked him about his treatment program.

"How many months have you been clean?" she said.

"I've been clean for ten months. You know...I've used drugs, alcohol and marijuana since I was eighteen. This is the first time that I have been able to have a complete positive thought." Tammy looks into his eyes. "And it feels good...baby," he said.

"I'm glad to hear that."

"I just realize the other day, I'm getting older and I need to settle down and do something with my life. Did I tell you I'm working again?" he said.

"No, you didn't tell me that."

"Yeah, I was sitting around the facility going through the classifieds. I saw an ad for pet groomer. I talked to my counselor Ms. Wilson about it, and she encouraged me to apply. The man hired me on the spot."

"Harry, that is so good."

"Yeah and he really likes me. He's an old white guy-the shops accountant. He just took a liken to me for some reason. And he knows I'm in treatment and everything. He's been doing the books for years on the place. The shop went through two managers, and currently they don't have a manager."

"Well maybe you can work your way up."

"I don't know about that. But, I like the job and so far everything is all good."

"What do you do?"

"I bathe-shampoo dogs and cats that come through there. Along with other miscellaneous stuff like keep the place spotless."

"Is that hard on you, I know you had that altercation," she says.

"Some days I feel sore. But for the most part, I try to hold the animals in a certain position that's not too strenuous on me. And I clean up when we're not busy. So it works out."

"That is so good."

"How about you?"

"I'm almost done with school, and I've been working on my business plan. It's just about done."

"Babe, that sounds good." The waiter asked them what they want to order.

"Have you decided," Harry said.

"I want the three chicken enchiladas plate."

"Sir, what about you?"

"Uh, I think I have the chicken quesadillas plate." He takes their menus. They both reach for the freshly fried corn tortilla chips. He loosens the wedges, dips it into the salsa, and takes a bite. Tammy does the same and bites into hers. Both are smiling at each other.

"How's the baby?"

"He's going to have to wear glasses soon and I have to attend a Down syndrome group when I can for support." Harry looks at her and puts his head down for a second.

"Tammy, I need to be in his life. Why won't you let me help you with him?"

"Harry, you're in treatment, how can you help me with him?"

"I'm talking about when I get out, but I can come and see him on the weekends. I get a regular pass you know?"

"Harry, remember in your letter when you said we could take it slow?"

"Tammy, it has been over a year, since we have been together."

"I know," she frowns. She feels he's pushing her too fast.

"Okay, Okay, have it your way. I won't say anything else about it. How's your job?"

"I don't want to talk about it."

"Why?"

"You may decide to go and beat up my boss. So to keep peace, I'm not going to say anything."

"You mean it's that bad?"

"Yeah…pretty much. I try not to talk about it. I'm just waiting to finish school, and then I'm going to look for something else then focus on my business.

"How are you going to do that?"

"I can work my own business on the weekends." He changes the subject.

"Does your grandmother still hate me?" She looks at him and grins.

"She doesn't hate you."

"Excuse me," he said. "She wouldn't even speak to me at the hospital that night. When I came to see you."

"Hey, you know how grandmothers and mothers are about their girls."

"Yeah, she's a trip!"

"Hey, don't talk about my Madea like that," Tammy says. They both snicker at the same time.

"Man, I thought she was going to jump on me the way she was looking at me. I told Papa, I said; let's get out of here…quick and in a hurry." Tammy laughs so hard, she almost urinates on herself. "Gee's she had me scared."

Tammy gets up and goes to the bathroom. On her way back she tries to keep a straight face.

"Harry, you are soooo wrong."

"What? Hey Tammy, you weren't there. I'm telling you what happened." She cackles and reaches for another chip. When their food comes, Harry blesses their meal. Tammy doesn't say anything. She stares into her plate then takes a bite. "Oh!"... "It's hot"...her hand fans her mouth to cool it off. Then she says, "Oh, you've found religion now?"

"What do you mean?"

"You blessed the food. I don't ever remember you blessing your food."

"Hey, I need God. He's the only one that can help me with my problems. You need him too!"

"Why do I need him?" she asks. He looks at her with amazement.

"I can't believe you just said that to me. Okay, number one, to help you heal in your thinking, the baby, work, school, and me...you see where I'm going with this?" he says.

"Hey, me and God are doing just fine," she said.

"Oh, so...you think, he wants you to run around here, mad at me?"

"Harry...Okay, let's change the subject. The last thing God needs is for us to be arguing about him." He takes a bite from his food. Neither speaks for a moment. She looks at Harry and smiles. Their waiter walks up to the table. "Is there anything else...I can get for you?" the waiter said. She wipes her mouth with a cloth napkin. "No, everything is fine," Harry said. The waiter leaves.

"Harry, I'm happy for you. I really mean that." He reaches for her hand and holds it a second. "Well, I'm glad you're here with me." After they finish eating, he walks her to her car. "Can I call you tonight?" he asked. "Why don't you give me a couple of days, and then call me," she said. He kisses her on the forehead and leaves.

Because of her good grades, she had landed a two month paid internship on the weekends. She had checked with the school's student services department for help, and Chef Dewey provided a recommendation for voluntary work placement. Her final course allowed her to do hands-on preparation of all outgoing food products for the schools catering operation. She and the other students also assisted in supervision of student hands-on activities in the kitchen. Her course is successfully completed with a cumulative final exam and completion of the Los Angeles County Health Department Food Service Management Certification.

Everyone has dreams, whether they are big or small, she thought to herself. Now she has the basics of what she needs for a new future. Skills in front-house management, hosting and cashiering, server training in alcohol responsibility and liability, along with setting up a detailed business plan for her catering operation. Every course helped to round out her new skills. She could now possibly run the restaurant if Mr. Schmidt allowed her too. But then she thought…*No, I want my own business.*

Culinary school had been a significant investment of time and resources. Often, she was too tired to pay attention. Nonetheless, she knew the experience itself was more than worthwhile for her. She had come a long way. As she looked back over her nine month course, she had learned to mix ingredients for green salads, mold fruit salads, vegetable salads, and pasta salads. How to prepare meats, seafood, and poultry, the right way with emphasis placed on advanced cooking techniques using cuts of meat, beef, pork, game, poultry, shellfish and finfish. There was also hands-on experience including roasting, grilling, braising, cooking to proper internal temperatures, and determining various degrees of doneness.

Now came the hard part, putting into action her plan to open her own business. Scared, feeling guilty, and now down in the dumps, her inner demons had surfaced again. *Why am I feeling this way?* she sits up in the bed and can't seem to get a move on it-this morning. It is her graduation, and she can't bring herself to get going. She takes a shower, walks to the kitchen and grabs a glass of orange juice. She sits down and tries to make her mind calm down. She closes her eyes and imagines herself running her catering business. *How do you feel…right now? I feel at peace and capable*, she tells herself. *The hard part is behind me. I can do this.* Another self defeating thought surfaces. *Girl, think good thoughts not bad thoughts. Put your attention on what you are trying to achieve.* She hits the sofa, *I can't.* Then she gets up and walks around. *Tammy brace yourself. You deserve this. Today is your day.* She walks through the house repeating this. Jittery, she can't sit still.

I wonder if he will be here, she thought to herself. Harry had told her that he would show up for her school graduation. But she didn't know if he was serious about coming. Finally, she dresses and leaves. As she stood among her family and friends, her grandparents, Evelyn, Ms. Williams, and Mr. Schmidt, there was no Harry. After the ceremony, Mr. Schmidt had asked everyone if they were ready to go. They all left to take Tammy to a nice formal dinner for a small number of guests. She was so happy, crying the entire drive to the restaurant. When she arrived at the restaurant, their table was filled with gifts for her and a beautiful cake.

The music was loud in the background. Everyone was having a good time. Madea and Papa got up to dance. Mr. Schmidt leans over and tells Tammy how proud he was of her, and before he left, he handed her a present. It was a gift card to a chef's warehouse that specializes in cooking equipment and gadgets where she could go and buy what she wanted, but couldn't afford to buy on her own. Tears filled her eyes as she hugged him. She had toughed it out for two years at his restaurant enduring all types of emotional abuse. He even offered her a promotion and told her to think about it. It was the best time of her life she thought, as she watched her grandfather slow dance with Madea. She chatted with a few friends met over the months from the "early intervention program" for mothers with Down syndrome children. That night before she left, they all held their glasses of tea and toasted her on her new beginnings.

After a couple of hours, everyone decided to leave. Madea had paid a babysitter to watch Ethan while they were out, so he would spend the night with her grandparents. When she arrived home she turned on the news and noticed a news story of a couple that was found dead. There was a robbery that had taken place in a familiar neighborhood. Brushing her teeth, she looked closer at the news story, the neighborhood and house of the robbery. The news reporter gave an address of the 9200 block of S. Harvard Blvd. She stopped in her tracks, and sat down to hear more. But the television broadcast only had a few details. *Isn't that the street Harry's grandparents live on?* she thought. Chills went up and down her arms. She grabs the phone to call the Wilkerson's. No answer. She tried calling Harry on his cell phone…no answer. "God, I hope that's not them," with phone in hand, she calls her grandmother.

"Madea"

"Yes baby!"

"I was watching the news and I think something may have happened to Harry's grandparents."

"What?" her grandmother shouts. "Oh Lord, let's pray that it's not his peoples."

"Okay, I'm going to turn in for the night but I'll call you tomorrow," she hangs up. She tries Harry's number again. Still no answer, she leaves a voicemail message.

The next morning, as she takes her shower the phone rings, but before she can get to it, the caller hangs up. On her way out, the phone rings again. The caller hangs up. She's in a hurry to get to work. Today, she's working a catering job, and her day is busy from start to finish with preparing and serving tea and coffee, and light snacks, while counting stock and clearing tables. On her way home, she can't help but think about Harry. Before heading home, she drives to the grocery store. He was heavy on her mind. *He has been trying to get back with me. But, still he's proven himself to be a liar. He didn't show up for my graduation, nor dinner and I couldn't reach him last night. He's probably off somewhere doing something he shouldn't be doing.* She had an attitude, and the only thing she could think of was that he was unreliable.

For twenty minutes, she sits in the grocery store parking lot. Then she goes inside to pick up a few groceries. Walking down each aisle, he kept popping up in her mind. She hadn't thought about him this way for a long time. *She remembers when he disappeared from the scene, and she hadn't heard from him in weeks*, she thought. After grocery shopping she places the ten bags of groceries in her car and heads over to

Madea's to pick up the baby. "Have you heard anything else?" Madea asked her. "No, I have not and I have not heard from him either. What address did the news station give, Madea?"

"Tammy, I don't remember."

"Well, I'm sure it was maybe one of his grandfather's neighbors. If it had been his grandfather he would have called me by now," she said, as she and the baby leave.

When she arrives home, she gets the baby settled and unpacks her groceries. She plops down on the sofa, suddenly, she begins to feel depressed, not knowing why. Her emotions had developed into patterns of up and down cycles averaging every two or three months, off and on. And then the next couple of weeks she was back to looking like her old self. She gets up and starts cooking dinner, while attempting to feed the baby. The phone rings…

"Hello"…there is silence. "Hello."…she's about to hang up, and she hears a voice say….

"Tell me right now, why I shouldn't use at this moment?"

"Harry"…she screams.

"Give me one reason why I shouldn't use right now," he starts to cry.

"Oh Harry…baby please don't," she screams.

"Tammy," he sobs uncontrollably. "Tell me"… "Tell me why not," he hangs up.

"Oh my God," she yells. "Harry don't! Please don't," she tries to call him back, but she gets his voicemail. The pot on the stove begins to boil over; she comes to herself when she hears it whistling. She runs to kitchen, grabs the handle of the pot and pulls it off the burner, back and forth she paces the floor then she picks up the phone…

Chapter 8

"Madea"

"Child what is it?"

"Harry just called me, sounding really funny like something was wrong."

"What do you mean?"

"He was crying, and he asked me to give him one reason why he shouldn't use."

"Oh baby! My Lord. Well there's nothing you can do but pray for him."

"Madea I tried to call him back and he won't answer his phone."

"Baby, I hate to say it, but that may have been his grandparents."

"Madea don't say that!"

"I know baby…it hurts. I know this is going to be hard, but wait until he calls you again. He'll tell you."

"What if he doesn't call?"

"Then I don't know what to say."

"Madea, his grandfather was always so nice to me," she sobs.

"I know baby, I know. Was he that man that was with him at the hospital?"

"Yes ma'am."

"Oh baby. Lord have mercy. Well, try to settle down and get some rest. We'll know pretty soon."

Monday morning, after making numerous calls to him, still, she had not heard from him.

She grabs the white pages and tries to find his grandparents address. Not knowing if it was or wasn't his grandparents tormented her. The television news station that aired the story confirmed the name of the older couple, verifying that indeed it was the Wilkerson's. In shock, she hangs up the phone. All at once, she feels sick to her stomach. She runs to the bathroom and throws up. Her head is laid on top of the toilet seat, she cries. Little baby Ethan had also begun to cry. At that moment, she didn't have the strength to go see about him.

His great grandfather was dead. How Harry must have been feeling right now. His grandfather was the only family member he had. He was good to him, especially making it a point to see about him these last two years. She cried for Mr. Wilkerson, his wife, and Harry. *How could life be so cruel to good people?* she thought. She calls into work and tells Dustin she doesn't feel well, and that she wouldn't be in today. He wanted to argue with her, but she hung up.

She musters enough strength to go see about the baby and calm him down. Then she gets dress and walks slowly over to her neighbor's Ms. Ross; house to ask her if she would come over and watch the baby for an hour. She drives to the Wilkerson's house and sees the yellow police tape surrounding Harry's grandparents' home. She gets out, a man from across the street, comes over to the Wilkerson's house.

"What happened?" she asked.

"Well, what I've been told, there were three young men, probably on that crack, broke in after dark to rob them. You know old man Wilkerson had a little money. He was retired from his city job, and his wife was a retired school teacher. They sure were nice people."

"I know but what happened?" she crosses her arms across her chest, with a blank facial expression.

"They kicked the back door in!"

"Why didn't they have burglar bars on the back door?" she asks.

"I don't know. Those people have been here for years, this area has gone down behind those drugs. Drugs are everywhere. Young folks don't care about anybody—anymore. They will even take your car away from you at the gas station. That's why I pack my pistol with me at all times. I hate to say that. But it has come down to either them or me. And it ain't going to be me." They both look at the front entry way of the house. He continued, "Wilkerson was old, and couldn't defend himself. They tried to take his large flat screen television but something went wrong. He did try to put up a struggle. After they shot him, they shot his wife who was hiding in their closet."

"Oh my God!"…Tammy burst out into tears.

"I know, such a sad way to go, for two of the nicest people I have known," he said.

Tammy gets into her car and starts to drive. Not wanting to go home she just wanted to drive and not-stop. She turns onto S. Western Ave, and then gets on the 105 Freeway, taking it pass Long Beach Fwy and drives until she's tired of driving. Meanwhile, Ms. Ross calls Tammy's grandmother and tells her that Tammy hasn't returned yet. "If she's not back within the next hour, I will come over," Madea tells her. When Tammy returns home, Ms. Ross is still there. "Child I didn't know what had happen."

"Ms. Ross, thank you for staying with the baby. I'm sorry. I had to run an errand, and it took longer than expected."

"I was getting worried. I called your grandmother."

"I'm okay…Thank you," she closes the door behind Ms. Ross. Madea calls her.

"Tammy Jean, are you okay?"

"Yes Ma'am."

"You didn't go to work today?"

"No, I needed a day off"…there is silence… "It's them," Tammy said.

"Oh my God!" Madea said.

"Why would God let this happen to them?" Tammy starts to cry again.

"Baby I don't know. He calls all of us at different times and different ways. Have you heard from Harry?"

"No ma'am. I can imagine what he's going through. This is enough to send him back to using."

"Well baby, I'm sorry to hear this. You've got to be strong... now...okay!"

"Yes ma'am."

"Okay, I'll talk with you later."

Tammy goes to work the next day. She tells Mr. Schmidt that she would like to switch back to the day shift, since she's out of school. "Mr. Schmidt, now that I have a baby, I have to make more money to take care of him. You don't offer health insurance, so I have to look out for me and the baby. I have checked around and prep workers make around $18,000 a year. Would you consider giving me this amount since I've gotten my culinary diploma?" Mr. Schmidt smiles. "Tammy you've been with me for over two years, and you have done more than average work. In the restaurant business, people come and go all the time. You know that we have gone through a lot of people. Yet you have stayed," he shuffles his seat around facing her.

"I know about some of the things that have happen here. Even though you may think I don't. You have showed determination, and I like that. You never gave up. How long have you been clean?" he looks at her with admiration while crossing his legs.

"Mr. Schmidt...nineteen months!" she drops her head, and lifts it again with a smile.

"See you can do it, yes I will give you what you're asking for."

She tucks her feet under her chair. "I can open the restaurant in the morning," she said. "Well why don't you plan on being here at 7:00am in the mornings and leave at 3:00pm." Her facial countenance changes to excitement. "Mr. Schmidt that works for me. I can continue making all the breads, the soups, sauces, and receive the product coming in. And work the hot line if needed."

"You don't want to work the cook line permanently?" he looks surprised. "No sir. I like the prep work better."

"Okay that sounds good...congratulations on your promotion." She hugs him and goes to her station.

That evening Tammy tries to reach Harry. Still no answer. She keeps getting his voice mail. Every morning, she buys a newspaper to read the obituaries to see if the Wilkerson's were in there. This morning she sees both their pictures and obituary. Their funeral is Friday, two days away. She makes preparations with Mr. Schmidt to attend and calls Madea and Evelyn to ask if they would attend his grandparents' funeral with her.

That Friday as they sit in the small church, the organist begins to play music. Next, some people get up to read scriptures and sing special songs. The minister had spoken some good things about the Wilkerson's and even mention Harry and his mother, and how the Wilkerson's loved them dearly. How they struggled with understanding when their daughter had died. And how sad they were when they lost contact with their grandson. "But they kept on praying and trusting God. Now God has called them home.

They both had run their course in this life, making life better for so many people. They were real special children of God"…he said. It was time to view the bodies. As Tammy walked up to both caskets she noticed…. *Each one looked beautiful, yet—cold and still*, she thought to herself. She couldn't believe they were gone. Funerals, she hated them and seeing people looking that way. As she goes back to her seat, she thought about when she first met Mr. Wilkerson, how nice he was. He took time to call her to see if she would come to the hospital to see Harry. *What did he think of me when I said no…*she thought. *He must have thought I was this horrible person. Still, he came to see me and the baby when we were in the hospital. Harry loved him.* Tammy held onto the bulletin, as she walked back to her seat. She would later contact the minister to see if he had heard from Harry.

As the pall bearers loaded the hearse, Tammy, Madeal and Evelyn got into Tammy's car to leave. They had decided not to go to the grave service. Tammy leaves the church parking lot and turns onto West 64th St. She sees Harry from her rear view mirror crossing the street. He hides behind the oversized tree near the parking lot, watching as the hearse pulls onto West 64th St. She stops in the middle of street.

"Gal! What are you stopping for?" Madea said, angrily.

"Madea there's Harry!" she blows her horn repeatedly.

"Tammy, you can't stop like this, keep going! Don't you see all these cars behind us?"

Tammy bends over the steering wheel and breaks down and cries. The baby starts crying from the loud temperaments in the car. "Evelyn, get up here and drive," Madea commands her. Evelyn hands the baby to Madea; she tries to calm him down from crying. Evelyn gets out, opens the driver's door and pulls Tammy out. She gets into the back seat and curls up into a fetal position...sobbing loudly.

"I didn't see him in the service. He must have been parked on the street waiting until the service ended," Evelyn said. She looks at Madea and asked, "Where are we going?" Madea pats the baby on the back trying to quiet him down. "Child please take me home! And you and that gal back there can do whatever you want to do."

"Tammy did you take off, all day today?" Evelyn asked. Tammy doesn't say anything.

They arrive at Madea's house. Tammy gets into the front seat and drives off.

"She's mad now," Evelyn said. Madea heads toward the front door. Evelyn holds the screen door open while she searches for her keys. "She will be okay," Madea said. Tammy goes to her house and puts the baby in his play pen. She sits on the sofa and watches television, hoping that the phone would ring and that it would be Harry. By 10:00pm that night, he had not called. The death of Ethan's great grandfather affected her in a shocking way. She was scared, thinking how life was short and that anything could happen to anyone.

It is November, and today's weather is clear, except for some fog in the air. Last month she had attended the Wilkerson funeral and was beginning to accept they were gone. *Harry should be getting out of treatment this month. If he was still there,* she thought while applying her make-up and getting dress for work. "Surely his grandparents' death was too much to handle. It would have been too much for even me to handle," she whispers. "Well, I can't think about him, he's a grown man, he can take care of himself. But, I would like for him to call on his baby's first birthday to at least say Happy Birthday," she mumbles. When she arrives at work, she tells Dustin she has a doctor's appointment and needs to leave a little early. "Since you have gotten your little diploma, you have started to get sloppy in your attendance," he said. She turns around and tells him, "Dustin…today is a good day for me. Not even you get to mess it up," then she walks back to her station.

That afternoon, she takes Ethan for his one year check up with his doctor. He is now crawling for the first time. The doctor checks his weight and measurements, gives him his next round of vaccines and performs the general examinations. Because he has Down syndrome he hasn't been able to say his first words yet.

The doctor tells her, "Pre-speech and pre-language skills must be learned first through imitating and echoing sounds, learning peek a boo, teaching the baby to focus on the speaker and objects, and by listening to music and speech for long periods of time. Then showing the baby to use his tongue, and move his lips. When you get a chance, make sure you work with the baby on his speech development," she touches Tammy's shoulder. Baby Ethan also has a sleep disorder; he has short periods of not breathing during his sleep. He awakens, briefly, each time only to resume sleeping. This keeps Tammy up at night and when he sleeps with her, sometimes he's restless, whiny, and difficult to calm down. It has had a negative impact on her moods at times. The fatigue and lack of sleep she experiences seems to compound the problem. Similar to when she was in school, when she didn't get enough rest. She was too depressed, to stay focused at times and was crying all the time. She wanted to sleep, but what she really wanted to do was die.

On her way home, she thinks about how hard her life has been and all the stress she has been under, depressed one day and manic the next. *Still and all, her final goal wasn't that far off*, she thought to herself. She needed to keep going in spite of her emotions. For nine months she has worked on her business plan, and this month it's completed. The first thing she does is call her local Health Department to check their regulations. She was told she would need to get a series of permits, insurance and inspection certificates. Therefore, she would have to rent the use of a kitchen approved for commercial food preparation and storage. The health department provided her with a list of approved kitchen facilities in her area. She locates a small local church in Inglewood and talks with the pastor about her concept. He tells her he would have to talk with the board about it and get back in contact with her.

Two weeks later, she gets a phone call from the pastor that her request was approved. It was their way of giving back to the community. And they would charge her half of what she would pay to lease a commercial space. She applies for her business license and food permit at the county clerk's office. She purchase's liability insurance specific for catering services through a business insurance provider. Business cards are printed. Monday through Friday after work, she spends one hour a day advertising her new business, handing out fliers and business cards in the better parts of the Inglewood area. She also mails fliers to every church in the area, telling them about the menus she is capable of offering to clients. Equally, she sends mailings to families with children in the Inglewood area.

One month later she is catering her first event to the early intervention group she attends. Her first event was so successfully for children born in December that she was booked for the month of January. Additionally, she would get phone inquiries from her flyers that were distributed. She was getting the hang of it and liked having her own business. By catering her birthday parties on weekends enabled her to work two affairs in one day, not jeopardizing her weekday job.

Back at the restaurant, a certain young woman has come in every Friday for the pass month, usually around 2:30pm. She has hopes of getting a glimpse of her mother. She waits patiently for Tammy to come out. Some days she sees her rushing to leave, and other times, she sees her standing around talking with some of the waitresses. However, today she has decided to follow her home. She finishes her lunch and waits for Tammy to walk out. Knowing where Tammy parks, she parks one row of cars over from her. Tammy comes out and throws her purse into the front seat of her car, and then leaves. She follows her to Compton and parks several cars away from where her car is parked. Thirty minutes later, Tammy comes out with a baby. She sits him in his car seat and takes off. "Whose house is this?" Hannah wonders.

"Whose child is that?"

Hannah follows Tammy to Lynwood. Once again she parks several cars down and watches her as she takes the baby out and goes inside. She waits twenty minutes or so to see if she will be coming back out. She drives by slowly to write down the address. "That must be where she lives," she mumbles out loud. The next week, she follows her again, and notices that she stops at both locations regularly. She wants to leave a note but doesn't. That evening Tammy gets a phone call from Harry.

"Hi…How are you and my son?"

"Harry!…Where have you been?"

"I'm okay. I called to see how you were?"

"The baby and I are doing good. I'm so sorry about your grandparents. Is there anything I can do?"

"Nah, I'm fine. I want to see you and the baby…soon, would you think about it?"

"Sure Harry. Maybe we can get together in a couple of days."

"Okay, I'll talk with you later," he hangs up.

Saturday morning Hannah drives to Tammy's house and leaves her a note. *I need to talk with you…signed Hannah.* Tammy comes home that night, finds the note and reads it.

"Oh!…My God"…she drops her purse on the floor, running through the house crying. "I can't believe this. My baby has found me." Immediately, she calls Evelyn and Madea to tell them about the note. Madea tells her to bring Hannah over when she makes contact with her. Several days pass, and she hasn't heard from Hannah. Tammy slumps into a deep depression. At night she had begun having auditory hallucinations and nightmares. For days at a time, she would have panic attacks and wasn't eating often enough. Even though she was glad to hear from Hannah, she didn't know what to tell her or how to tell her the truth about her being taken away from her when she was a baby. Depressed and scared she knew she had been neglectful as a mother. "What does she think about me?" she contemplated.

One Friday afternoon, Hannah was seating in a booth near the restrooms. She sees Tammy getting ready to leave. "Tammy!" She hears someone calling her and turns around to see a tall beautiful "medium brown" complexion—young woman, with waist length small black micro braids, approaching her. Tammy looks at her... "Hannah?" Hannah walks closer to her... "Yes it's me." Tammy gasps and screams out, then covers her mouth. She hugs Hannah. Customers in the restaurant are looking at her and Hannah. "Oh, let's take this outside," Tammy said. "Hannah, Oh my baby," she hugs her again. Hannah pulls away. Tammy begins to walk in a fast pace to her car. "So, baby how have you been?" Hannah stares at her, but doesn't answer.

"Hannah?"

"Tammy, I'm okay."

"Oh baby! It's so good to see you."

"I wanted to meet the woman that gave me up for adoption nineteen years ago."

"Hannah," Tammy touches her face. Hannah jerks away.

"Hannah lets go to my home and talk."

"What!...Do you mean that dump you call a house in Lynwood?" Tammy looks at her, with shock and refrains from getting angry.

"Hannah, I know you're upset with me."

"You're #@% right...I am!"

"Baby!"

Hannah steps back, "Stop calling me baby, I'm 24 years old now."

"I know, I know, you're a grown woman now. But can we please talk, let me give you my home number." Nervously she searches for a pen and note pad in her purse. She scribbles down her number. "Would you please call me tonight? Maybe you'll let me take you out to dinner, and we can talk." Hannah looks down at the piece of paper, takes it and walks off. Tammy sits in her car, fidgeting her hands and feet, while chewing the inside of her mouth. "God, Oh God," she looks up into the rear view mirror to see if she could see what direction Hannah had walked to. She watches Hannah pull off in her Red sports car.

Tammy goes to her grandmothers to pick up Ethan. When she walked in, Madea could tell something was wrong. "Tammy how was work today?" Tammy walks over to the baby and starts to play with him. "Oh, it was okay." In deep concentration, she looked like she had lost her best friend. "Did you ever hear from Hannah?" Tammy sits down and places her hands up against her face.

"Yeah, and she hates me," breathing in and out she sighs.

"She hates you, what did she say?"

"It wasn't what she said; it was what she didn't say. Madea she wouldn't even hug me, and then she told me I lived in a dump."

"These young folks today are so disrespectful." Madea begins to rattle pots and pans as she is washing dishes.

"Why has she come back into my life?"

"Huh?"…Madea yells out.

Tammy gets up and walks into the kitchen. "I said, why did she come back into my life?"

Madea turns around and looks at her. Then said, "You know I have mixed feelings about children finding their parents. They have a right yes. But if they do not want to forgive their parents but taunt them, then it would be better for everyone if the child doesn't come around. When you lost her and her siblings, you were a different person at that time. We can't change mistakes like that. We have to move forward. I hope a good family has taken her in and provided for her. How did she look?"

"I almost didn't know who she was. Tall, beautiful, high maintenance, and she drives a expensive fancy red sports car." Madea reaches for a kitchen towel. "Oh yeah, either she has a family that has been good to her or she got some kind of sugar daddy." Tammy takes down a bag of chips and eats from the bag. "That's what I'm saying, why come back now?" Madea finishes drying the pots and pans and places them into the

cabinets. "Baby, I don't know what to tell you. But it will reveal itself...
sooner or later."

"Okay, I'll keep you posted," she hugs her, and Tammy leaves
with the baby.

That night at home, she thought about how she didn't want to
crash into depression and end up, filling remorse and horror at the
mean things that Hannah had said. Or what she would say to her, if
things got out of hand. She didn't want to spend a lot of time "cleaning
up" after herself, explaining, apologizing, and trying to make it up to
her.

The next night, when she gets home, Hannah calls, and asks her
if she is available tonight for dinner. "Hannah, I just walked in the door
and I'm tired tonight, could we do it maybe tomorrow?"

"I wanted to talk to you tonight," she snaps at her.

"Hey Hannah...wait a minute, first of all, I don't appreciate you
being disrespectful to me. You call here and you don't even say hello,
you just start right on in."

"Never mind"...Hannah hangs up. Tammy slams the phone
down.

"Who does she think she is?" she begins to clean up the house,
picking up toys and clothes from the week, with clothes in hand
she starts a laundry of clothes. The phone rings. She can't hear it
because of the washer. It rings four times. Tammy stops the washer to add additional clothes; she hears the phone and runs to answer it. "Hello, Hello," no one's there. She had missed a call from
Harry.

Two weeks had come and gone, and she hasn't heard from Hannah. But one night, Hannah calls in the middle of the night to apologize. She asks Tammy if she would like to meet Sunday for lunch at a
buffet restaurant. Tammy agrees.

That Sunday, Tammy meets her at the restaurant. Hannah looked
tired. "Baby why you look so tired?" Tammy asked her.

"I just finished school and I've been celebrating."

"Hannah! That is wonderful. What were you studying?"

"I got my bachelors in nursing."

"Hannah, Tammy begins to cry. I knew you would make it." Hannah stares at her. Tammy wipes her face with a napkin. "Is there anything wrong?" Tammy said.

"What do you mean?"

"Well, why and how did you find me?"

"I wanted to see why you gave me up and what you did for a living. I have some unresolved memories of our times together as a family before joining my adoptive family. It is important for me to talk about them."

"You were a baby. What memories do you have?"

"That's why I'm asking you, to see if what I remember is right," Hannah snaps at her.

"But Hannah...Why?...Why rehash all that pain?"

"Because I need to know the real reason why you gave us up." Tammy throws her napkin on the table. "Let's get some food, and I'll answer your question." They get up, and head to the buffet. Once their plates were filled, Hannah takes a bite from her taco.

"Is that all you're eating?"...Tammy asked her.

"Yeah, I'm not really that hungry," Hannah says.

Tammy takes a bite from her salad, and wipes her mouth. "Hannah, during the time we lived together as a family." Hannah rolls her eyes back. "Hannah life is hard!" Tammy said.

"What?...Tammy, I mean, didn't you love us?"

"I'm trying to answer your question." Hannah takes another bite from her taco.

"Those were some crazy times for me. My life was a mess. I admit that. But I did and still do love you and your two sisters. Just some things happen. Wrong choices I made caused me to lose my kids. And, I'm sorry for putting you through that...Can you forgive me?" Hannah doesn't say anything. Tammy takes another bite of her salad.

"I saw you with a little boy...Who is he?"

Tammy smiles, "He is your baby brother, and his name is Ethan."

"Aren't you a little too old to be having children?"

"Well it wasn't like it was planned." Tammy pauses, "He is a special needs baby."

"You mean he's retarded?"

"Why are you being so mean?"

"I'm not being mean. He's retarded, that's all I'm saying."

"Okay, let's talk about you. How have you been? Tell me about the people that have adopted you?"

"What my mother?"

"Okay Hannah."

"It's a white family, they take good care of me."

"A white family?" Tammy looks puzzled.

"Yeah," Hannah said.

"Do they have any children?

"No." Hannah gets up, goes back to the buffet table, and comes back.

"What are their names?"

"I rather not say."

"Okay," Tammy said.

"He even brought me a sports car."

"What kind is it?"

"Saturn Sky-Red Line. When I turned sixteen he taught me how to drive and I have had nice cars ever since."

"What does she do for a living?"

"She doesn't have to work, she volunteers."

"Oh! Well, sounds like they have taken good care of you."

"Yeah. I have the best of everything."

"Well that's good to hear Hannah." Tammy puts her head down, and then excuses herself from the table. Five minutes later she comes back. You could tell she had been crying. "I bet you were a good student, making all A's," Tammy said.

"No not really. I had to work with a lot of tutors."

"How come?" Tammy asks.

"I don't know."

"But you finished high school and college, that says a lot."

"I guess so."

"Are you looking for work?"

"Not really. I just got out of school, and I'm taking it easy. My rent is covered, and I live in one of the school's apartments off campus, been there four years."

"Where?"

"In Carson, but my parents want me to come and live at home again until I find work, and save up money to get my own place. My adoptive father has even told me he will help with the down payment on a house."

"That sounds good," Tammy moves her water glass over. "I'm curious how did you find me?" she has a curious look on her face. "I used registries, worked with the case worker that handled my adoption, and the hospital. I was allowed to petition the court to receive identifying information for medical reasons."

"Medical reasons? Are you okay?" Tammy looks at her suspiciously.

"Yeah!"

Tammy takes another bite of her salad. Puts her hand up to her mouth. "Do you have a boyfriend?"

"I have an on again off again boyfriend."

"What does that mean?"

"It's too complicated."

"Oh!"...Tammy said. Hannah tosses her braids back.

"Who stays in Compton?"

"Your grandmother's, mother."

"How old is she?"

"She's in her late sixties."

"Huh," Hannah said.

"She wants to see you. It has been years since she last seen you. You were a young baby, and I'm sure Auntie Evelyn would like to see you, she has two daughters."

"We'll see." Hannah catches hold of the table ends.

"Well thanks for lunch."

"Is that it?... You're leaving?"

"Yeah, I'll call you."

"Hannah can I at least get a hug?" Hannah looks at her and walks off.

That evening little Ethan was discontented and withdrawn, un-responsive not just to Tammy but to Madea, as well. He was crying a lot, appeared apathetic and listless, had problems eating, sleeping and he wasn't growing normally. At times, Tammy was pressed to be a good mother, and other times, she found it hard and difficult to bond with him. She had begun to not pay attention to his signals or at the other extreme; she could be overly intrusive and hostile toward the baby. By the ends week, she was exhausted and didn't want to be bothered with him.

Her two jobs kept her busy and she missed not being able to have me time for herself.

Now, there was Hannah back in her life. She knew ultimately she would have to try to mend their relationship.

Some days, Hannah would pop into the restaurant unexpected to have lunch before Tammy's shift ended. This day, one of the wait-resses notices her and tells Tammy that she has a guest. Tammy walks out to her table with a smile on her face. "I was thinking about you this morning."

"Oh!...How come?"

"Do I have to have a reason to think about you?" Tammy sits down across the table from her. Hannah takes a bite of her beef tips and homemade noodles. "What did you do today?"

"Pretty much nothing."

"Boy I wish I had that luxury," Tammy grins.

"You get off from work at 3:00pm every day?"

"Yeah. Have you started looking for work yet?"

"No."

"When were you planning on starting? Or better still...what are you planning to do with your life...baby?"

"I told you the other time, that I just finished nursing school. So that means, probably I will be looking for nursing jobs," Hannah snaps at her. Tammy frowns. "Well, being that it's a new year, you should start looking for work now. Since everyone is looking for work in January." Hannah stops eating.

"I'm in control of my life. You can't tell me what to do so don't even try. Anyway how would you know?...You're an idiot."

"Excuse me, are all your little friends talking to their mothers like this?" Hannah looks at Tammy with a blank stare. "Well, I have to pick up the baby, and you seem to be in a bad mood."

"You mean your retarded child?"

"Hannah...I need for you to watch your tone with me. I don't care anything about you being 24 years old." Tammy gets up from the table. "When you want to talk to me with respect...then call me." In a hurry she walks out the door. She was trying to hide her emotional pain she was holding inside. She had to become a good actress. Smile, even laugh on cue when dealing with Hannah. At home though, she would fall apart and sink deeper into her depression.

Hannah doesn't trust anyone. Her and her siblings went into the foster care system when they were very young. Hannah was five years old and the oldest. She has been tossed around through the system for years, finally ending up at a prominent white family home who could not have any children. Her adopted father "John Paul Freeman" is a well known prominent chiropractor and board director at a specialty hospital in the community.

Her adoptive mother, "Piper Freemen," is pensive, brooding, and contemplative. Because of her husband's prominence, she has the luxury of buying whatever she wants and not worry about the everyday essentials. She's cultured and stylish, buying only designer labels and top of the line products. Involved in charity events and philanthropic causes, she's a socialite. Over the years while living with them, Hannah has picked up a snotty and disrespectful attitude. However, secretly she feels she does not truly belong anywhere. She views Tammy's lifestyle as impoverish and doesn't respect her, in spite of Tammy's recent accomplishments.

Harry stops by to see Tammy and the baby. But they're not there. He leaves a note on her door. When she arrives in, she looks at the note. "I missed him again, he needs to give me his new cell phone number" she mumbles while, opening the front door. An hour later, Evelyn calls. "Hey, whatcha doing?"

"Girl, I just got in, another note from Harry."

"Where is he?"

"I have the faintest idea. I keep missing him. It would be interesting to see what he's doing. The last time I spoke with him, he wanted for the baby and me to meet him. You have any ideas about where we could go as a family?"

"Hmmm"…Evelyn thinks for a moment… "Hey, I've got an idea. There's a place in Pasadena called…wait a second…what is that place name?" she yells out to her daughters. "What is that place in Pasadena that we went to that you liked so much.…Kidspace children museum. That's it…Sis…Kidspace. It's on N. Arroyo, on the west end of Brookside Park, near the Rose Bowl stadium. They have a really creative learning indoor exhibit and even outdoor learning environments for kids. And we saw quite a few toddlers there when we went."

"You know…Sis, we may go there. When he calls, I will bring it up to him." That following week Harry calls, and they make arrangements to take the baby to Pasadena. Harry wasn't the same since his grandparents' death, not wanting to talk about their death at all. He was very quiet not talkative, and deeply sad. She could tell there were a lot of things going on in his mind. He was having a hard time thinking clearly and his decision making, seemed impaired. Maybe because he was still in a state of mourning. She could see that he was hurting. He watches Tammy and the baby throughout the entire trip. But he doesn't say much.

He had thought he needed to settle down and buy a home. He didn't know how he was going to do it. But knew it was the right thing to do. He wanted to make sure Ethan had him around at all times. His grandfather words of wisdom were beginning to make sense. He need-ed to stand up and be a man, responsible for his son. Tammy had told him that her daughter was back in her life, and she needed to spend time with her to mend their broken relationship. And, that she wouldn't be spending a lot of time with him. *That may have been what he needed...he* thought. It would give him a chance to get his act together. After their outing he takes Tammy and the baby home.

Day in and day out, at work, she continues to perform her ev-eryday tasks. She felt confident about her job, and knew that she didn't have to worry about losing it, even if, Dustin went on one of his firing rampages. Mr. Schmidt had made it clear to him that he was proud of her and that she was an asset to his business. On the weekends, she con-tinues to work her catering job, with sometimes catering twenty affairs a month. The church that allowed her to use their kitchen also provided volunteers occasionally to help cook the meals for her. Tonight, Tammy is at home cooking dinner and the phone rings. It's Hannah wanting to talk...

Chapter 9

"HELLO TAMMY, HOW are you?"

"I'm great…how are you?"

"Oh, I was planning on going out with some friends."

"Okay, are you 'all going to a movie or what?" Tammy asks.

"Probably a movie."…Hannah pauses…"Can I ask you a question?"…Hannah said.

"Sure what is it?" Tammy opens her oven to check the temperature on her meat that was baking.

"Why is it, all of a sudden you have this motherly drive?"

"What do you mean Hannah?"

"I mean, why didn't you fight for us?"

"Hannah I have always loved you and my other kids. When I moved into this place that was one of my hopes and desires, that one day, I would be able to see my kids and make amendments with them."

"Well, now you have your baby."

"Stop saying that!…He's your brother."

"Hey Tammy, I was talking about…your kids, not the baby."

"Hannah, I'm trying to be the best mother I can."

"You're trying to be the best mother? You weren't a good mother then, how has that changed?" Tammy slams the top down onto her sauce pot, "Hannah, Hannah…Alright, Alright…Did you want to talk about something else?"

"No. Thought I would call to say hello. Now that I've said hello… I will talk to you later," Hannah hangs up. Tammy looks at the phone receiver. "I can't believe her. How could she have this much hatred for me?" After her conversations with Hannah sometimes, she would sit in her chair and gaze at the front door, her emotions frozen. Those were the times when her depression would come on suddenly. Her depression could be so gripping, at times it was hard to walk out the door and leave the house. She didn't know what to do and didn't want to ask for help. In a strange place emotionally, at times she thought she would never get out of it. Some days she never even showered. Here was her first born, who hated her. That was hard to deal with.

While in school, Hannah was diligent about her studies. Occasionally, she would hang out with her friends on the weekends at different bars, mostly to meet guys. Her girlfriends were the complete opposite of her. She was temperamental. It is hard for her to trust anyone—the adults in her early years, for whatever reason, did not meet her emotional needs. Her daily struggle is with serious low self-esteem. On the other hand, her two girlfriends are funny, wild, adventurous, and love to party. Hannah feels like she fits in with this group. It is the acceptance that she gets, that keeps her connected to them and this lifestyle.

One evening, several days later, Hannah stops by Tammy's home. Tammy looks out the peep hole, sighs, and then opens the door. "Hi. I was in the area and thought I would stop by. Can I come in?" Tammy looks at her… "Sure baby come on in." Hannah walks around her home, going from room to room as Tammy watches her. "May I use your restroom?"

"Sure it's right there." Hannah takes off her light weight evening coat, and lays it on the chair. Tammy starts to pick up the clutter on her coffee table. Hannah sits down in the living room. "I was on my way to an art exhibit and thought I would stop by."

"They have an art exhibit in Lynwood today?"

"No!...In Los Angeles."

"Okay...Hannah, did you want something to eat or drink before you go?"

"No...thank you."

"You look nice in your black silky dress."

"Thank you, John bought it for me. It cost $450.00 dollars."

"Whew...girl who can afford that type of money for a dress? Anyway, who is John? Is that your boyfriend?"

"No...silly!...John is my adoptive father, I wanted to look glamorous tonight." Tammy puts her newspapers in a bundle stack. "Well sugar, you do look that way." Hannah was wearing an elegant long sleeve form fitting silky black dress. It had a lightning bolt, rhinestones design weaved through the bodice and into the top of the floor-length, flowing skirt with side-slit.

Tammy goes to the kitchen and grabs a glass of water. "Are you sure you don't won't anything to drink?"

"I guess I could take a glass of water." Tammy cleans out a glass and fills it with cold water and brings it to her. Hannah starts to cry. "Baby what's wrong?" Tammy puts her arm around her. Hannah is weeping and screaming one minute, then giggly the next. "I'm okay."

"Are you sure?"

"Yeah...I'm excited about tonight. There's going to be some big name rich people there, a lot of celebrities. Then we're going to go partying after it's over."

"Hannah...what's going on with you?" Hannah puts her glass down and stands up. "Tammy, I owe you no explanations of what's going on in my life. Remember you gave me up years ago."

"Hannah, then why come over here? Why are you playing these games with my mind?"

Tammy begins to cry, "Can't you see how you're hurting me?" Then she shouts at the top of her voice, "I can't change the past...I can't change the past...Hannah...But I'm still your mother."

"You never attended any PTA meetings, you were not there when I got on the bus to go to camp, and you never threw a birthday party for me, should I go on? No...Tammy. You're not my mother. A mother is someone that raises you, is there for you when you're hurting, and takes care of you. You haven't done that for me, or my sisters." Hannah walks out, gets into her car and drives off.

Tammy paces the floor, back and forth. She takes a pillow off the sofa and hits the top of the sofa. The phone rings and its Evelyn. Hysterical she screams... "Yes, what is it?"

"Sis...what's wrong?"

"Evelyn, I can't talk right now. Hannah just left here and"...she breaks down, crying hard.

"Sis, do you need me to come over?"

"No...I'm be okay. I just can't take this."

"What is she doing?"

"She's trying to make me feel bad about not being there for her."

"Ah! Sis. That is so sad. I mean why is she doing this? Does she know and understand what she's doing? She's causing emotional disruption in your life, damaging both herself and you."

"Sis. I can't handle it. The more I try to reach out to her. The worst it gets."

"You're going to have to tell her not to come around anymore if she can't be respectful to you. That's it."

"I don't know. I've got to figure something out."

"Have you told Madea?"

"No. I don't want to upset her. It'll be okay. Maybe with a little more time, things will turn around."

"Okay...well, if you need me, let me know, I love you!"

"I love you to Sis," Tammy hangs up. She had begun to compare feeling depressed with the feelings of a five-year-old who didn't know how to look after herself in this "big bad world." She needed someone to take her by the hand, cuddle and hold her until it felt better.

Later, that night Harry calls. Upset, she doesn't want to talk. He becomes concern. "Hey did you need me to come over there and cheer you up?" She laughs. "No, I'll be fine. It is this daughter of mine. I really would like for her to meet you." He sounds surprised. "Tammy, after everything you have told me about her, you still want to continue on trying to make it work with her?"

"Why not...Harry? She's my family, my blood. Definitely a problem child but that's something I have to work through," she turns up the TV volume. "Girl, you are amazing. Well let me know when you want for all of us to get together. How's my son?" She chuckles. "He's fine."Okay let me know...when and where," he hangs up.

With working both her restaurant job and catering business, she's never at home anymore, except at nights. "If I can work both of these jobs until I can save up a nice down payment, me and Ethan can move into our own home. Let's see how many months I would need to save," she gets out her calculator and adds up her business, and personal expenses. "Man, I'm looking at a while before...I will have the money to pay twenty percent down on a house," she leans back into her dining room chair, with her head down and hand up against her head. "Man I've got to stay focused."

Three months had passed, and she was sitting outside on her front porch, thinking about how she hasn't heard from Hannah. Six months ago, when Hannah came to see her, she was so happy that her grown-up baby had taken the initiative to find her. Yet each time they spoke, she always felt so much pain and sadness. Nevertheless, she gave birth to her and wondered where she was and how was she doing. She didn't know how to ease Hannah's pain, and Hannah wasn't making it easy to bond with her. Her phone rings, she runs inside to answer it. "Hello, Tammy"...the voice on the other line sounded down. "Hannah?" Tammy listens closely for a response. "Yes, it's me." There is silence. "I was sitting on the porch thinking about you."

"Oh...that's nice. Tammy, my best friend father has been abusing her sexually for years.

I feel really sad for her. The other night, she asked me.... what should she do? Tell her mother or what?"

"Someone needs to be told about it!"…Tammy said angrily. "It's not you is it?"

"Didn't you just hear me say, it was my best friend?"

"Ok…Hannah. Well, like I said, she should talk to someone about it. And try to get out as quickly as possible. Does she have anywhere to go?"

"No."

"Maybe she could go to a shelter or something."

"A shelter?…Did I hear you say a shelter?"

"Yeah…they have all types of shelters for women in distress," Tammy says.

"No. I can't see that happening."

"Hannah, people will do whatever they have too, to survive, if they are old enough to make the right decision."

"Ok, well I thought I would call to say hello."

"When can I see you again? …. Maybe you, me and baby Ethan can do something soon?"

"How soon?"…Hannah whispers. Startle, Tammy smiles.

"Whenever you're ready," Tammy says.

"We could go to the mall and walk around," Hannah said.

"That would be hard to do with a baby," Tammy said.

"I love-shopping," Hannah, said. Tammy laughs. "Well"… "Maybe."

"C'mon, Mom!"

"Ok, what about Saturday evening? I will have my sister to keep Ethan."

"That would be great; I'll talk with you before Saturday." Tammy sits back down on her porch. "Maybe, she's trying to come around," she whispers. A couple of days later, late Saturday afternoon, Hannah calls. "Tammy, I am ready to meet you when you are."

"Ok, where do I meet you?" Tammy said.

"Let's meet at the Mid Wilshire District near Third and Fairfax—The Grove."

"You want me to meet you at the Grove?"

"Yeah!"

"Ok…Hannah. Where inside of the place?"

"Chico's clothing store."

"Ok, I'll try to find it."

"What time will you be there?" asked Hannah.

"Give me at least an hour."

"Ok"…Hannah hangs up.

Tammy gets into her car, and she rushes over to the mall. She wanted to arrive early, to give herself sometime to find the clothing store. Inside Chico's she looks around at the different clothing. Five minutes later Hannah approaches her. She looked different from the last time she had seen her; three months ago. She had on a pair of narrow leg denim stretch jeans with a graphic tee shirt that said; "Love is the answer." Multi-color flat shoes, a muted pink color head beret, trimmed in vintage velvet flowers, hiding the roots of her waist length black micro braids. "Hannah, you look beautiful as always." Hannah tosses her braids back. "Thank you," she said.

Today, she wore a sad countenance. Tammy didn't want to ask her any questions, fearing it would trigger an explosive argument. They look around the store and Hannah picks out two outfits, a leopard print dress and a mesh style-open weave cardigan, animal print tank top, light taupe denim boot leg jeans, along with matching jewelry and earrings. In all it cost Tammy over $300.00 dollars, it was more money than she had planned on spending. But it was Hannah, her daughter.

They leave the mall and have dinner at the Avocado Grill on N Larchmont. Tammy chose this place because the food was fresh and inexpensive. The two talked for two hours, mostly Tammy, filling in Hannah about her determination for getting her diploma in culinary. "So, you're officially a chef now?" Tammy sighs… "Yes, I guess you could say that, I own my own catering business."

"Really?"

"Yeah. It's brand new and I only do a small number of clients per week." Hannah doesn't say anything. "Have you found any good nursing jobs?" Hannah looks down at her food. "I've applied at several places, but I'm still looking for the right job."

"What is the right job?"

"Good money and flexibility. I have a lot of options. So, I'm taking it easy."

"Hannah how are you able to support yourself?" Hannah looks around the restaurant.

"John, my adoptive father helps me out with everything. He has spoiled me…I guess you could say." Tammy picks up her fork and takes a bite of her food. "What about your adoptive mother," then she separates her food on her plate.

"We started having problems four years ago, she decided it was best for me to go to college. So, I've been out of the house living in a campus apartment the whole time. John comes by every week to see me and gives me money." Tammy doesn't say anything, taking it all in.

"Sometimes he takes me on day trips on the weekends."

Tammy leans back into her seat, "What are day trips? Tammy asks.

Hannah looks at her with a puzzled expression, "They're short distance road trips. Sequoia National Park, Vasquez Rocks, Catalina Islands, places like that. Usually you can drive back in a matter of hours."

"Does your other mother go with you?"

"Her name is…Piper…no she doesn't go. She does her own thing. I think they're married for convenience sake. They sleep in the same room but that's about it. Anyway, why should she care? He is rich, she doesn't have to be bother with him and she can spend his money anyway she wants too. I guess it's an invisible contract." Hannah takes a napkin and wipes food off her blouse. "They've been married for a very long time. I would like to have that kind of marriage."

"What does he look like?"

"He's chubby but solid; maybe twenty-five pounds overweight, but says he's cutting back on his meal portions, and he has started an exercise regimen." Hannah smiles. "He is kind hearted, gentle, has a good sense of humor, has brains, and treats us well." Hannah takes a sip of her fountain drink and sits her glass down. "Well Tammy, I need to leave. Later I'm meeting some friends for drinks, so I need to go home and change."

"Oh Hannah, Ethan's' daddy would like to meet you!"

"Why me?"

"We thought it would be nice to have a cook off, and that you would come, Evelyn and her girls will be there, sort of like a family get together."

"Sure. When?"

"What about next month—June? That will give me a chance to organize it and make sure everyone can come."

"Did you need me to bring anything?" Hannah asks.

"No...just yourself." Tammy stands up, they both embrace for what seemed like a long time... "Baby, take care of yourself," Tammy said.

"Thank you for everything," Hannah said, and then she leaves.

Tammy stops by Evelyn's on her way home to pick up the baby and tells her how the outing went. "She was a little sad today, I could tell. I didn't want to pry in her business, so I left it alone. But when we went to grab something to eat, she opened up a little about her life. She didn't go into a lot of detail. But her adoptive father seems to cater to her needs and wants. I'm a little concern about that."

"Girl, you know that's how white people do it. If they've got money. They spend it on their kids. Do they have any children of their own?"

"Hannah says no."

"Well see, there you go. They're trying to make up for not having any kids."

"I don't know Evelyn...Piper."

"Who's that?"...Evelyn interrupts.

"Hannah's other mother. She didn't mention anything about them being close or doing things together. It was always about the father coming around."

"Girl don't worry about it. The most important thing is they have helped her to get in school and she's finished with it now. Is she working?"

"That's the other strange thing about this. He's paying for everything."

"Tammy, that's what white fathers do!"

"I take it she doesn't have to work. Or, she has the leisure of taking her time in finding a job," Tammy says.

"Sis, don't worry about it. She's opening up and that's a start. I would love to meet her.

Why don't I cook dinner this next weekend, and you and her both come over?"

"That sounds good, but let me check with her. Her mood changes instantly with no predictability. She's bossy, harsh, critical, and aloof. Let me see. I'll talk to her about it." Tammy picks up the baby and leaves.

A week later, Hannah calls Tammy. "Hey, while I got you on the phone, Evelyn, my sister, is cooking dinner on Sunday afternoon, and wanted to know if you could come?"

"Yeah. What time?"

"I don't know. Maybe around 3:00pm. Would that be good for you?"

"Yeah, I don't see why not."

"Ok, I'll tell her, and if you want to you can bring your boyfriend."

"Ah!"…."We're off again." Tammy chuckles. "Oh! Oh! He's in the dog house…huh?"

"Pretty much."

"Well still come."

"Ok! Where do I come?"

"Why don't you come to my house and me and the baby can ride with you over there." "That will work"…Hannah said.

The next weekend, Hannah stops by, and they drive over to Evelyn's home. Hannah pulls up to the 2800 block of Griffin Ave,

"Okay turn into here," Tammy said. They get out and ring the door bell.

"Hey!" Greeted by Evelyn and her daughters. They walk in and Hannah sits on the sofa next to the mock fireplace. "If you want to, you can come into the kitchen. I'm waiting on the cornbread to finish baking." Hannah gets up and goes into the small cramp kitchen. "Um, not much room to move around," Hannah says. Tammy looks at Evelyn. Evelyn laughs. Tammy takes the baby into the girl's room. By that time, Evelyn and Hannah are sitting at the small breakfast table, having small talk while waiting for her. Tammy walks in, opens the refrigerator and grabs three cans of soda.

"Hannah, it is good to see you. The last time I saw you, you were three years old."

"Really?"

"Tammy tells me you just got your bachelors in nursing."

"Yep." Hannah takes a sip of her soda.

"Well that's good." Not knowing what to say, she's gets quiet.

"What do you do for a living?" Hannah asked.

"I'm a home health aide. I take care of elderly people."

"Oh! So you're sort of in the health profession?"

"Yeah, you could say that."

"Do you like it?"

"I have good days and some bad days."

"What are your bad days?"

"Oh!...Like when I've been working with someone for a while and they die on you.

That's always hard, especially if you have developed a bond with them."

"Does it happen often?"

"No, but when it does, it's hard. I cook their meals, make sure they're taking their meds, wash their clothes, and take them to doctor's appointments...things like that. Yeah, I have been doing this, since I was eighteen, right after leaving home. I had to find a way to support my babies." Tammy gets up and goes to the bedroom to check on Ethan. Evelyn then gets up and checks the cornbread.

"So, what have you been doing all these years?...Ms. Hannah."

"Huh? Oh!...Just trying to make it." Evelyn laughs with a roar, so loud that Tammy comes back into the kitchen. "What?...Did I miss something?" Tammy says.

"I asked Hannah what she had been doing all these years and she said...Oh!...Just trying to make it." Hannah laughs also.

"Girl, you're silly"...Tammy jokingly said. "No...Tammy, I'm serious," then Hannah breaks out into insuppressible laughter. *It was wonderful to see Hannah smile*, Tammy thinks to herself as she looks at her affectionately.

"So, Ms. Hannah...Do you have a boyfriend?" Evelyn asked.

"Yeah...sort of."

"What does that mean? Either you do or you don't."

"I guess that means I don't...for right now."

"You want to talk about it?"

"No...not really. My studies took most of my time. I've dated around but haven't been intimate with any of the guys."

"Oh, that's good, so you're still a virgin?"

"No!...Not hardly." Tammy looks at Evelyn, and then opens the pantry door to throw something in the trash. Hannah changes the subject. "What do you and Tammy do for fun?" They both laugh.

"Your mother and I have been so preoccupied with the kids. I help her also with her catering business? Did you know about that?"

"Yeah, she told me."

"I'm real proud of her. In a short amount of time she's come along ways." Hannah doesn't say anything.

"What do we do for fun? When we do get out, we go over to your great grandmother's house and check on her. We mostly spend a lot of time there...sometimes. Do you remember her?"

"Vaguely," Hannah groans.

"Well she's up in age, but still spunky. I'll call her in a bit and let you talk to her."

"That would be great," Hannah said. Tammy looks at Evelyn with a smile. "Tammy what do we do for fun?"

"Huh." Tammy thinks for a minute. "Honestly, nothing outside of family and work."

"Tammy do you have a serious boyfriend?" Hannah asks.

"Baby, I'm like you."

"What about the baby's daddy?"

"Oh...he's around, we have started talking again."

"Do you love him?" Tammy...thinks about her question for a while.

"Well, I guess you could say...yes. He's the guy I was telling you about."

"C'mon on mama, tell the truth," Evelyn laughs. "She couldn't stand him, but they are working it out."

"I would like to meet him. Is he good to you?" Hannah said.

"Yeah, you could say that. I mean, during our abrupt break up, he always stayed in contact and when he started back working. He would send the baby things; diapers, clothes, toys, and money for formula, food...you know things like that."

"Child, I tell you. Most men, when they get you pregnant that is it. You don't see that joker at all. Or if you do see him...he tries to do very little," Evelyn said. "Isn't that the truth"...Tammy said.

"You just make sure you don't get pregnant Hannah. You've finished school, and can make something out of your life. When you have a baby...it's hard. It can be done. But it's hard...ask Tammy"

"Oh. I'm not planning on getting pregnant."

"You don't want any children?" Evelyn asked.

"No. I don't."

"Well, you are the only one in our family that has gotten a bachelor's degree. That says a lot, so if you can, don't mess up by getting pregnant." Evelyn screams for the kids to come to the table. "I can help you set the table"...Hannah said. "Baby that would be nice, Thank you. Look in that top drawer next to the sink for the silverware." Hannah sets the table. Tammy fixes the plates while Evelyn gets the kids settled at the table. They spend the rest of that evening, talking, eating, and watching movies. "Well…Sis, we are going to leave. I'm full and I've had a great time."

"Hannah, you know where I live, don't stay a stranger."

"I won't. I thought you were going to call your grandmother?"… Hannah said.

"Oh shoot that's right." Tammy takes out her cell phone and calls her grandmother. Madea!…Madea! She can't hear me well. Hey I got somebody I want you to talk too."

"Hello…how are you?" Hannah says.

"Hannah?" Madea says.

"Yes."

"Child, you are a big girl now. It's good to hear your voice. You have to come over sometime-soon."

"Yes. I will," she gives the phone back to Tammy. "Madea, I'll call you tonight." Tammy hangs up as they walk out the door. Evelyn walks outside with them. "Who's that boy staring at us?" Tammy asked Evelyn.

"Child. That's the neighbors' son. He sees this pretty gal, and well, you know how they are. He ain't working on nobody's job, but trying to pick up somebody." They all laugh. "Tammy I'll call you later." They get in the car and head back to Tammy's place. On their way there, Tammy decides to ask Hannah if she wanted to spend more time together. "Hannah did you want to spend the night with me?"

"No Tammy, but thank you for the offer."

"Ah! I was hoping you could stay."

"Maybe next time. I have to go home."

"Okay, well I've enjoyed your presence," Tammy said. Hannah reaches out to her, giving her a hug. "Thank you, baby I needed that from you," Tammy says. Hannah leaves.

As soon as Tammy gets the baby settled, the phone rings. "Hey baby, well how did it go?" Madea asked.

"We had a good time."

"Well that's good. Did she behave herself?"

"For the most part. But she did comment on Evelyn's kitchen being small."

"Young folks, I tell you"...Madea said.

"Madea, she doesn't have a steady boyfriend."

"You think she's gay?"

"Madea...please. No. I think it's strange though."

"Well someone her age, you would think she would," Madea said.

"Yeah, that's what I'm saying."

"Or maybe she doesn't want to be bothered."

"Yeah. Maybe that's what it is," Tammy says.

"Ok. I'm checking on you to see how it went. I'll talk with you later," Madea says.

Hannah calls Tammy, two weeks later. "Tammy did you and Evelyn want to go to the Los Angeles Zoo Botanical Gardens?" Tammy's shocked and happy that she asked.

"Hmmm...baby that sounds fun."

"I thought it would be a nice outing for everyone. If you can't...I understand."

"I don't see why we couldn't. If Evelyn can't make it, certainly...I can."

"We can take the Safari Shuttle train for a quick trip to the back of the Zoo. And then we can work our way back down the hill toward the main entrance. Plus, there are six different stopping points. We can get off and get back on as often as we like, and it would only cost a few dollars."

"Hannah, I've never been to the zoo. That would be fun. Let me check with Evelyn and see if she wants to come and I'll let you know. By the way, what's your phone number?" Hannah gives her, her number. "I'll let you know something soon."

The next day Tammy calls Hannah and tells her it's a go, that Evelyn would love to come and will bring her two daughters.

That Saturday afternoon they all meet at the zoo in the Animal section. While the kids screamed and hollered at the different types of animals, Hannah took some photos on her portable camera. From the California Desert Tortoise, Old World Rabbit, Elongated Tortoise, and Colombian Rainbow Boa there were enough attractions to keep everyone happy.

After allowing the kids to play at the Neil Papiano Play Park; with its animal-themed climbing sculptures, large play structures, and water misters they decided to grab something to eat. Everyone voted on eating at the Mahale Café for burger baskets and kids meals. Tammy was enjoying the view of the zoo's exotic animals. Even baby Ethan couldn't resist pointing at the animals and trying to imitate their sounds. Once they finished eating, they rested for about thirty minutes and visited the World of Birds Show of rare and exotic creatures before leaving.

"Hannah, this was a good idea. I've had a good time," Tammy said, after taking a piece of her niece cotton candy. "So have I," Hannah said. "We have to do more of these get-togethers," Tammy said.

"I agree"…Hannah said. They hug each other, before each one head to their cars.

Although Los Angeles, is known for its great weather, mostly sunny and warm days; however, there's a haze over the city-today. It's a week later, since Tammy last spoke with Hannah. She calls Hannah, to say hello, but gets her voice mail. She leaves a message. That night Hannah returns her call, "Tammy, did you want something?"

"No, not in particular. I called to see how your day had gone. Have you found work yet?"

"I've narrowed it down to two places," Hannah says.

"That's good, you're making progress. I also wanted to tell you that Evelyn said she might be able to get you on at the company she works for. They use RN's to go and visit their elderly clients."

"Really…hmmm. Thanks, that's something to think about."

"I don't know what the pay is. I'm pretty sure it would be good. Since RN's make good money. But maybe it would be a good start for the first two years of your career and then you could move up to somewhere else."

"Well let's see how the other options work out," Hannah said.

"That's what I had to do. No one would hire me after I was released from prison. But one restaurant owner took a chance on me. In a couple of months, I will have worked there almost three years."

"You were in prison, Tammy?"

"Yeah, I thought you knew that."

"No, I didn't. Wow! That's kind of deep. May I ask what for?"

"Hannah, sweetie...let's not go into that. That's my past and it's behind me. I only brought it up to make a point." Hannah clears her throat. "Sure...Tammy, if you don't want to talk about it, I understand. Were you up to another outing soon?"

"What did you have in mind Hannah?"

"Have you been to the Hollyhock house?"

"What is that?...The name sounds funny." Hannah laughs.

"It's a public art park. And the Los Angeles Municipal Art Gallery is also located there with art from all around the world. Since you work your business on Saturdays-the best time to go would be on Sundays, around 1:30pm," Hannah says.

"Where are they?"

"They're on Hollywood Boulevard."

"Okay...Hannah, I can do that."

"You might want to leave the baby with your grandmother. He may get a little antsy."

"Oh...I don't know if she will do that, that's right about the time they're on their way to eat after church."

"I guess you could bring him, if you had no other choice."

"Yeah, I better bring him."

"Okay, that's fine. And if you have to leave that's okay too. So are we on for this Sunday?"

"Yes Ma'am. Ok...Ms. Hannah, I will talk with you Sunday morning."

That Sunday morning, Hannah comes over to Tammy's and takes her to Hollyhock. "Boy, I keep forgetting this is a small car," Tammy's trying to get herself settled inside Hannah's car. "Are you and the baby settled?" Hannah touches the baby's face. Ethan smiles. "Why did you name him Ethan?" she stops at a red light.

"I like the way the name sounds," Tammy says.

"Does he keep you up at night?"

"Yes, but sometimes he sleeps through-out the night. Then there's other times when he doesn't sleep well."

"You know I could babysit him sometimes and not charge you anything. I mean, before I start working."

"Hannah, you would do that for me?"

"Sure...why not?" Tammy looks at her. "You've got yourself a deal."

"Yeah...Tammy, just let me know when." They arrive at the Hollyhock house. Tammy gets out with the baby, and Hannah locks her door. They walk around and look at the various art works. "Boy there are so many talented and gifted people in this world," Tammy said.

"Yep"...Hannah said, she plays with Ethan's finger. "Can I hold him?"...Hannah asked.

"Sure." Tammy takes him out of his stroller, hands Ethan over to her. He cries for a second and then smiles up at Hannah. She rocks him back and forth then holds him up in the air.

"He's a heavy baby."

"Yes ma'am. He knows how to eat. Be careful with him. I don't want his glasses to break."

"What are they, Bifocals?"

"Yeah."

"Is he a Down syndrome baby?"

"Yeah, he is." Tammy checks him to make sure he didn't have a urine accident. "I have met some Down children. With the new advances, a lot of them live good quality lives."

"That's what his doctor said to me. But you know, it's different. I'm finally adjusting to it after some time. His second year birthday isn't that far away."

"Were you disappointed when you learned your baby may have a genetic issue?"

"I mean, who wouldn't Hannah? Every woman wants her baby to be born healthy as possible with no or less medical issues."

"I understand." Hannah tries to position Ethan upon her breast area. "Do you want me to take him?" Tammy asked.

"No, he's fine."

"But, I'm learning, children are a reward from God. When he was first born-I'm not going to lie. I was scared. Just like I was when I had you and my other babies. I'm older now, and it's different. Let me put it this way. Now, I have some sense. This would be the best time for me to raise a baby."

Hannah is quiet. "Do you think about your other children?"

"Every day, I wonder how they turned out. If they hate me. If they would speak to me, if they saw me. What about when I get old. Would they have thought about me? And make the effort to find me. It's best to leave things as they are. I don't want to intrude on their life." Hannah walks slowly, listening to her every word. She turns and faces Tammy,

"Well, I'm glad I found you."

Tammy eyes, wells up. "Baby, I'm glad that you found me too," she puts her arms around Hannah and the baby. They walk a little further, then the baby starts to get irritable, and they decide to leave. "Did you want to meet Madea?"

"Sure, why not?" Tammy calls her grandmother and tells her they're on their way over there for Hannah to meet her and her husband. "We can't stay long, the baby's acting up. But I wanted her to see you." They pull up at Madea house, the street seems quiet. "They have not been to long getting back, this is when they take their nap," Tammy said. She, Hannah and the baby go inside and meet them. They stay about fifteen minutes and leave then Hannah takes Tammy and the baby home. She pulls up in the drive way, and helps Tammy with the baby.

"Can I use your restroom?" Hannah rushes to the bathroom. "Sure baby. You don't have to ask me. Just go on in there." Tammy sits Ethan on the floor and turns on the television. Hannah walks out, hugs and kisses Tammy, "I'll call you," Hannah says.

"Hannah, don't forget next-Sunday, we will have the barbeque dinner. Are you still planning on coming?"

"Yeah. I'll be there."

"Okay baby...I love you," Tammy said. Hannah closes the door behind her.

Chapter 10

TAMMY SITS ON her sofa, next to Ethan while watching television. She thinks about Hannah and Harry. One year ago, Hannah had entered her life unexpectedly. She had such a hard time forgiving Tammy, and now she's coming around. Then she thinks about how she has treated Harry even though he constantly reached out to her. She had been self-ish. And was getting back the same treatment she dished out to him. *It hurt, really bad,* she thought. Now, I understand how Harry must have felt when I treated him so poorly. She begins to recognize the power and value of forgiveness.

The essence of the importance of forgiving your perpetrator, piece by piece, she broke down every demeaning act or words she had spoken to Harry. How she had reacted, and how it has affected her life, health and well-being. Within her heart, she knows it is the right thing to do—to forgive him. In the haunting darkness of her depression and troubles, she now was able to come to terms with, just maybe, God would hear her prayers. In a humble way, she makes her requests. "God, when I think back over my life, I have said and done things that have hurt others. I'm sorry. I need to forgive people that have hurt me. Like you have forgiven me. One person that comes to mind, I can't even speak his name...my supervisor, but I'll whisper it...Dustin. I forgive him too." Then she speaks out loud, "I'm no longer a victim, I release the control and power of negative thinking about my situation being all

Harry's fault. I had a part in it too. After all, he didn't force me to do drugs or sleep with him. I took that chance when I—made the choice. Some choices or good and others, you have to suffer the consequences. I can't blame him-that's not fair to him."

At that moment it was as if a huge burden had been lifted from her shoulders. She could feel the presence of God. His peace, his love. Her grudges had begun to melt away. *It felt real for the first time,* she thought.

"I need to have compassion and understanding for these people, and my prayer is that Hannah will do the same toward me"...she whispers.

Harry calls, and wanted to know if they could get together this weekend. "Harry, I have a wonderful idea. Sunday we're having a barbeque. Hannah will be there, along with my sister and her kids. I would love for you to meet Hannah. Can you make it?"

"What? How are you going to fit everyone into your tiny house?"

"Don't worry about that, can you make it?"

"Yes ma'am, I will be there. What time?"

"Around 2:00pm...will that work?"

"Yep. Okay see you then."

That Sunday afternoon, one by one, people were showing up. First Evelyn and her kids, Hannah and a girlfriend of hers, and then Harry and his 12 step sponsor and wife. It was cramped but she arranged it so everyone had a seat. Tammy had put the kids in the room with Ethan, to watch and play with him, while the adults talk.

She has her back yard decorated in bright happy colors, appropriate for October, one of the best months of the year. It was a beautiful warm day. She decorated the outside with sprinkles of greenery plants; hanging flowers, a few 4ft Cedar Spiral silk trees, and Green Pony Tail Palms in white ceramic pots for the table display to compliment her theme. And a nice flowered table cloth covered the large folding table for the food, so guest could help themselves buffet style.

Tammy had marinated and refrigerated all meats the night before to allow the seasoning to sink in. She slowed cooked the meats from low to high heat. She had gotten up early that morning to start cooking the ribs, grilled shrimp, steaks, cod and the sweet bake beans, potato salad, and grilled veggies. Not wanting to rush, she wanted it to be a fun and engaging time for everyone.

As the guest arrived, she offered them non alcoholic beverages, banana strawberry smoothies, apricot tea, or their choice of sodas. To get the party started she chose two hours worth of jazz music and some old artist's from the seventies, beforehand.

Harry introduces himself and his guest. Hannah shyly introduces herself and her guest. The music was loud and everyone was in a conversation. *That's a good thing...*Tammy thought, laughing to herself. Hannah watches her every move as she cooks the food. She gives the responsibility of grilling the veggies to the men. "Tammy, Hannah and I can help you with something, what do you need done?" Penny, Hannah's guest, said. "Well I pretty much have it under control. I want you all to sit down and enjoy yourself." Harry comes into the kitchen and kisses Tammy on the cheek. Hannah sees him, smiles quickly, followed with a frown. Then she looks at Tammy from top to bottom and back up again.

When Harry goes back outside, she corners Tammy and asks if he is Ethan's daddy. "Yes, that's Ethan's daddy.... You like him?"

"I don't even know him?"

"Well go talk to him," Tammy says.

Meanwhile out back, Evelyn and Jim, Harry's sponsor get up and dance to a tune playing. Hannah sits back down and talks to Penny and Vanessa, Jim's wife. She watches Harry; how he relates to Tammy then she gets up and follows Tammy around. Whatever she sees that needs to be done, she does it before Tammy asks her to, then, Tammy sits down at the table outside. Hannah sits next to her. The conversation is about, does a person's personality change as they get older. Harry yells out, No! Evelyn disagrees with him. Then Jim said, "According to one researcher notes I read on the subject, he feels there is no evidence that our overall personalities changes as we grow older." Hannah jumps into the conversation, then Jim's wife. They argue, laugh and give examples from both perspectives.

The conversation changes to the current events from the United Nations, Japan, Africa and other events. Opinions were flying—but respectfully so. Meanwhile, Tammy shouts to everyone, "Come and get it, the food is ready." The men allowed the women to fix their own plates—first and then they came after them. Jim tells, Tammy... "You did a good job." She places the silverware on the table. "Thank you... Jim, cooking runs in my family."

Jim says, "Harry...this woman knows how to cook, she's going to make some man, a good wife." Tammy blushes and laughs.

Harry jokingly asked Evelyn where her man was. "Hey if you got any friends that are looking I'm available. I'm a good cook too." Everyone laughs. Vanessa interrupts and tells how her and Jim met and married. "Believe it or not, we met at a bar. I took one look at him, and walked up to him and said you're going to be my husband." He turned around, looked at me and said, "Woman you are crazy, bartender put this woman out of here." There was an outpouring of laughter. Evelyn asked her how did you make it happen. "I kept going to the bar to see him. Then I gave him my phone number, and he called me." Jim laughed.

"Was it one of those nights when you were lonely...Jim?" Harry asks. Everyone laughed.

"Yes and no. I saw something in her, she was fun and aggressive."

Vanessa jokingly interjected, "He likes his women aggressive." Then Jim finishes his sentence, "But after...I don't know...talking to her a couple of times we started going out to dinner together. I ended up in the 12 step program, and then she got involved shortly after I did. That was twenty five years ago and we're still together."

"Man, that is outstanding," Harry said. "I hope me and my wife can make our marriage work that long." Tammy gets up and goes to the kitchen. Harry laughs. She comes back and sits down. "Hannah how is your food?" she said, trying to ignore Harry.

"I like it; it's divine," Hannah said. Her friend, Penny wasn't talking to anyone. Her eyes were closed as she took each bite. Every now and then she would look up and smile. Everyone ate until all of the food was gone. They talked, played games, and danced. "It is a good party," Vanessa tells Tammy. Around 6:00pm the party had begun to wind down. Hannah and Penny helped Tammy clean up and put away the trash. Tammy thanked everyone and promised next year they would do it again. On their way out, each guess is hugged and thanked for coming as they leave.

Friday afternoon, a week later, one of the new waitresses tells Tammy to come up front, there was a delivery for her. When she steps out front the florists brings to her a stunning long-stem arrangement. The vibrant red roses were gracefully large with open blooms, nestled among fresh, delicate greenery. Accompanying the roses was an artistically designed stylish elegant silver footed vase. With hands up to her face, she stands there in shock. The waitress yelled...

"Boy those are gorgeous, who sent them to you?"

"I don't know." Tammy smells them and smiles. Gently she touches the shape of each rose. "Read the card, read the card," the overly enthusiastic waitress said.

"Well um, let's see," she takes them back to her work area and sets the arrangement down. She opens the card and it says...*Tammy please meet me tonight in Inglewood at 300 East Florence Avenue...signed Harry.* "East Florence Ave?" she said. "What is over there?"

"Maybe some type of restaurant," the waitress said.

She couldn't wait to see him. Her grandmother is called, and she asked her if she could keep the baby overnight. She takes off early, goes home and cleans up. Days before, Evelyn and her grandmother had pitched in to give her a surprise makeover by a professional at the mall. Then they took her shopping for clothes appropriate for her age. After all, she had graduated from school, and it was time for a new look and image.

That evening, she takes out the outfit they had bought her. Her favorite black and white Anne Klein tweed jacket, an orange and red sheer silk top—peppered with a shimmering gold print design, and her black wide leg stretch pants. She looked beautiful. Her hair had been relaxed, and brown based highlights added. Because of her work schedule she only wore her hair in a ponytail. But tonight she wanted to look glamorous, wearing her hair down. Her brown tone highlights complimented her black hair and her "mocha brown" tone complexion. She looked flawless, with her red shimmery lip color. *"Not bad looking for a 12W plus size beauty*, she jokingly thought to herself.

When she arrives at the restaurant she sees Harry's car parked. She walks in not knowing what to expect. It was a casual restaurant setting with booths, a cozy and relaxed atmosphere, with ethnic music playing in the background. The decor was comfortable and there were only a few other people present.

There was Harry sitting alone waiting for her. When he sees her, he stands up. She runs over to him and squeezes him so hard that neither wanted to let go of the other. Trying to keep tears from falling from their eyes. He grabs her hands and tells her that he wanted to talk with her at the barbeque. But he could never seem to catch her by herself for very long. She reaches up and touches his *"Cafe Latté"* colored complexion, he smiles at her. The waitress walks over to their table. "Would you give us about 10 minutes and we'll be ready to order?" Harry says…. "Sure, my name is Cynthia, let me know when you're ready." Harry breaks his silence about the night of his grandparent's death.

"Tammy, right then, I was dealing with some heavy emotions. It was like I was just numbed all over—for a long time. My mind was going back and forth from confusion, fear, guilt and anger, that's just a few of the things I was dealing with. All of this stuff bundled up inside of me. I feel like an adult orphan." She touches his hand. "Baby "I'm so sorry about your grandparents."

"Thank you!…Baby," he moves his napkin around on the table. It was still an uncomfortable subject for him. "Are you okay?" Tammy said.

"Yeah, I'm still clean," Tammy reaches over the table and grabs him, while crying.

"Baby, I just knew for sure that, if there was anything that would drive you to use that would be it, after you hung up that night. I just knew it was all over. But I tried to pray for you. When I saw you later, I figured when you were ready you would tell me everything. That's why I never pressured you."

"You prayed for me?…Huh."

She looks into his eyes and smiles, "Yes .. I did."

The waitress comes back and asks if they were ready. She opens the menu, "Everything looks good on here. What would you recommend?"

"The jerk chicken and curried chicken are favorites."

"Okay we'll have that. Oh Harry, I'm just ordering for you."

"No it's okay," he grabs Tammy's hand.

"You know that was the saddest day of my life. It happened a month before my release from treatment." He drops his head down for a moment, talking in a low voice. "He was the first person that taught me how to tie my shoes. And when I was a little boy, a bully at school would always mess with me, beating me up. I was tired of it and scare to go to school." He tries to hold back his tears…

"Um"… "And my step father was abusing me. So as a kid, I had a lot of anger that I carried over for a long time. I'm lucky I didn't end up in prison." He lifts his head and looks at her. "I remember telling my grandfather about it, and one day he met us after school, as I was walking home. This bully and his friends caught up with me. It seemed my grandfather came from out of nowhere at the right time." He stops briefly…

"When that boy hit me and knocked my books out of my hand. My grandfather ran up to us, and told me to hit him back, and I did. I ended up kicking that boy's behind, and I never had a problem with him again." Tammy starts to laugh. "He was my best friend when I was a little boy. Every weekend I would go to their house," he reaches down beneath the table, fidgets with his pant leg. "But then, when my stepfather came on the scene, within no time that changed. Less and less, I was going over there, and then one day my step father stopped me from going altogether, and threatened my mother. He didn't want us to have any contact with my grandparents. I was so afraid of him...I couldn't even tell my grandfather what was happening. He threatened that he would kill him and my mother. I didn't want to see that happen to my grandfather. He was a good man. When my step father told you he would do something...he meant it."

Harry begins to shed tears. "He would be proud of me. I have been clean for two years," he stops and closes his eyes. "But what kept me going was my 12 step sponsor—Jim. He let me stay at his home with he and his wife. They treated me like gold. I drew my strength from God and from their support."

"Are you still working?"

"Yep. Never missed a day since I started except for that day you saw me at the funeral."

"Harry that is so wonderful." He wipes under his eyes with the napkin. Smiling, he said, "He even promoted me to running the place. Yeah, I work six days a week now...with a half day on Saturdays."

"Harry," her voice is high-pitched. "Baby that is great."

"Yeah, I do everything. I have another shampoo boy that helps out. But I...run the place, and clean it at the end of the day, long hours sometimes, when we are busy."

"How about you?" he said.

"I have never told you this but...I got a promotion," Tammy says.

"A promotion, girl look at you."

"Yeah, he pays me about $1500 a month to do the prep work, and on weekends, I cater two to four kids' birthday parties at least."

"Girl you're rocking, look at you."

"Yeah, I told you I would have my own business. But you know what?" her eyes wells up with tears. "It has been soooo freaking hard"... she gets choked up on her words. "Between work, my jerk supervisor, school, the baby, I thought I was losing my mind." Harry gets up and slides into her seating area. "Sometimes I didn't think I was going to make it.

The baby cried most of the time. He kept me up at nights. I could barely focus at school, and still somehow, I manage to get good grades." Harry puts his arm around her. "I hate to say this, God forgive me." She pauses, "But sometimes, I found myself hating my baby. I know that's evil and wrong to say. I need to be honest with someone. I couldn't understand how he could be born like this. He is behind on most of his development milestones." Both of her arms are on the table, and then she puts her head down into her hands. "I wanted a baby, that could talk, catch on easily, play with his toys, sit up without any help, and crawl," she wipes her eyes. "He has progressed, but it has been slow. Madea keeps him most of the time. I don't know how she does it. Sometimes, I would just leave him with her for days at a time." He rubs her face. "Then my crazy supervisor, he has made my life a living hell ever since he came there."

"What's his problem? Harry asks angrily.

"I don't know."

"You know restaurant jobs are tough. All kinds of people come through there," he says. "Yeah, we've had so many people to come and go." Harry looks at a couple that walks in. "Messy lives. Everyone has some type of mess and drama in their life, and they bring it to work with them, taking it out on others. Are you going to still work there?"

She leans back into her booth. "I've been there three years, and would like to stay another year. Just long enough to get my business really going." The waitress brings their plates. "Watch it, these plates are hot," the waitress said.

"Ummm boy that smells good," Harry said.

"Yeah!" she said.

"I remember when you first got that job. Man that seems like a long time ago." Harry blesses the food. They each take a bite of their food and smile at each other. "Ummm…. it's flavorful and tender and the vegetables are fresh, sauté and seasoned right," she said.

"I know, you know, good food when you see it."

"Um huh."

"What did you think about the flowers?" She drops her fork unto her plate.

"Baby they are beautiful," she kisses him on the jaw. "No one has ever given me any flowers. Thank you!" He hugs her with his free arm and continues eating.

"Tammy I have something to ask you." She stops eating. "I would like the baby to be christened at my grandfathers church. They have been good to me these last couple of months."

"Is that where you are going?"

"Yeah, I started going back there and would like you and the baby to come to service with me sometimes. Maybe, if you like it enough, you may join." With tears in her eyes, she looks up at him. "How would he be christened?"

"Well, I've already spoken with the pastor about it. We would have to reserve the service date and time for during regular Sunday service. We would have to choose Godparents to take over the responsibility of the baby, should anything happen to us, while Ethan is a minor. And we would need to get him a cream colored kind of gown for the event," he said.

"We could get one from a department store, Wow...Harry!"

"What's wrong?

"Nothing's wrong, I'm just taking all this in."

"On that Sunday, you and I will stand with the baby in his gown and with the baby's godparents at our side. The minister will perform the christening by sprinkling water on Ethan, while saying, *'I baptize you in the name of the Father, and of the Son and of the Holy Spirit.'* That's it, the ceremony is over. That means we raise him as a Christian." Tammy starts to cry into her food, she doesn't say anything.

"Okay, let me ask you something, number one, I don't know anyone I could ask to handle that type of responsibility. I have not been in church for many years. Who did you have in mind?"

"Well the pastor at the church, I could ask him, since he and my grandfather were friends."

"Okay, I don't have a problem with it. Just let me know if he says yes or no. If he says yes, then I need notice to arrange for my family to come. They may agree to an earlier time, if so we can move the date up after you find out on your end." Harry excuses himself, and goes to the men's room.

The waitress comes by and asks if they want dessert. "Yeah, two peach cobblers would be fine. Thank you," she says. Harry comes back and hugs Tammy. "I ordered two peach cobblers for us."

"Okay. Whatever you want, when she comes back, we need a re-fill on our fountain drinks." Tammy clutches her arm into his, and leans on his shoulder. The waitress brings back their desserts. "Um, and can we have refills on our soda?" Harry asks.

The waitress smiles, "Sure."

"Where have you been staying, at your grandparent's house?"

"No, I had the church members to go in and take what they want-ed and whatever was left it was donated to an organization that helps people. The only thing I had them to get for me was their china din-nerware, old photo albums with family pictures, my grandfathers col-lection of religious books and his gold necklace with a cross…this one that I have on."

Tammy reaches up to his neck and touches the crucifixion cross. "Baby it's beautiful." He grips the cross with his right hand. "That way I have a remembrance of him. The church members cleaned up the house, and I paid them a little something to do it." The waitress brings back their sodas.

"Are you working tomorrow—Saturday?" she asked.

"Yep, I have to be there at 9:00am."

"What time will you get off?"

"Saturday's are our busiest days, maybe around 3:00pm."

"Are you working tomorrow?" he asked.

"I have to cater two birthday parties, and then I'm done for the evening. Harry gets up and moves across the table from Tammy.

"Hey…what do you think about me?"

"Is that why you moved, so that you could ask me this?"...she says jokingly.

Harry wasn't smiling, he had a serious look on his face.

"Harry, I've always loved you, even when I thought I hated you."

"You sure did take a long time in letting me back into your life," he looks at her. "Life is too short and we need each other. I want my son to have a father. I think I have proved this to you. Haven't...I?"

"Yes, you have."

"I mean, even when I was making nothing, I made sure to send him diapers and little outfits...right?"

"Yeah...Harry, I give you that credit."

"Do you want me in yours and the baby's life?"

Tammy is silent, and she then asks, "Harry why ask me this? You already know the answer."

"Tammy, I need to hear you say it."

"Yes, I want you in our life. I want us to try again."

That moment, as she takes a bite of her dessert, he reaches into his pocket. "I've been wanting to do this for a long time," he takes out a small "cherry wooden" double ring jewelry gift box. He grabs her hand and asks her to marry him.

"This is for you," he opens the box and turns it toward her. Inside the gift box was a 3/4 ct. Marquise diamond center stone-bridal set with diamond accents, and matching band, totaling, 3 cts., within a 14K gold setting.

She jumps up from off her seat, running and crying really hard, as she enters the ladies room. The manager of the restaurant had to go in behind her to see what was wrong. After about fifteen minutes, she walks back to their table and hugs Harry. Then she kisses him for what seemed to be a minute.

She looks up at him, "Yes!" Harry, I will marry you. Where did you get the money for this? I mean how could you afford this?" still shaking her head in disbelief.

"My grandfather left me in his will. I am his sole surviving relative. I sold his house, because I just couldn't take living there after what happened. I still have not gone by there, it's way too painful. The house was on the market for $300,000 but I had the agent to drop the price to $249,000, and it sold."

"What?"... "Harry, I can't believe it," she places her hands up to her face.

"Yeah, it's true. Hey girl you were kind and good to me. You didn't even know me, but you took a chance on me. You were my friend, and you understood my pain, my secret that I couldn't share with anyone. I know we both said some horrible things in our craziness. Still, I kept thinking about us all this time, how you were then and how concerned you were about me. Now, we have a special needs child together," he stops and looks at her tenderly...

"With all that you have been through, I think you deserve this."... She kisses him again. Then rests her head into his chest and cries. "I know your grandmother talked about me bad...but you can show her that miracles do happen." She playfully hits him, and leans back into his chest. The manager comes over, learns of the engagement and offers champagne for a celebration. "No, we don't drink," he said.

"Why don't we take care of the tab for you?" Tammy looks at Harry. "Hey, man that's alright with me. Hey baby see, good things do happen!" Harry leaves a tip for the waitress and thanks the manager... again.

Outside the restaurant, she tells him she doesn't want to go home by herself tonight.

"Well um, why don't we go to my place so that you can see your new home?" he said. Tammy shakes her head. "My new place," she liked the sound of it. "Where is it?"

"I'm in Inglewood."

"Man, that's where the kitchen is that I use for my catering business. I can't believe this."

Back and forth, she walks up and down on the entry walk way.

"Well did you want me to follow you home to get some change of clothes, and come back to my place?" he asks.

"Yeah, yeah, that will work." He walks her to her car.

"Okay, I'll follow you home," he tells her. When they arrive at her house she gets out of the car and runs over to his car. "Were you going to come in?"

"No...I'll wait for you, don't take long." Inside, she grabs her toiletries, and a couple of outfits and baby clothes. Her messages are checked, and she sees where Evelyn and Madea have called. "I'll call them from over at Harry's," she turns off the lights and gets back into her car. When they arrive in Inglewood, he stops at a convenience store to buy a large bottle of orange juice. Finally they arrive at his well manicured neighborhood. "Oh! This is nice," she said.

Harry turns right onto Thoreau St, makes a left onto Willkie, and then makes an immediately turn right onto the 2300 block of Van Wick St. "Lardy, Lardy," she chuckles. "Look at this neighborhood." Harry pulls up into the driveway, and she parks behind him. Eagerly she gets out of the car. "Baby, this is sooo nice."

"I was hoping you would like it," he puts his arm around her, and opens the front door.

The first thing she notices is his old furniture. "Baby, we are definitely going to have to get some new furniture," Tammy said.

"What?" he smiles. "You don't like my furniture?"

"C'mon, baby," she kisses him.

"Man this looks like something from the Goodwill," jokingly she says.

"Guess what?" he catches hold of her waist. "It came from a place just like that. Hey, let me show you the rest of the house."

"Harry this is soooo freaking nice."

"As you can see it has hardwood floors and a fireplace."

"Yeah...I see that."

"It's a 4 bedroom, 2 1/4 bath home, the kitchen and all bathrooms has been updated, with new carpet in the bedroom areas. And it has a formal dining room and eat in kitchen with built-ins," he guides her through each room. "The open kitchen has a new stove, dishwasher, cabinets, and granite counters. The entire interior has fresh new paint. You probably noticed. It has a detached garage enclosed by a brick fence. So far the neighborhood has proven to be quiet," he walks back to the entry door and looks out into the street. "And it's located in a well-maintained neighborhood."

"Man, this place is nice. I love the golden oak color cabinetry and black granite countertops. This is a spacious kitchen. I can do a lot of cooking and entertaining here." He grabs her and puts his arms around her. "Boy this is something, Harry." Then, she opens the refrigerator. "We need to get some groceries," she says.

"Well what about Sunday?" he says. She checks the freezer. "There's enough in there until then," he said. She takes out the baby's food and places it in the refrigerator. He washes out their glasses and pours them orange juice. All worked up, she goes and looks at the bedrooms again. He brings her, her glass of orange juice.

"Baby this could be the baby's room."

"Um huh," he holds her closely.

"And, the master bedroom I could fix it up a little more. I can bring some of my furniture over here and add to the different rooms. We can go to some of those inexpensive but good quality furniture places and get the rest."

"When did you want to do all of this?" he asked.

"Why don't we shoot for next weekend? I will take off from work that Saturday, and I'm off on Sunday. Can you take off?"

"Yeah, as long as I have someone to cover me. I would have to go in and check on everyone, open and close the place you know," he takes her hand and leads her into the living room. She looks at her ring. "Baby I'm in a dream right about now. This ring is so beautiful."

He leans over and kisses her. "We need to talk about a couple of things before we retire for the night," he tells her. "First, so you will know the house was bought at a foreclosure price. I bought it for 30% less its asking price. I contacted the bank directly because there wasn't a listing agent available. The previous owner couldn't meet their payments on the house. Since the bank owned it, they were motivated to sell the home at an attractive price."

"Well, how much are our house payments?" she scoots around on the sofa.

"We don't have house payments," he said.

Bemused she looks at him, "We don't have house payments?"

"No, I paid cash for it."

"Uh, Harry," she pauses. "How were you able to do that?"

"Remember when I told you my grandparents had left me in their will?"

"Yeah."

"Well it turned out they left me a good chunk of money. Not only was I able to pay cash for the house, I also bought the pet grooming place."

"What?" her mouth is open. "What?" she gets down on her knees—facing him. "You bought out your employer?" Harry laughs.

"Yeah."

"How did you do that?"

"The old man was tired of fooling with the place. Besides, he has a lot of money. He has been nice to me, sending me to adult education computer classes and all. I guess he was grooming me for the job. Anyway, when he would come up to the shop we would talk for hours at a time.

I think he sold it to me, to help me make something of my life. I mean, he said I could always come to him for help with any questions about the business. He even went as far as to help me establish all my necessary paperwork. He's a good old white guy," he picks up his glass of OJ and takes a sip. "Hey Tammy it's just a small steady business. I treat the customers really good, and we have good pet groomers."

"How many?"

"Uh about four women, and one shampoo boy outside of myself. It's not a hard business. But it is noisy. The dogs bark all the time." She gets back on the sofa, lays her head into his lap. He strokes her hair, and she kicks off her shoes. "We do good work, shampooing, grooming, cleaning the pets ears, trimming nails, brushing teeth, and shaving the animal's coat into a style."

"What are your prices?"

"We charge about $30 to $90 per pet depending on what needs to be done. Usually the customers leaves good tips. The shampoo boy places flyers at pet stores and veterinarian offices, and animal shelters. And we even offer our services to the local animal shelter. If they like our work, they refer people to us. So we always have to be available for appointments. This means more office work for me." She turns over onto her back, staring at him with amazement. "Um, um, um," she shakes her head as she clears her throat.

"How much did you buy it for?"

"He sold it to me for practically nothing."

"What's nothing?"

"About $40,000 including fixtures and everything.

"Lawd, have mercy," Tammy sits up. "Your grandfather would be so proud of you."

With glass in her hand, she takes a sip of orange juice. "Um, Um, Um...Man, God is really real. Madea said she has been praying for me and for you. Man, this is crazy," she gets up and goes to the bathroom, comes back and turns the TV on low. "Boy!" she said, as she sinks into his arms. Harry chuckles. "Missy, we need to talk about some sensitive subjects."

"Okay, go ahead," she smiles.

"Have you been making your doctor's appointments for the HIV and the baby's doctor appointments?

"Harry, I love life too much not to at least get a regular check up. Yes, I have gone to the doctor frequently."

"How frequently?"

"I don't know. Maybe every two months. But I take the baby often."

"Have you been going?" she asked.

"Yeah, once I got clean, and started to think straight, I started going regularly too. I want to be there for you and my baby."

"What about sex?"

"What do you mean?" he asks.

"How does that work since you and I both have the disease?"

"My doctor told me that using a latex condom with only water—based lubricants, like K-Y and Astroglide can help protect us from other sexually transmitted diseases, as well as other strains of HIV which may be resistant to anti-HIV medications." She bends forward and puts her head down. He rubs her back. "You know, we can be vulnerable to infections. The best way to keep us safe is for us to never miss taking our meds," he snug's her in the side. "Even at work I have to be careful at all times," he says.

"What do you mean?"

"To lessen my exposure to germs, I have to avoid cleaning out the cat litter boxes."

"So, every time we want to have sex, we have to use a condom?" she asks.

"Pretty much!"

"Where are your candles?"

"Look in the pantry," she lights two candles and turns off all the lights.

"You know that really sucks," she says.

"We have to do, what we have to do," he said.

"I know, I know, I'm just saying...."

"Hey, work with me. We're going to have to be responsible or we may not be around to see Ethan grow up."

"Harry I'm just saying when a person gets in the mood, they're not going to want to do all that!"

...Harry laughs. "We're different...we have to," he kisses her on the top of her head.

"What about our wedding?" she asked. "Did you want a small wedding or what?"

"Tammy if you want one that's okay with me. But if you want my honest opinion, going to the court house would be fine." She tilts her head. "You know what?" then she smiles. "That will work for me too. I don't need a big fancy wedding. Whatever money we have, we need to save it for emergencies, in case you, I, or the baby gets sick."

"Right," he said.

"But we do need a three day honeymoon in San Diego," she says.

"Why San Diego?" he laughs.

"Their downtown is so clean and beautiful. I just love how nice the place is," she said.

"You've been there before...I take it?"

"Many years ago. I went for a visit on the bus. I loved it," she said. "Okay, so when... Tammy?

"Would we have to go to the courthouse together and obtain the Marriage License?" she asks.

"Yeah...like thirty days before the wedding, or something like that," he said.

Chapter 11

He gets up and goes to the kitchen. "What do you think?"...he yells back into the living room. Tammy gets up and goes into the kitchen. "I'm pretty sure there is a fee. I'll call next week and fine out all the details. Do you have two people in mind that could be a witness for us at the ceremony?" she asks.

"I could ask my sponsor and his wife."

"I don't think, I'll tell Madea, Evelyn, or Hannah as of yet."

"Why?"

"We'll wait until after the wedding. It will be better to tell them then," she changes the subject.

"We can go furniture shopping next weekend. How does that sound?" she asked. Harry doesn't say anything. They walk back into the living room. He changes the subject. "I will be making enough money to support us. Why don't you consider only working one job? I don't want you to get down sick."

"Harry! Please, Please don't ask me to choose yet."

"All I'm saying woman is we can make it on my salary and your part-time salary. I think you need to spend more time with the baby."

"Harry, Ethan is emotionally draining. Yes I love him," she rubs her eye. "But I need to get away sometimes."

"Hey Tammy, please think about it. I much rather have you alive and sober than not have you, because you've overworked yourself." She kisses him on the forehead. "Are we done?"...she asked.

"One more thing," he said. "Ethan, what's going on with him, his health?"

"He's wears bifocals now and he has a slight hearing problem," she puts her hands clasped behind her back. "A therapist has been working with him. The program provides all types of therapy for Down syndrome children. Since he's just turning two that means next year he will be old enough to enroll in a preschool program for children with disabilities."

"So, he has to be three before they can take him?"

"Right. Currently he has at home visits at Madea's, when I'm at work. I hope he will learn to play with his new friends, and develop some new skills, like listening and following directions from people, things like that," she said.

"He'll be fine," he said.

"Yeah, I've heard some good results from other mothers about their child's development."

He rubs her shoulders. "It will be okay"…he tells her.

He picks up the remote control to watch a scene from an Abbott & Costello movie. Costello is in a room with a prize boxing fighter whom the police are looking for. They think he killed his boxing manager, and he is hiding from them until it can be proven he's innocent. He had taken a portion that makes him invisible. When he turns invisible before Costello, Costello almost has a heart attack. He becomes afraid and hysterical as the man disappears right before his eyes. They laugh at the scene.

"Harry…why don't we wait until our honeymoon to sleep together?" He looks at her, and grabs her. "Whatever you want. Are you going to pick up the baby tomorrow?"

"Yeah after work. I'll stop by the grocery store and pick up a few things for us, and bring the baby back with me." Tammy stretches her arms out, "I'm tired, let's go to bed." Harry turns off the television and they both get dress for bed.

She lays in bed thinking about Hannah. Even though their relationship had been troubled, just maybe they could all become a family.

How would Hannah react to her getting married? Better yet—how would Madea react? *No, I won't tell anyone—not even Evelyn until after the fact.* She thinks about the more serious issues. *What if the business failed? Would I really be able to trust Harry to provide for us? What if Hannah needed a place to stay sometime later in her life? Would Harry be comfortable with her living with them? Would he really know how to be a good husband and father?*

Tammy and the baby officially moved into Harry's place. She tells only Evelyn and Hannah. Immediately after moving in their life began to change. Harry was working long hours, and she was barely seeing him. When he arrived at home, he was too tired to talk or play with the baby. Sometimes he wanted to eat and go to bed or lay back in his big chair watching whatever was on television.

Tammy has also been working long hours between work and her catering business. She wants to save as much money as she can. However, lately she has been spending more money on Hannah, taking her shopping often to spend more time with her and to make up for when she wasn't there all those years. Harry has a problem with it, and they have had confrontations about it.

The strain of both jobs is wearing her down. But she refuses to let go of either job. After work, she goes and visits Evelyn. They talk for a couple of hours and run errands together.

"How's the relationship with Hannah going?"

"Sis it's better than it was at the beginning. There are still a few little problems. But I think in time our relationship can heal and be like it was meant to be."

"Has she brought up the other children?"

"No."

"What about you…have you thought about them?"

"Evelyn, how can I not think about them they are a part of me? I can't do anything about the past. Hopefully they're with good families. Who knows maybe they will come and find me."

"What about you looking for them?" Tammy turns and looks at her, "Sis, I can't intrude on their life. If they wanted to see me they would have found me. Besides, I'm pretty sure they don't want to know me. Let's change the subject," Tammy tells her.

That evening at home, Tammy couldn't seem to get Ethan to settle down. He had fallen off her lap and was in a crying frenzy. She tried spending alone time with him in his room, and then she would take him into the master bedroom to lay down with her. Still, this didn't help. Angry, she was starting to feel less attached to him, less affectionate and less sensitive. "Why won't he shut up!" she said. She was tired of trying to make him be quiet. Harry comes in and sits with him until he calms down. Tammy walks into the kitchen and grabs the vinegar bottle, and then she picks up some old newspapers. She uses the vinegar to clean all the mirrors in the house. Harry approaches her while she's cleaning the bathroom mirror.

"Baby why was he crying like that?"

"Harry, I don't know what's wrong with him."

"Do we need to take him back to the doctor?"

"No. He'll be fine. He just goes through those spells. Sometimes he's a good baby, sleeps through the night, and other times he cries all the time and keeps me up through the night," she finishes the bathroom mirrors, and then goes to the refrigerator to clean it out. "Do you want this lasagna?" He looks at her. "How long has it been in there?"

"Several days."

"No!" he said. She dumps it along with some other things in the trash, to clear out space.

"Tammy are you okay?" She grabs her towel and mixture of baking soda and water to wipe down the inside of the refrigerator. "Harry, I'm tired, but okay."

The next morning Tammy goes into work and is told that she has to fill in for the other prep cook that didn't come in. The restaurant was busy and they had one cook that was out. She was ripping and running non-stop all day. She even had to stay and work over time to finish up her prep work. That night she was too tired to cook for Harry. "Did you want to order a pizza or something?" he said.

"I'm not hungry but if you want to that's fine," she said. He orders a pizza and they watch a movie together and she falls asleep on the sofa. Harry and Tammy were beginning not to see much of each other. Even on Saturdays, Tammy would cater parties all day, and Harry would work practically all day. By Sunday, they both were worn out. They rarely got a chance to talk anymore.

Hannah calls Tammy and wants to meet for lunch on Sunday afternoon. Tammy wasn't up to it but agreed anyway. They make arrangements to meet at a Chinese restaurant and then they go to a movie. She doesn't get home until late and Harry's upset about it. She opens the door and he's watching TV. She walks up to him and kisses him on the head. "Did you have a good time?" he asked.

"We did."

"Are you feeling better about your relationship with Hannah?" She pauses and thinks for a second. "Harry I grew up feeling different, knowing I felt things deeper than the normal person. I don't know why, but I always felt bad about myself, couldn't connect with people and had trouble forming close friendships. I'm making a special effort to be there for Hannah. I sense she's the same way. You may not understand this. But, I'm asking you to work with me. I'm trying to love her and I need to make up for lost time," she walks into their home office and begins to divide her important business papers into categories. Then she files her incoming papers after opening the mail, placing the things that need their attention in a mail tray. Harry walks in behind her chair and commences to massage her neck and shoulders. She touches his hand after he's done. She looks up at him and tells him…"Thank you."

Hannah decided that Sunday's should be her and Tammy's day. Harry would have to watch the baby. Sometimes Evelyn would meet them with her girls and they would stay out until eight o clock or later that night. But when Harry wanted to go out with some of the guys from the 12 step program, Tammy always had a problem with it. They would argue about where he and the boys were going, and how long they stayed.

"Excuse me…but don't you, Evelyn and Hannah meet every Sunday afternoon and do you' all girl thing?" he snaps at her. "Harry that's not the same," she said.

"Give me a break, will yah? Why isn't it the same Tammy?" She dry mops the floor, while talking to him.

"Because that's my family," she kids around with him. "Well these guys are like my family. We all have something in common… recovery. As a matter of fact, you should come to some of our meetings. You have not been to a support group meeting in a long time." She playfully hits him in the stomach and walks toward the kitchen. She takes a dish clothe, cleans out the sink, washes down the cabinets, and loads the dishwasher. He walks over to her and kisses her on the lips before heading out.

The next weekend Tammy decides to stay at home and relax. Evelyn comes over with the girls. *How could she tell her she's tired?* she thought. The kids were screaming and having a good time, running around playing in the back yard. She just wanted to see everyone happy, so she brought out games for everyone to play. The house was filled with fun, games, and lots of screaming. Harry comes home turns around and walks out. Tammy runs outside to catch him. "Harry Jones, where do you think you are going?"

"Hey," he yells. "It's girl's night. I'll be back," he gets into his car and goes over to Jim's, his sponsor's home. When he returns, she is pouting. "How was your outing?" she said, while picking up Ethan's toys and putting them away. "It was good," he smiles. She turns on the vacuum cleaner. "Did you and the girls have a good time?" he tries to yell over the roaring sounds of the vacuum cleaner. She turns off the vacuum cleaner with her foot. "What were you asking?" she said. "I wanted to know if you had a good time with your family."

"Yeah."

"I thought so, you' all have taken over my home."

"Correction," she said. "Our home," she gives him a blank stare. "You're being amusing to me right about now," she tells him. She vacuums the master bedroom floor and puts up the vacuum cleaner.

The next day at work, Tammy learns she is needed to work the dinner shift until the restaurant can replace the head cook. She quickly learns the job is hectic; she has to be quick and think on her feet. What she had learned in culinary school has prepared her to at least wing it for the most part. Extreme temperatures, fumes, dirt, smoke, loud noise, and unpleasant odors is what she has to work around. Everything that could go wrong in the kitchen went wrong that day. She burned herself while taking a chicken out of the oven, not watching what she was doing when talking to a worker. Then another cook forgot to add water to the Mac and cheese. He burned up the noodles and it left a terrible smell in the kitchen.

Later on that week, she needed to help another worker put out a fire that the worker had started, that same evening another worker slipped and fell because of spilled liquids on the dining room floor. And, then there was another worker complaining about his repetitive strain injuries from chopping vegetables. When her shift was over—she just wanted to take a hot bath and go to bed. Once at home, she learned the baby had been crying nonstop again. Harry was annoyed because it distracted him from his TV programming. "How long are you going to have to work evenings?" he asked her. "Until they find a replacement cook," she takes a cleaning rag and cleans the top surfaces of their coffee and end tables, and bookshelves. "Have you and the baby eaten?" she makes her way to the bedroom. "Yeah, we both have," he yells into the bedroom. She undresses and gets into the shower, then changes into her comfortable clothes to settle in for the night.

Around midnight there's a knock at the door. Harry gets up and answers it. It's Hannah. Tammy gets up. "Hannah do you realize what time it is?".... he asked.

"Yeah, but I was in the area and wanted to know if it would be alright to spend the night? I didn't want to drive back to Carson." He looks at Tammy.

"Hannah, come on in," she said. Tammy hugs her and shows her where the guest bedroom is. Harry goes back to bed. The next morning, Hannah gets up early and fixes breakfast. The smell of maple flavored sausage woke Tammy up from her sleep.

Harry was on his way out to work. He stopped by the kitchen to take a sausage with him.

Tammy sits down at the table, while Hannah tries to feed Ethan. "These eggs are good Hannah."

"I mixed cheese in with them."

"Ummm," Tammy said, while taking another bite. Hannah had made eggs, sausage, and toast and poured a glass of orange juice for Tammy's breakfast. "Where were you coming from last night?"

"I was hanging out with my friend and didn't want to make the drive home to Carson," she takes a bite of her toast. "Tammy what if I spent the weekends with you, that way I could see more of you and help you with the baby." Tammy gets up and goes to the refrigerator to get a small bottle of jelly. "I could babysit on the weekends and then Sundays. I wouldn't have to drive in, I would already be here."

Tammy looks at her lovingly. "Hannah that is a good idea. But I don't want you telling Madea that I'm living with Harry...promise me that."

"Sure, no problem." Hannah gets back on her subject. "Would you need to talk it over with Harry?"

"No, I 'm sure he wouldn't have a problem with it."

"I could even help you with groceries. You would just need to make a list and I will take care of everything for you."

"Okay, you've got a deal." That night after work, Tammy comes home and Hannah's not there. She walks into her room to see how she had left the room and if she had left a note.

"Where is Hannah?" He puts his feet up on the ottoman. "She left a while ago."

"Did she say where she was going?"

"Baby I don't know, maybe home," he gets up and places a exercise mat on the floor and lies flat on his back with his knees bent, feet up on a chair. "Do you need me to help you?" she said. "No." He sounds almost out of breath. "No, I got it." Tammy sits on the edge of the sofa watching him work out. He pushes the small of his back down into the floor, raises his head and upper back off the floor, looking up at the ceiling with his arms crossed across his chest.

He makes sure his head and upper back are already off the floor. He lifts his upper body higher off the floor, contracting his abdominal muscles, while holding to a beat and returning to his starting position. "Well she's supposed to stay with us on the weekends." He stops for a moment.

"Tammy you told that girl she could stay here?"

"She's not a girl…Harry, she's my daughter."

"Hey!"…he sits up on the mat. "Come here for a second," he looks directly at her. "Baby, she's twenty five and wild. This is not going to work."

"Why not, Harry?"

"Because she's a troubled young lady. I could tell that from the party you had a couple of months ago."

Tammy gets up and goes to the bedroom to undress. "Harry, why are you doing this?" she grumbles.

"Doing what?" he stops to catch his breath. "Tammy, I know what you're going to say. You feel guilty…right?" he says. She doesn't say anything. "Baby you can do whatever you want. If you want her here, she can stay here. But I'm telling you this isn't going to work," he says.

That weekend Hannah brings her weekend clothes and settles in. Most of the time, she spends her time in her room listening to music and talking on her cell phone. At dinner time she comes out and cooks for everyone. Saturday night, they all sit down for dinner. Harry wanted to know what her plans were. "Have you found work yet?" he asked.

"I'm still looking."

"Well, what are you waiting for?"

"I'm waiting for the right job." He laughs… "You may be waiting a long time. You know how many people are out of work and are looking for jobs?"

"Duhhh!…What does that have to do with me?" she says angrily.

"Okay, nothing Hannah, if you don't get it by now." Tammy laughs. After dinner Hannah cleans up the kitchen and goes back to her room. An hour later, Tammy knocks on her door and asks her if she wanted to watch TV with them. She hears Hannah screaming at someone on the phone. Hannah opens the door and tells her no, that she's getting ready to take her bath and go to bed. Tammy sits on the sofa, and thinks about Hannah, Harry and the baby. How pleased she was about her family life now coming together and that she couldn't ask for more.

The next night, Evelyn and the girls came over for dinner. Tammy cooks the dinner while Evelyn and Harry sit down on the floor, to play the word game—Scrabble. Hannah turns the music on and helps Tammy in the kitchen. "Evelyn that's not a word"…Harry shouts.

"Why not? It is too," Evelyn says.

"C'mon, Sis." Evelyn rotates the game board to view her next move. "Hey, there you go!" she gets up and does her dance before going to get a drink. "Ah, come on back here. The game is not over yet." Tammy lets out a hardy laugh as she's frying chicken. Meanwhile, Hannah smashes the potatoes to make mashed potatoes. "See sis, your man thinks he's smart…but I got this. I'm going to win this game," Evelyn laughs. She takes out two bottles of water and takes one to Harry. "Don't say I never gave you nothing," she laughs and sits back down.

"Hey, yeah sit down, so I can show you how to play right." Harry spells out his word and earns points. "Uh, No!" Evelyn panics, "Where's the dictionary?" Evelyn screams out. "Where's the dictionary?"

"Woman that's spelled correctly." Evelyn laughs. Now it's her turn. She spells a word and adds up her total score. "Hey wait a minute Evelyn, new words must use one of the letters already on the board. And you can't use words requiring a hyphen or apostrophe."

"Man, be quiet," she tells him. Harry laughs with a belly roar, falling backward onto the floor. After an hour of playing, Harry stands up and boasts about him winning. "Baby I took her down," he tells Tammy. Tammy's laughing in the background. "Wait a minute what's

your total?" Evelyn asked him. "Ah, Evelyn don't be a sore loser."
Evelyn laughs, "Sore loser—right!" she mumbles to herself.

Harry goes into the kitchen to check on the food. "Man, you're
doing some serious cooking in here. Hannah, how's it going?" Hannah
smiles, after she dips her spoon into the mashed potatoes. Harry hugs
Tammy, and then yells out to Evelyn, "What movie do you want me to
put on after dinner?"

"My favorite movie, *Play Misty for Me* with Clint Eastwood,"
Evelyn yells out to him. "Yeah, I like him. He's a good actor," he said.
Hannah sets the table and grabs the kids from Ethan's bedroom. Tammy
fixes everyone's plate. They wash their hands, sit down and say their
grace, and begin eating. There's a knock on the door. Harry gets up and
opens it. It's two of his guy friends from the 12 step group. "Hey, man,"
he extends his hand to both. "Come on in. We had just sat down for
dinner. Are you hungry?" Tammy looks at Evelyn, and Hannah laughs.
"No man, we're alright."

"Hey, I can't let you sit in my house while we're eating in front of
you. That would be rude. Come on, at least get something." Both men
laugh. "Alright man." They follow Harry to the kitchen. "Hey wash
your hands," he gives them the paper towel roll. Tammy gets up and
brings over two more chairs. They sat down at the table, "I'm Phillip,
and this is David."

Immediately they started talking about football, going into a
lengthy discussion. After everyone had finished eating, the men finished talking and the women got up and cleaned up the dining room
table and kitchen. Hannah takes the kids back into Ethan's room and
comes back and sits down in the living room.

Harry, Philip, and David go to the living room to watch the game
on television. Tammy, and Evelyn join them. "Hey Harry I thought we
were going to watch a movie?"…Evelyn asks.

"Hey man"…Harry signals to the guys, "I promise Sis, I would
watch a movie."

"Hey man, it's your house, you watch what you want to watch."
Evelyn feels guilty and says, "That's alright, turn on the game." The

men are yelling and screaming at the TV while the women sit back and watch. David attempts to break down the game into quarters and calls out the winner of each quarter, points scored in a quarter, number of fumbles, number of interceptions and so on. After the game, the guys and Evelyn get ready to leave. Evelyn hugs everyone and heads home with the girls. Even though Hannah has been staying with them on the weekends, they barely saw her. She's always gone by Saturday night and mostly Sunday evening.

Back at work, it's another week, and Tammy is still working the dinner shift. Tempers have begun to flare at work because they're busy. At the end of the day she's ready to leave. When she arrives home, she learns Hannah had stopped by and left again. Hannah and Harry are beginning to bicker at each other constantly. When Hannah moved in she was helping with house chores, but now, she spends all of her time in her room playing her music loudly. She also has become competitive in her affections toward Tammy. It is as if, she is trying to sabotage their relationship. Tammy doesn't know what to do about it. She loves Harry and Hannah and tries to keep their schedules filled with activities when possible. But Harry doesn't want to be around Hannah. He has made that clear to Tammy. Still, out of respect to Tammy, he is congenial to Hannah.

Hannah sees how Harry treats her mother and becomes jealous. She thinks to herself that she has to think of a way to get him out of her life. She tells Tammy that the reason she hasn't been staying there much is because Harry watches her when she comes out the bathroom and it makes her feel uncomfortable. Then she tells her that Harry has made passes at her. Angry, Tammy doesn't know what to think. A few days later, she is down emotionally again. This time, she started having anxiety and panic attacks and was beginning to think that she may not be well emotionally.

How could Harry, the one that said he loved me, do this to me? It never crossed her mind that Hannah was lying. Each time she looked at him, she became angrier. But she would never ask him to confirm or denied the allegations. *Why?* she asked herself. *Maybe fear of losing him.* Then one evening, she asked him to walk with her. "Harry there's something I need to ask you. I just need to know the truth." He looked puzzled. He walks slowly while listening. "Have you made a pass at Hannah?" He stops, waits a moment to gain his composure. Then he said...

"Tammy I'm going to take you to the doctor and have your head examined. Do you really think I would sleep with your daughter? C'mon ... now. You should know me, better than this." Tammy breaks down and cries.

"See, this is why I didn't want her here. I knew she was nothing but trouble, spreading these lies, filling your mind with who knows what. Look, listen to me! I'm not going to deal with this in my own house. She's going to have to go back home. You can meet her on weekends. But not here."

She wipes the tears from her face. "Harry, No!—She's my daughter."

"Look!...I see where this is going. Either you put her out or I will," he stands face-to- face with her. "Which is it going to be?" She is quiet as she walks slowly down the street. "Well?" he said. She wouldn't respond. Harry walks back to the house, goes to the garage, takes the lawn mower out. He mows the lawn for thirty minutes and comes back in—to shower.

Tammy gets up and embraces him on his way out of the bathroom. "Harry I do believe you. But please don't make me choose between you and my daughter." He looks at her and slams the bathroom door. He walks into their bedroom and changes clothes. "Tammy, I'm going to do this because I love you and my baby," he opens one of the dresser drawers. "But I'm telling you, if that girl doesn't get her act together, she's out of here. Do you understand me?" he yells. Tammy smiles at him...and whispers, "Thank you."

That night Hannah comes in. Harry and Tammy both acted like nothing has happen. Tammy's waiting to see where this is leading to, if Hannah is going to tell more lies or what other manipulative things will she do? She knows she's bossy, controlling, and rude. But she didn't know that she would try to sabotage her relationship. Hannah walks to the kitchen and opens the refrigerator.

"Hey, have you' all eaten yet?"

"I fixed some sandwiches for us. That's about it," Tammy says. Hannah looks around to see what she could put together for a snack. "Hey, Tammy a friend of mine is having a get together this week at her home. Would you both like to come?" Harry gets up and walks toward the front door. "I don't think I'll be able to make it, I'm busy that night," he said as he walks outside. "When is it?" Tammy said. "Saturday night starting around 7:30pm."

"How long is it?"

"It's just a get together. You can leave when you want to."

"Sure I'll go—but I won't stay long. Why do you want me to go?"

"I want to show you off to my friends," Hannah grabs a banana and heads back to her room.

The next morning, Tammy spends the morning going to doctor appointments for her and Ethan, then she visits her parents support group for Down's children. She drops Ethan off at home with Hannah, and gets dress for her work shift. At work, all week long, Mr. Schmidt had brought in different prospects for the head cook position. Today, he has allowed a young woman to come in and work alongside Tammy, to learn the job. He wanted to see what Tammy thoughts were on her work. Tammy likes her, and her work is quick, and creative. He pulls Tammy into his office, and asked her what her thoughts were. "I like her; she's friendly, helpful and catches on easy."

"That's good to hear, between you and I, Dustin was fired. I would like to promote her to his position after ninety days or so."

"You fired Dustin?" Tammy dropped her mouth open. Mr. Schmidt laughs. "A lot of people didn't like him. And I was getting complaints after complaints on him from staff and customers. Later, I found out he was stealing from me."

"What?" Tammy sounds surprised. "It was only a matter of time," he said. Tammy crosses her legs while sitting down listening to him.

Then someone knocks on his door. "Yes?" he yells out. "Mr. Schmidt we need you out front."

"Mr. Schmidt I wish the best for him," she stands up to follow him out. An answered prayer she thought. He had been so nasty to her, and all her suspicions about him were right. But it was his antagonizing ways that pushed her to move forward. That was the only thing she would give him credit for.

Harry comes home and sees Hannah car. *Oh God! She's here*, he moans. He walks in and speaks to her before looking in on the baby. He changes into his work around the house clothes and goes outside to work in the yard until dusk. Then he comes in and grabs a glass of water.

"Harry, I'm leaving. I'm meeting some friends and we're going to the mall."

"Okay Bye!" he said. He takes a shower, cleans up and brings Ethan into the living room to watch TV with him. Tammy arrives in, looking tired and exhausted. "Hey babe, how was work?"

"Busy as usual," she takes their food into the kitchen, walks over to him and kisses him and Ethan while attempting to play with Ethan. "What's in the bag?" Harry asks.

"I brought some food home for us. Where is Hannah?"

"She left, saying she was going shopping. For someone who's not working, she seems to spend money at a drop of a hat."

"What do you mean Harry?"

"You know, she's always shopping, and partying."

"She's irresponsible right now," Tammy said.

"Why did she even go to school, if she was not planning on working?" he said. Tammy walks back into the kitchen and takes their food out the bag.

Then brings it into the living room and sets it down on the coffee table. "Hold that thought babe, let me change into my comfortable clothes." Moments later, she comes back into the living room and grabs Ethan from Harry's lap and sits him into hers. She opens the food containers. "I got the Sirloin Steak Tips dinner for you. The meat is grilled

with onions, it should be good. There's buttered corn and mash potatoes with it. Harry would you get us something to drink." He set his
food down and gets two glasses of tea and brings it back. "Here you go."

"Thank you, babe."

"What did you get?" he asks.

"I got the seasoned tilapia, topped with sautéed mushrooms, onions, diced tomatoes, and Balsamic glaze, plus a salad and broccoli," she
takes a bite from her broccoli. Tammy pauses. "Harry about Hannah,
I can't answer your question. I don't know her. Remember it has been
years since I've seen her, and I'm sure the people who have raised her
have had a great affect on her and her attitude."

"Sounds like they spoiled her," he takes a bite form his Sirloin
steak tips. "Oh it's that obvious?" she laughs while feeding Ethan a piece
of broccoli. "You know," he takes a sip from his glass of tea. "There are
a lot of twenty something women that are responsible," he said.

"Yeah but there are those that are just like her. You know what,
I don't want to talk about her tonight. Let's just sit here, eat, and enjoy
ourselves," she takes a bite from her tilapia and gives the baby some.
"Anything new going on at your job?" she asked him. He pauses.

"No not really, but I had to hire another shampoo boy to help
me."

"You're that busy?"

"No, the other one left, decided to go back home to Michigan."

"How is he or her?"

"It's a...he. He's doing well. I have no complaints. The previous
owner stops by to see me often and helps me with the books."

"How is he doing?"

"Ah! He's getting up there in age. But he still gets around. He's
fun to talk too, and he's sharp. I like that in old people." Tammy smiles.
Harry finishes his dinner and throws the container in the trash. "Did
we have any plans for tomorrow or this weekend?" he asked. Hannah wants me to go to some party with her. "Babe...you're doing too
much," he said.

"I know. After this party, I think, I'll just stay home on the weekends after my catering jobs. Every now and then, get out—but you're right, it is becoming too much for me."

Friday night, Tammy and Hannah are on their way to Hannah's friend's party. They each take their own cars in case Tammy wants to leave early. When they arrive, there are about ten people there. Some are sitting in the living room and others at the breakfast table. Hannah introduces everyone to Tammy, and she starts to socialize among the different people. One of the guests had made a comment about Tammy's jacket. She wanted to know if it was a designer label, and she looked at the jacket back tag. Oh, it's not designer, the female said. Tammy doesn't say anything, but moves around and tries to mingle with the other guests. When the pizza arrived, the delivery guy takes it to the kitchen and sets it down on the partial island along with the salads. The hostess had placed the additional food, hot wings and litter soda on top of the oven surface. Most of the guests got up to get their slices of pizza and other foods. Tammy waited until everyone had fixed their plates, then she goes into the kitchen to fix her something.

While at the oven, she picks up two pieces of chicken wings. The pizza box flaps were open and hanging over the island near the stove. She accidently bumps into one of the open pizza boxes, trying to get out of the way of another guest trying to open a litter bottle of soda. She almost knocks the almost empty pizza box over. Hannah looks at her with a hateful glare as to say...you idiot! Immediately, Tammy noticed that Hannah's personality had changed for the worst. Tammy goes into the living area and sits down to talk with three guest. Hannah comes in wanting to be the spotlight of the party, she pulls up a chair.

As Hannah takes a bite from her pizza, she looks at Tammy with hate and anger in her eyes. Tammy could see her dislike for her as she sat there talking to her and the others. Forty minutes later, Tammy gracefully thanks everyone and leaves. On her way home she cries—quietly. She didn't know why she was crying. But she knew that Hannah didn't like or didn't think much of her as a person, and that is what hurts her the most. While driving she turns on the radio and hears one of her favorite songs. She listens to the lyrics and rolls down the window for some fresh air. She thinks about there has to be a change. Weeks before they were getting along and she could see progress in their relationship. "Maybe it's not meant to be"…she whispers to herself.

Back at home, slowly she gets out of the car and walks inside. There she finds Harry dozing off in his big chair. He awakens from the touch of her hand. "Hey, you're home…huh?"

"Yeah, is the baby asleep?"

"He's in his room. I guess so, I don't hear him crying," then he dozes back off to sleep. Tammy checks on the baby and sees that he's asleep. Quietly she backs out of his room, goes to her bedroom and changes into her night gown. She sits in her wing chair near the bed and picks up her favorite book to read. She fumbles through the pages and puts the book back on her night stand. Tonight she wasn't in the mood to read. She was thinking about how she had failed as a mother. Her mind raced with thoughts of when Hannah was a little baby, and how she half took care of her.

Today she's a grown woman who is vengeful toward her. She picks up the phone and calls Evelyn, she wanted to talk to someone. "Hey Sis…were you sleep?"

"Oh, I had dozed off. What about you?"

"Oh nothing."

"OH! OH! When you say that, something's on your mind." There is silence on the line. "Is it Hannah? Or Harry?"

"Sis, this relationship is not working."

"With whom?"

"Hannah."

"What has she done now?"

"She asked me to go to a party with her."

"Why you?"

"She claims she wanted her friends to meet me."

"How did it go?"

"Honestly, I am soooo hurt right now. She made me feel like a klutz in front of her friends. I mean, me and someone else were standing in the same spot; I was getting food and she was getting her drink, and I accidently backed up against the pizza box and it almost fell off the counter. Thank God there wasn't a whole pizza in there, maybe one or two slices left. But Sis, when I looked at her…I could see hatred all in her eyes toward me."

"What? Are you serious?"

"Yes, I am. Then one of the females made a distasteful comment about my jacket. She said it wasn't a designer jacket and Hannah laughed."

"She what?"

"Yeah. Now…how would you feel, if someone had done that to you?"

"Girl, Girl, Girl. Hannah definitely has some issues."

"I mean…even Harry is beginning to notice her behavior."

"You know girl…mother and daughter relationships can be a mess. Look what Madea had to go through with us when we were younger. And, our mother, bless her heart, she really sent Madea through changes."

"I know Sis. I can't figure out why she came back. She asked me if she could stay on the weekends with me. I agreed to that, even when Harry disagreed. Yet, she's never here; mostly she's out and about running the streets, shopping. And, she still doesn't have a job."

"Is she looking for one?"

"Evelyn I don't know and don't care at this point. My mind is confused, upset, and ambivalent and I feel silly. At the same time, I am relieved that at least I can see her." Tammy pauses… "There are so many things going on in my head which don't make sense."

"Hang in there…Sis! You've got to be strong."

"Anyway, I thought I would call and talk. I don't want to keep you from your beauty rest. I'll talk to you tomorrow."

"Okay. I love you," Evelyn says.

"I love you too."

Sunday morning, Tammy lies in bed reading a book not wanting to get out of bed.

Harry has gone to church and will attend a 12 step meeting afterwards. He's taken the baby with him to give Tammy a break. She gets up, showers and grabs a snack from the refrigerator, and then gets back into bed. *I'm not getting out of this bed at all today,* she tells herself. She turns on the TV and watches a religious program then changes the channel to a movie. She finishes her snack and dozes off to sleep again. Several hours later the phone rings. It's Harry wanting to know what she wanted to eat. "Hey, you can pick me up a chef salad are something like that with Catalina dressing?" An hour later, Harry shows up with her salad, Ethan's meal and a burger combo for himself.

"Are you going to get up today?" he asks.

"No!" she pulls the covers back over her head. Harry brings her food and closes the bedroom door. Then he sits with Ethan, making sure he eats all of his meal. Tammy gets up to check on them both. "Babe that salad hit the spot. It was good," she plays with Ethan for a moment then goes back to bed. Harry comes in and changes clothes, then goes back into the living room to get Ethan. They get into bed with her. He cuddles Ethan into his arms while he attempts to read to him. Ethan watches him as he turns his head to his daddy's voice. Next, he sings to Ethan. "Harry I never heard that song before."

"I got a lot of skills you don't know about"…he hits her on the behind. "That's a silly song," she said.

"Well my little man likes it…see he's smiling." Tammy turns over and sees Ethan's eyes light up. "Besides he doesn't care if it's silly. It's a lot of fun for him," he plays with Ethan's feet. A few minutes later, she tells him… "Hey you' all are making too much noise."

"Come on Ethan…let's go. Your mommy is grumpy," Harry walks Ethan, while chatting to him, explaining things around the house to him. On the floor, he plays roughhouse with him while looking him in the eye continually. Minutes later, he takes the baby and puts him in his playpen, playing with him until he falls asleep. Tammy gets up around seven o clock and wants to know if he wanted her to cook dinner. "It's whatever you want to do babe," he's watching sports on TV and doesn't want to be disturbed. Tammy sits near him and watches a little TV with him, and then she goes back to bed.

Monday morning she gets ready for work and then drops Ethan off at Madea's. The buzz around the kitchen was that Katie the new girl had been hired to take Dustin's place as head cook/manager. Because Tammy and the staff liked her, Mr. Schmidt decided to go ahead and take a chance on hiring her. She would be in charge of the entire kitchen from ordering food and scheduling of the kitchen employees. In addition, making sure the quality of the food products were right, as well as consistent. He also made her responsible for purchasing food at local markets early in the morning before the restaurant opens. He also hired a new line cook that would work underneath Katie at his assigned station, as a griller. He would cook the food as orders come in. Tammy's food preparation responsibilities would happen before the restaurant open and wouldn't change that much, which was fine with her. She was just glad to be back on the day shift-permanently. That afternoon she stops by her grandmothers to pick up the baby. Hannah calls while she was there, to tell her that she had gotten a job offer as a RN, she was excited.

"Hannah, that is great. Where is it?"

"The job is at a medical center in Long Beach. I signed up with a healthcare organization that's one of the largest employers of clinicians. They work with RN's just out of college. I would be working in their dialysis department, caring for all the hospitalized patients as prescribed by physicians."

"What is the pay?"

"I was told $27.00 an hour starting out."

"Hey, baby that is some good money."

"Yeah I'm happy."

"Okay here is Madea she wants to say hello to you." Tammy hands the phone to Madea. She asked her, why haven't she seen her lately. Hannah tells her that she has been busy and spending time with Tammy at her new house. "New house...what new house?" Madea asks.

"Didn't you know? Tammy moved in with Harry several weeks ago." Madea hands the phone back to Tammy. "Tammy Jean why didn't you tell me you moved in with your boyfriend?"

"Madea, I didn't want you to get upset." Madea picks up the remote control and turns up the volume on the TV.

"Madea it's a nice place."

"Tammy Jean you're not ready for that"...she hollers at her. They get into a heated argument, and Tammy grabs Ethan and leaves. That night Tammy's in the kitchen cooking dinner. Harry comes home and walks into the kitchen. She places pork chops into the skillet to brown before putting it into the oven to bake. He grabs an orange and begins to peel it. "What are you cooking?...It smells good."

"I decided to focus on us eating more whole grains and lean protein sources like: chicken breast, fish, and extra lean cuts of pork and beef. Tonight we are having pork, legumes-peas, sweet potatoes, a salad mixed with nuts and seeds."

"Hmmm sounds good," he said. She reaches into the cabinets to grab a baking pan. Then stirs together the celery, and uncooked rice. She places onion slices over the rice, then adds the pork chops. "I love watching you cook." She turns around and winks at him. "Well guest what?"

"What?"

"Hannah started work today."

"It's about time," he takes a bite from his orange.

In a 2 quart saucepan, she adds her ingredients to the boiling water and stirs to dissolve, then she pours the mixture over the pork chops. "Boy, got that out of the way," she wipes her forehead.

"I'm glad to see she has found work. She's making good money too."

"How much?" he asks.

"About $27 an hour-fulltime."

"Well that's good, she can start paying us rent for staying on the weekends," he laughs while taking another bite of his orange. Tammy covers the baking pan with aluminum foil, to bake until the rice is cooked and the pork chops are fork tender. I'll top the pork chops with green peppers when they are done."

"Seriously baby, she needs her own place," he said. "Hmmm, I'm wondering if her adoptive father is going to help her get a home? At least that's what she told me. But I haven't heard much about that anymore." Harry goes outside to change the oil in his car. He takes an old pan from the garage to catch the wasted oil and a funnel to pour the old oil back into the canisters for later disposal. He reaches into the passenger side of his car—for the car's manual and begins to read it. Tammy walks up to the car. "What are you doing?"

"I'm getting ready to change the oil."

"Well check mine too please, when you finish with yours," she looks down onto the ground for a second. "What's wrong?" he asked.

"Oh, I told Hannah when she asked me if she could move in. Not to tell Madea—I had moved in with you—yet."

"And?"

"Well, she told her today." He slams his car door that was left open. "See!" his face turns red. "She needs to get out of our house."

"Harry I can't throw her out she's my daughter."

"Tammy, I'm telling you, she's troubled. Now why would she do that after you asked her not to?"

"I don't know Harry?"

"You know...Tammy! She's trying to be vindictive that's why."

"I've got to check on the food," she goes back inside.

The phone rings and it's Hannah, sounding emotional. "What is it Hannah?"

"Tammy I need some money?" Tammy turns on the water to wash off her fruit for the salad she's making. "For what, Hannah?" Hannah's quiet...then she whispers..."For an abortion."

"What? You didn't tell me this earlier when I spoke with you."

"I know. I didn't want to say anything while you were at Madea's."

"Hannah what happened?" she screams.

'Tammy, I don't want to go into it on the phone."

"I can't pay for you to do that. I'm sorry. We can work together on planning out what direction you should take. But I can't do that."

"Okay, fine." Hannah hangs up. Tammy tries to call her back but keeps getting her voice mail.

Three days later, after countless messages that Tammy has left, Hannah, returns her phone call. "Hannah....we need to talk. Can you come within the next hour?"

"Yeah. Will Harry be there?"

"Yeah...But he usually works in the yard before dinner. So that's not a problem."

That night, Harry sits in the living room watching television. "Baby, Hannah is on her way over," Tammy says softly.

"Ah Man!" he slams the remote down, "For God's sake, why?"

"Harry, I need for you to work in the front or back yard until she leaves...okay?" He looks at her with a disgruntle expression.

"Yeah...Tammy."

Hannah comes over about seven o clock that night. Hannah sits down, and starts to cry.

"Hannah did you have the abortion?"

"Yes."

"Who paid for it?"

"John."

"Your adoptive father?"

"Yes."

"Is it his baby?"

"Tammy," Hannah stands up and walks around the house. I don't know if it's his, or someone else."

"Oh my God. You've been sleeping with him?"

"Yes, John told me that I couldn't tell anyone."

Chapter 12

"Does his wife know about it?"

"I don't think so. But she has treated me badly for the last five years."

"Did she start out that way?"

"No. We were close, and then one day she changed."

"That's why he has been buying you all this stuff. I have the good mind to call the police on him."

"Tammy, please don't. If you do, I'll never speak to you again."

"You'll never speak to me again. I'm your mother." Hannah sits down on the sofa. "Well I'm not pregnant so it doesn't matter."

"Hannah, you are a grown woman. You have to get out of that house, and get your own place, support yourself for a change. You're working now, and you can do it. I will help you with getting an apartment until you can save for a house."

"Tammy. I will be okay. Give me a couple of days to think about it. I need to go." When Hannah leaves, Tammy is so mad, that she tries to locate John's phone number. "What did she tell me their last name was?" she looks in the phone book. "Freeman, that's it. John Paul and Piper Freeman." Hannah had let it slip that she lived in Carson. So she calls directory assistance and asks for the Freeman residence. The phone rings for a long time. Then someone picks up...

"Hello"

"Mrs. Freeman?"

"Yes."

"This is Tammy Brown, Hannah's biological mother." Piper doesn't say anything. Then she said, "Ms. Brown, How are you? What can I help you with?"

"Don't be smug with me"....Tammy shouts. "I know your perverted husband has been sleeping with my daughter."

"Stop!...I won't listen to this"...Piper yells back.

"Oh you will listen, I'm going to call the police and the news channel and report both of you. Then, I'm going to call the case worker that handled your adoption and tell them about it. How could you let him sexually abuse my child?...Huh? How could you? She trusted you! Hannah has told me how nasty you have been to her. You've been covering this up for a long time...haven't you?" Piper hangs up.

Tammy grabs her keys. "I need to go over there and really give her a piece of my mind." She gets in her car, starts the engine...but stops. If she harms anyone, she will be back in prison. *What would happen to Ethan? Harry would leave her. Is it worth it?*...she thinks. She hits the steering wheel..."@*%$"..."I don't believe this." For a moment she sits in the car, too cool off. *Calm down*, she tells herself. *It will work itself out.* She doesn't want Harry, Evelyn, or anyone to know. It's Hannah secret. She will wait to hear from Hannah. If she doesn't she will take matters into her own hands.

The next night, Friday evening, Harry comes in late from work. Tammy's cooking while Ethan's asleep. "Hey baby," he walks over to her, for a kiss. Tammy jerks away. "What was that about," he said, as he heads to the bedroom to undress. Tammy doesn't say anything. "Here we go, another pouting session," he takes a shower and changes into a t-shirt and his bottom pajamas. After he comes out, she approaches him. "Did you want something to eat?" she said. "Nah, I'm fine." Tammy slams the refrigerator door. Harry sits down in his easy chair. She walks over to him. "Harry I'm beginning to feel I'm doing all the work around here."

"Tammy please don't start that again tonight. I take out the trash, and help around the house." With both hands on her hips, she screams at him... "Harry, I work two jobs, cook, clean and care for the baby. When I cook I expect you to eat it. I could eat at the restaurant and not cook."

"Tammy don't I normally eat when I come in?" Her eyes glare at him. "I don't feel like arguing tonight,"...he turns up the television. "All I'm saying is, would you do more to help out with the household chores and the baby?" Harry gets up and goes to the bedroom to lie down.

The next morning Harry is gone before Tammy gets up. The alarm goes off, she hits the snooze button, and goes back to sleep. The phone rings, it's Evelyn calling wanting to know why she was still in bed. She jumps up, dresses her and the baby and takes him to her grand-mothers. They have three catering jobs today. Depressed she doesn't feel like going, but forces herself to go. That evening, Harry asked if she wanted to go with him to rent some movies. On their way out, to the video store, Hannah calls. Tammy has decided that she will not tell her that she called Piper. "Tammy I need to borrow some money."

"For what Hannah?"

"One of my girlfriends is willing to let me roommate with her. I have not been home; instead I've been staying here."

"Have you talked to Piper or John?"

"No not yet."

"How much did you need?"

"She's charging me $900.00 dollars a month."

"Where is it?"

"It's on S. Virgil Ave near Beverly Blvd."

"Okay...What's the name of the place?"

"Emerald Terrance, Tammy, are you going to help me out or not? You were the one that said I needed to leave home. I found a place...I just need some money."

"Okay, Hannah. We are on our way to the video store but will be back within an hour. I will stop by an ATM machine and draw the money out."

"Thank you, Tammy."

Harry loads the baby into the back seat of his car, and waits for Tammy to come out. At the video store, she asked him what movies he wanted to see. "I like action movies."

"What if we did action, comedy and romance?" she asks. "That's fine," he said.

"Oh before I forget, we need to stop by an ATM."

"Why?" he asked. "Hannah called and has an emergency."

"Just about every time we see her, she's asking for money. Didn't she ask you for money at the barbeque that you had? We're not a money tree," he pulls a video case from the shelf.

"Doesn't she work?"

"Harry, she's not going to have a paycheck for a while."

"Yeah, but she can't just spend her money on clothes, shoes, and eating out, then expect for everyone to bail her out. We can't help her all the time!"

"You're beginning to sound like a broken record...Harry." They get into a heated discussion. "Harry, I didn't ask you to give her any money. I'm her mother, if she can't get it from me, who will she get it from?" Tammy walks toward the checkout counter. He follows behind her. "Who was she getting it from before you came back on the scène?" She throws the video cases onto the counter, for check out.

On their way back, they pull up into the driveway and see Hannah waiting with a friend. Tammy hands the money to Hannah and tells her to call later. That night, she couldn't sleep; she goes to the living room to watch television. With the sound muted, she watches the images flashing before her face. She thinks about Hannah, and her own regrets about not being there for her children.

The next week, Tammy comes in from work, relaxes, and starts to clean the house. In the bathroom, after cleaning it, she adds a new shower curtain, and decorative accessories. Exhausted, she takes a break, falling asleep in the chair. Harry comes in and accidently pees on the floor and leaves the toilet seat up. Tammy goes in later, sees the stain on the floor, cleans it and let's down the toilet seat. Disgruntle she walks over to him... "I just cleaned that bathroom and would like to keep it clean, for a couple of days." Harry turns down the television, "What did you say?"

"I...said...I just cleaned the bathroom and you left pee stains on the floor. Plus, I need you to let down the toilet seat when you're done. I don't want to fall in during the middle of the night when I get up to use the bathroom." Harry doesn't say anything. Tammy goes into the kitchen to fix dinner, and then she starts a load of laundry. As she goes through his pants, she sees a business card with a female face and name. She holds it up to him. He turns around and looks at the card. "Who is this...Harry?"

"Tammy, I don't know who that is. It could be anyone. You know people do leave me their business cards and they leave them in the fish bowl on the counter at work. Tammy!...Hell...I don't know. Leave me alone!!!"

A few days later, right before the wedding. They decided to pick up a few items from the supermarket. She tells the butcher... "I would like four lean cut porterhouse steaks." The butcher weights and wraps the steaks, she looks into Harry's eyes.

"Do you respect me?" she asks.

"Tammy...I've had about enough of this. What is this really about?" he's trying to get Ethan to sit down in the buggy. "Boy would you please sit still," he yells at him.

"Why are we always fighting now?" he asked. The butcher hands her their package, and walks away. "We can't seem to agree on any-thing—anymore. What do you mean...respect you? Baby, all I did was answer your question. You asked me what meats we needed to get. I told you I liked tenderloins sometimes. You have made a big issue about nothing. If you wanted porterhouse steaks, then just say it." He throws the steaks into their buggy. "I tell you what, get whatever you want!" he said, angrily. He pushes the shopping cart further down the aisle.

On their way home—neither says anything. When they arrive home, he opens the door and comes back to carry the groceries inside. "Where do you want these bags?" he asks.

Tammy frowns, "Hell!"... "Harry, just sit them down, anywhere, I don't care," she snaps at him. Harry brings in all the bags of groceries. Ethan starts crying, because Tammy won't let him stay up and play. She wants him to take a nap. By this time, Ethan's hollering and crying at the top of his voice. Meanwhile, Evelyn calls and she holds a long conversation with her, ignoring Ethan's' cries.

"Tammy," Harry yells out to her. "Baby would you go see about the baby?" Tammy ignores him. "Tammy, the baby is crying," this time his voice elevates. "Hey Sis, let me call you back, this boy is acting a fool." Harry and her get into an argument. "Hey," he catches her arm. "Hey...wait a minute. You said at the grocery store you wanted to be loved and respected. I asked you to get off the phone and see about the baby, see how you treat me."

"Harry, you did not ask me to get off the phone."

"Tammy"...he steps back. "You know what...I'm leaving."

"Where are you going?" she shouts out, as he heads toward the door.

"Tammy, you're playing games with me, at least that's how I'm seeing it."

"What?...How am I playing games with you?"

"Okay, let's go at it this way. The baby's screaming in the background, who wants to be hearing all that hollering."

"Excuse me, he's your son too," she said.

"That's not the point. Why didn't you tell Evelyn you would call her back?" he yells.

With a startle look she stares at him. "Because I didn't want to," she blurs out. "You see what I have to deal with. I've been dealing with this for over two years all by myself!"

"So, now you're saying—I haven't helped you with the baby?"

"All I'm saying Harry is, he's a handful. I need you to help me! I know you take care of him but I'm talking about you being around more, you and us as a family." Harry walks out to the car, slams the car door and comes back in.

"What do you want me to do...Tammy!" he looks at her, angrily. "Just tell me and I'll do it. What is it?" angrily, he asks.

"That's okay...I got it now," she said. Harry goes out back and starts mowing the back yard. Later, he takes his shower and changes clothes. *Is he changing his mind about us?* she thought to herself.

Later that week, Harry pours himself a glass of tea, and sits down in his favorite chair.

Tammy walks over to him and sits in his lap, he almost spills his glass of tea. "Hey watch out!" he said. "I'm sorry," she kisses him. "Is there anything wrong?" she asks.

"No...why would you ask me that?" he said angrily. "I don't know," she tries to snuggle into his arms.

"Tammy, I can't watch the television." She jumps up... "So that's what's important to you, television?"

"Hey, hey...C'mon...don't do this!"

"Don't do this, Don't do this," she yells back at him. "Harry what's wrong? You're changing on me."

"Woman you're tripping. Go over there and sit down," he yells. "Excuse me! Harry don't talk to me like a child," she storms off into the bedroom and slams the door, while waking the baby. "Ah man!... Now the baby's crying. Tammy!...Tammy!...Get the baby." Ignoring him, she doesn't come out of the bedroom. "Tammy, get the baby!" he says. In the bedroom, she lays on the bed crying. He goes to the baby's room, picks him up, and takes him to the living room. Then he talks to the baby while rocking him back and forth, soon Ethan settles down. He turns the television back up and mopes.

Tammy comes out of the bedroom and goes into the kitchen, slamming dishes around.

She approaches him. "I need to know one thing." He looks at her. "Are you sleeping around on me?" He sighs, "Woman...you've lost your mind...get away from me."

"Harry," she yells... "I don't see you anymore, until night."

"Tammy you know that I work from sun-up to sun-down. Someone has to be there for my clients pets, when the pet owner isn't going to be home. You know the place has to be cleaned up for the next day. Why are you nagging me? What do you want from me? Do you want me to sell the business? How would we live? Is that what you want?" he yells at her. The baby starts to cry again. "Give him to me, I'll take him," she takes the baby back to his room and rocks him asleep. Harry gets up, slams the front door and leaves.

Their wedding was two days away. Yet they have been fighting like cats and dogs. Every week, she counted on her hand, they would have at least two to three fights. First it started out with disagreements, escalating to full blown arguments with either her or Harry leaving for a few hours. And to add fuel to the fire…. she was having to deal with Hannah's issues. It was draining her mentally. In like manner, her grandmother is upset and won't talk to her for moving in with Harry.

Madea threaten Tammy by telling her that she couldn't come back to the house she had allowed her to live in. She was on her own. Her grandmother would continue to keep the baby while she worked, but she wasn't going to help her with anything else. She was still upset with Harry about infecting Tammy with HIV and getting her back on drugs. In her grandmother's mind, she thought that it would be a matter of time before they both would be using drugs again. Madea's mind was made up; she wasn't going to go through that anymore.

Meanwhile, John Freeman had made contact with Hannah, putting her out of their house in Carson. He tells her that Tammy called and threatened him and Piper. "Everything, I have given you, you've paid me back this way. First, tracking down your biological mother without telling us, then you tell her I was sleeping with you," he said to Hannah.

Hannah goes to see Tammy the day before her wedding. Loudly, she bangs on the front door. Tammy rushes to the door and opens it. Mad and crying, she screams, "I trusted you. I asked you not to say anything to them about the abuse. But no, you had to open your big mouth."

"Hannah, wait a minute."

"Don't tell me to wait a minute!"

"Who do you think you are?" Tammy said. By this time, Harry has pulled up and could hear the yelling from outside. He rushes inside to see what is going on. "Tammy, what's going on?" he asked her.

"Harry, I've got this! Please, give me a minute with Hannah." Harry walks around the house, and then he goes to the bathroom. "Hannah, I did it to protect you. Anyway you have a place now."

"That's suppose to make it okay, what you've done? Tammy I trusted you. Now he could go to jail and lose everything," she screams.

"Why do you care? He deserves to lose everything. Both of them deserves to go to jail, what is this about; you no longer have a money tree?"

"You *@%$+"...Hannah screams out.

"Oh no...missy. You won't talk to me that way," Tammy says angrily. Hannah looks at Tammy, sobbing maniacally.

"I have been molested all my life from as young as I can remember. Going from one foster care family to another. Each one abusing me, and I had no one...not no one, to protect me. I cursed you each time those filthy old men touched my body, and when I cried, they just told me to be quiet. It's your fault Tammy!"

Tears begin to flow from Tammy's face, putting her hand over her mouth, as if to throw up. "You think you're a good mom, you ain't %*@$. You tell me which is better, having someone to take care of you or having someone in your life that's HIV positive? That's right I know about it. I checked it. Remember I'm a nurse. You're no better that he is. You're a #*%@ junkie." Harry comes out of the bathroom.

"Hey! Hey! Don't you talk to her like that. Get out of my house Hannah! Get out now!" he runs and opens the door. Hannah walks toward the door, turns around and tells her,

"I don't ever want to see you again." Harry slams the door, on her way out. He embraces Tammy, and tells her to sit down for a minute. "That girl is a trip! She has some serious psychological problems," he says angrily. Tammy rocks back and forth crying. Harry tries to comfort her. But she shoves him away from her. "I'm okay. I'm okay. Just give me a minute," she goes out to their backyard crying ferociously, as Harry watches her. In one of the patio chairs, she sits down, with her head down between her legs. "Oh Hannah," she softly whispers as she cries her eyes out. "Oh Hannah," still wanting her to be a part of their lives. All of her problems had hit her at that moment. Her and Harry arguing, little Ethan's health problems, Harry wanting her to work only one job, better still not work at all, her health—now Hannah.

The truth of the matter was everybody was stressed. Knowing, Harry takes very seriously trying to be responsible. She has never had a man in her life that looked after her. His point of view made sense on some things, and others things she didn't agree with...like not having to work, because of the baby. *Could they make it?* she thought. *Was this what marriage life was suppose to be like-day end and day out?* She didn't know what she should do. *If she left him, where would she go?* Madea was very serious about her not coming back to the house. She was forty one years old, and was tired of starting over again. *Could her and Harry resolve their differences before it was too late? Would she and Hannah resolve their differences?*

◦✲◦

Friday afternoon, Harry is at the LAX Court house waiting for Tammy. Stuck in traffic, she shouts out, "C'mon man," to the other driver that cuts her off. She blows her horn then switches from lane to lane when the driver before her can't make up his mind to drive normal or slow speed. She reaches for her purse, and realizes she doesn't have her cell phone. "Shoot, where is that phone?"

Underneath the front seat, she looks around as she tries to steer her car. "I can't believe this, where is my phone?" she yells out. "I need to call him and let him know, I'm on my way. God please help me to get there on time. C'mon...people!...let's go!" One of the drivers gives her the finger.

"Forget him! He's not going to destroy my day."

She could see the Courthouse from the 105/405 freeway intersection. Ten minutes later she arrives at the court house.

When she arrives at the building she was surprised, up close it didn't look like your typical courthouse. The front had a glass facade and looked nice. The parking was more of a challenge though. The parking lot is relatively small for the building, so she had to park in the lot adjacent to the courthouse.

On the six floor, where she is supposed to meet Harry, she signs in and is told to be seated in the waiting area until their name is called. Harry's sponsor Jim and his wife Vanessa, walks over to her and congratulate her. "Well looks like you and Harry, finally agreed to get married. I told you at the barbeque bash that he needed to marry you." They all hug and laugh.

He tells her that Harry went to the men's room. Then, moments later Harry steps out of the men's room. "Wow," Harry smiles. "Hey baby, you look beautiful," he says. Tammy was dressed in a below the knee flattering white draped, short strapless form fitting gown, contouring her body into an hour glass shape. Its coordinating ruffle neckline shrug added glamour and coverage to her dress. With her hair up in a bun, she added a large white feathery flower with a small sheer net veil hanging slightly over her eyes down to her nose. "Do, I?"

"Yes," he said

"For a moment, I thought I was at the wrong place. I couldn't call, to tell you—I wasn't far away. I must have left my cell phone somewhere."

"It's okay...calm down"...he whispers to her.

"Look at you!.... You look nice!" she said

Harry was wearing a three button black tuxedo suit, white shirt with a burgundy red vest, and tie. "Thank you, baby!" he responds. The justice of the peace comes in to begin the ceremony. Their name is called, and they all head back to the justices work area. They see his staff members working, paperwork everywhere on their desks; she tries to keep from being distracted. He starts the ceremony, with Tammy starting her vows. They turn and face each other.

"I, Tammy choose you Harry to be my husband, In the presence of God, to respect you in your successes and in your failures, to care for you in sickness and in health, to nurture you, and to grow with you throughout the seasons of our life."

"I, Harry take you, Tammy, In the presence of God, to be my partner, loving what I know of you, and trusting what I do not yet know. I welcome the chance to grow together, getting to know you as you grow, falling in love with you a little more every day. I promise to love and cherish you through whatever life may bring us."

They exchange rings. The justice then said.... "Because Harry and Tammy have desired each other in marriage and have witnessed this before God and our gathering, affirming their acceptance of the responsibilities of such a union and have pledged their love and faith to each other, sealing their vows in the giving and receiving of rings, I do proclaim that they are husband and wife in the sight of God and man." They embrace each other with a passionate kiss, and then he holds Tammy for a few seconds. "Congratulations'" the justice says. Harry's sponsor and his wife hug both of them. Then everyone in their group is asked to stay and sign off on some legal documentation.

They look at each other as they sign their documents. The last month had been trying for the both of them. Tammy had even thought about not going through with it. But, she loved Harry, and he loves her. They drove to Wal-Mart to have their wedding pictures taken then met Harry's sponsor Jim, at the restaurant for dinner. Nothing fancy, a small cozy dinner for four, before driving to San Diego for their honeymoon.

Jim and Vanessa had planned a nice early dinner for the two at a restaurant in Manhattan Beach. From there Harry and Tammy would drive into downtown San Diego and check into their honeymoon suite. The upscale restaurant offered Mediterranean and Asian influenced dishes. It was especially interesting to Tammy. She has always been open to trying new and different entrees. Harry was in her life permanently, they both were sober, had good friends, and most importantly, the bickering, intense arguments, and crisis had made their love stronger for each other. *Life was good as it could be*, she thought.

All four toast their new beginning with a savory flavor ice tea. After an hour and half of talking and eating, they headed out to San Diego. "Jim and Vanessa, what would I have done without you guys?" Harry said. "Yeah, Thank you for being his friend and now my friend," Tammy said. They kiss and hug, and Harry and Tammy leave.

Harry gets on the freeway heading to San Diego. He has brought along his favorite collection of music ranging from Tammy favorites from the seventies, to his favorites, jazz and old school music. He puts on a favorite of his by Lenny Williams… *"Cause I Love You."* Tammy listens to the lyrics, sinks back into her seat and thinks about the meaning of love. Harry rubs her left hand as he drives. He sings to her at different breaks in the song. She touches his face, and then she cuddles with him, while stroking his leg.

She looks at him and begins talking about her feelings. She tells him about her personal challenges for the day, then she is quite. "Did you get everything out?" he asked her. "Yes," she laughs.

"Do you feel better?" he asks.

"Honey, I felt better the moment we said…I do." He places his hand on her leg and begins to rub it. "I have something special for you tonight. It will take your mind off of Hannah, and anything else that's bothering you." Smiling, she said, "Are we staying until Sunday or Monday?"

"Our registration is booked for three nights through Monday afternoon 12:00pm. If you want to stay longer, then we will have to talk with the front desk."

"No, three days is good. I'm so excited I can hardly wait."

"We'll be there shortly," he said.

"What did you think about the food at the restaurant?" she said.

"My lobster chowder was really good, and the filet mignon, mashed potatoes with asparagus was awesome. How about your food?"

"I loved the baby spinach salad and all natural salmon. We should go back to that place on our own," she said.

"Next time, we will have Evelyn or your grandmother to watch Ethan, and then we'll go there."

Tammy would watch Harry as he maneuvers through traffic. "I love the way you grip your steering wheel. You're a good driver baby."

"Thank you…babe," he reaches over and kisses her. Two hours later, they had arrived in San Diego.

"This place is so clean…I love it," she said. Harry pulls up to a hip luxury hotel immersed in the dynamic energy of downtown San Diego. The heart of the lively Gaslamp District. Valet parking men welcomes them. Harry reaches in the back and grabs the gift basket he had bought for her and gives it to her. The night before, he had placed it in the trunk of her car, unbeknownst to her.

"What is that Harry?" he grabs their luggage.

"It's a surprise." She smiles as they enter into the hotel. "Baby this is going to be a vacation of a lifetime, celebrating our new life together as a married couple," he said.

"Oh Baby!"…she whispers, as she quenches his arm.

They check in and go to their room. As they approach their room door, he tells her to wait a minute. He unlocks the door, and picks her up and carries her in. She looks around the artfully designed room. Its color palette was aqua blues and browns, with dark mahogany stained seating, and a comfortable chair that occupied the small living area. The bedroom area was separated by a beautiful light color taupe wall. "Baby, this is beautiful," she runs up to him and kisses him. "I'm glad to see you like it," he said.

"Look at that flat screen television," she said.

"Yeah, there should be two flat screens in here. One in the living room and another in the den of love," he laughs. She runs over to the king size bed and falls into its plush linens.

"Ah! This is heaven."

"There is even a CD/DVD player," he said.

"Look Harry!" Tammy notices the animal print plush robes. She softly strokes them… "Oh this is smooth," she sits up and tells him to sit down next to her. He puts their luggage in a corner and sits downs.

"Baby this is beautiful. You've really made me feel special." They embrace and kiss for a long time, and then she pulls away from him. "I tell you what, why don't we go on a sightseeing tour of the hotel, come back order a pitcher of orange juice with two champagne glasses, and then take a hot bath together."

"That will work, but let's unpack and get settled in before we do this…is that okay?" he said. "Okay sure," she said. He places the luggage on the bed. "I'll let you have the honors. I'm going to the little boys' room." Tammy eagerly takes out their clothes, humming as she places them into the drawers. She hangs up their trousers, his shirts, and her favorite blouses. He comes out of the bathroom.

"What does it look like?" she asked.

"Go see"…he tells her. Inside there is a Fuji soak tub plus separate shower. "Man this is too nice. Baby you did a good job." Both change into comfortable clothing. They walk up to the pool side terrace. Tammy clutches her mouth. "Oh my God! Baby this is so nice."

"Yeah it is," he said.

The terrace was beautiful and large, decorated with bright colors and beautiful lounge chairs. "We could come out here maybe Sunday morning or late one evening. It would be perfect for relaxing. Let's check out the restaurant," she said. He grabs her hand, as they walk. The restaurant has an upscale decor with several cozy pattern booths. "I like this Harry."

"Yeah we can eat here or we can eat downtown, when we get out," he said.

"Speaking of downtown did you feel like walking around downtown tonight," she asks. "No baby," he embraces her. "Why don't we go back to our room and relax. We can sightsee some other time. Tonight, let's just relax and not think about anything else. This will be a fun time for us…okay?" he kisses her on the lips. "Okay, handsome," she touches his lips with one of her fingers, and they head back to their room. On their way back, they stop off at the front desk and requests for a pitcher of orange juice with two champagne glasses and a bowl of strawberries dipped in chocolate to be sent to their room.

Back at their room, Tammy runs their bath water. Harry turns the TV to a movie channel. Room service knocks at the door. The room attendant sits down their pitcher of orange juice, glasses and bowl of strawberries. Harry tips him, closes the door, and undresses. He goes into the bathroom and gets into the tub while the water is still running. Tammy undresses and gets in, while turning off the water. She lays back into his arms. "Who would have thought we would be here together at this place and at this time in our life."

Harry sighs… "Yeah, you're a pretty tough cookie." Enjoying the moment, she smiles to herself.

"When I first saw you woman. I knew you were going to be my wife."

"Really," she sounds surprised.

"Yep…I had that gut feeling."

"I'm glad you didn't give up on us," she turns around and French kisses him on the lips. They wash each other with the hotel spa products and then rinse each other off. "What is in your gift basket? Looks like a lot of beauty products."

"I'm not going to tell you. You have to wait and see. But I promise, you will like it," he puts his arms around her. She stands up, reaches out her hand to help him get up. He moans, as he's getting out of the tub. They dry each other off and slip into their robs. Out of curiosity, she opens the gift basket and sees scented oils, instructional DVDs, relaxation music, candles and incenses.

"Boy, talk about the perfect ambience," she says. As she takes out the scented candles, she lights them, and puts in one of the relaxation CDs. Harry jumps onto the bed. He takes out the scented massage oils and begins to rub it onto her arms, her legs, her feet, and wherever he missed a spot. She takes a handful and rubs it onto his feet, his legs, his arms, and tells him to lie on his stomach; she rubs the oil unto his back. She then rubs his hands, going in between his fingers, one by one. Then she rubs it into her hands and fingers, but rubs off some of the oiliness with a napkin. Harry gets in under the sheets as she pours the orange juice. She hands him his glass then brings the bowl of strawberry dipped chocolates. She picks up one and bites into it...she looks at Harry while he watches the TV. "Harry...you remember these?" He looks at her and laughs...

"Yeah, that's how we got baby Ethan." Tammy laughs so loud that she wondered if the neighbors could hear them. She slides into bed underneath the sheets and begins to feed Harry strawberries. "What are some of the things you like to do?" she asked him. "You mean now or in general?"

"In general Harry," she laughs.

"Nothing can replace the sensation of biting into a thick, juicy, bloody steak, and watching highlights of the NFL Primetime game, I've just finished watching."

"Okay what else?"

"Uh...let's see, yeah a comfy chair"

"Okay, what else?"

"My remote control"... Tammy looks at him. "Yeah...I like my remote control."

"Anything else?" she asked.

"Oh Yeah...I like to have a radio in the bathroom, air fresheners, along with my books, when I'm in there." They both burst out laughing... "Hey, didn't you just ask me what I liked?" he asks. She was laughing so hard, she couldn't answer his question. "Come here," he pulls her over close to him. "Okay tell me what you like?"

"I love romantic movies, and treating myself to a spa bath."

"What else?" he asked.

"Cooking you a romantic dinner."

"Really?" he said. Then he rubs her hand, moving his hand down her leg, he pats her on the leg. For two hours they laugh and talk about things that had happen in their lives, and about times they shared together that were special. Tammy looks into his eyes and tells him that she appreciates him. She kisses him on the forehead. He turns the television off, and she turns off the lights. Snuggled in each other arms they lay for the rest of the night. That morning, he awakens her with a kiss, tells her she's beautiful. He strokes her hair, and enjoys her body scent.

He embraces her and tells her, that her skin feels so soft and silky next to his.

"Harry?"

"Yes," he answers as he kisses her neck.

"You always know exactly what to do and where to touch me," she moves her legs… "Mmmm, sweet," she responds to his touches.

They make passionate love. Saturday and Sunday, they stayed in bed all day, ordering room service, talking, laughing, watching movies and joking around with each other. Monday they both call their jobs, and she calls Madea to let her know she was still out of town but would be back soon. Monday morning, they get out to visit the different areas of the city. Harry had made arrangement to stay later since they arrived late Friday night. Tuesday morning they get up early for breakfast and to sightsee in downtown San Diego. Then once back at their room, they pack and check-out at noon. "Baby, this was really nice," he tells her.

"Well, I guess we're on our way back to Los Angeles," she mumbles. "Yeah, not unless you want to move here?" he said. "Boy would I like to," she says.

Back in Los Angeles, a young female, borderline tipsy-drunk heads to her car, she had been out drinking with her friends, for half of the night, and decided to go home. Saddened about her situation with her adoptive father and not willing to accept having to be responsible. She thinks about her life, her mother, and her last conversation with her. Suddenly her red sports car is plowed into by someone that has run a red light. Her car swirls around, and stops at an angle, embedded into her air bag, her blood-soaked face. Her body is still and almost lifeless. Traffic stops to a haught. People get out looking. But only one man walks over to her car to see about her.

He calls 911 and tells them there has been a bad accident. The ambulance sirens could be heard as it approaches her car. She is placed on a stretcher and taken to the emergency room. She goes into unconsciousness. The medical team is trying to contact her family. They identify her as Hanna Brown Freeman and identify her parents as John Paul and Piper Freeman.

The phone call is made to them at 11:00pm, that their daughter was in critical condition and may not make it. John refuses to come to the hospital. Yet Piper races to her bedside. When she arrives, she asks if she can see her. She goes in and sees her mangle up body on life support and barely breathing.

Piper runs out of the room, holding onto a wall, trying to catch her bearings. Not able to constrain her endless flow of tears. She didn't want to do it, but she needed to call her biological mother—Tammy. *What would she say to me? Would she curse me out? Blame me and John? Or both?* Piper knew if she didn't make the call she could never live with herself. She dials Tammy's number, the phone rings, but there is no answer. She leaves a message along with her cell number. "Oh God… where is she?" Thirty minutes later, she calls again…Still, no answer, another message is left, this time with urgency in her voice.

Harry and Tammy had stopped over at Madea's to pick up Ethan. When Madea answers the door she is shocked to see Harry. Tammy flashes her wedding ring to her. Madea hugs her and Harry and tells them to come in. Tammy's grandfather stands up to take a look at him.

"So you're Harry? Where have you and my granddaughter been?" he reaches out his hand to him.

"We were married over the weekend and went on our honeymoon," he said. Madea sits down and shakes her head. "I don't believe this. I don't believe this," Madea says.

"Madea," Tammy laughs… "What is it that you don't believe?" Madea hesitates, "That you married your baby's father. I hope this marriage last and I wish you both the best." Harry laughs, "Madea it will last. I love Tammy and she loves me." Tammy interrupts… "Madea we came over to pick up Ethan and then we have something we need to do. Where is he?"

"In that back room. Tammy where else is he going to be? That's his little room with all his stuff." Tammy goes to get him. Madea looks at Harry. "Harry you have done right by granddaughter and that's all I can ask of you," standing, she reaches out and hugs him. "Thank you!" he said. Tammy walks back in with the baby, "Madea 'I'll call you later."

"Does your sister Evelyn know?" Madea asked. "No—not anyone but you," Tammy smiles at her. On their way home, Tammy kept looking in the backseat at Ethan. Harry asked her why she kept looking back at him. "Honey, I don't know, I guess making sure he's okay."

"Why wouldn't he be okay?"

"Harry, I got this gut feeling that's something not right."

"With whom?"

"That's just it, I don't know. It could be Evelyn or the girls." Quiet and still, she ponders her feelings. They pull up to their home and Tammy takes the baby out. When they walk inside she notices that the red message light on their answering machine is blinking. Tammy puts the baby in his room and leaves his door open. Harry checks the messages and calls Tammy.

"What?" she runs into the living room. "Some white woman name Piper has left you several messages. Sounds urgent." She plays back the message and notes down her number. She calls Piper, and she tells her that Hannah is in intensive care, and that she needs to come quickly. "Oh my God," she throws the phone down and rushes to her car. "Hey, baby what's wrong?"

"It's Hannah. Stay here, I'll drive."

"No I'll drive," he grabs the baby from out of his room, loads him into the car and drives them to the Los Angeles hospital. Tammy runs to the nurse's desk to inquire about Hannah. Piper overhears their conversation and knows it must be Tammy. She walks up to them and introduces herself, a tall slender woman with strawberry blonde hair and green eyes. "What happen to my child...Piper?"...Tammy yells.

"Tammy, Hannah has been asking for you, she was in a tragic car accident." The doctor at first, didn't want to let Tammy in to see Hannah. "This is my child and I want to see her." Piper whispers something to the doctor and he allows her in for only a few moments. Tammy walks in and sees all types of tubes going into her body. She caresses her braids and calls out her name.

"Hannah, Hannah...Can you hear me? Hannah, I'm here, please say something."

Hannah looks up, sees Tammy and smiles. "It's going to be okay sweetie. It will be," she rubs her face tenderly. Hannah looks into her eyes, "Tammy, I'm sorry."

"I'm sorry too," Tammy said.

"Would you forgive me?" Hannah whispers.

"For what? I need to ask you to forgive me for not being there all those years." Hannah looks up at Tammy and closes her eyes. The life support machine makes a sound indicting she has died. Piper cries and clutches her handkerchief, "No! No!" Tammy catches Piper by the arm and walks out with her. "Piper it's okay, she's gone, she's gone, we can't bring her back."

Tammy places her hands up to her face. "Ah…this is unbelievable," she goes to the waiting area where Harry is and tells him Hannah just died. He rubs her shoulders with one hand. "Baby I'm so sorry," he says. Piper walks over and asks if she could talk to Tammy alone. Tammy signals to Harry that it's okay. She sits down next to Tammy. "You were right. My husband has molested her all these years. I didn't find out about it until she was eighteen.

One day I walked in on them, but they didn't know I was there. Her bedroom door was cracked. I could see and hear him"…she stops and puts her head down. "I'm so ashamed," Piper cries out. "I didn't do anything to stop it. I sent her off to college thinking if he didn't see her often maybe he would lose desire for her. But he was going to see her as often as he could. Buying her all types of things to keep her quiet." Tammy just looks at her. Piper catches Tammy's hand. "I'm really sorry." Tammy pushes Piper's hair back from over her eyes. "Your husband is a sick man and needs help. But right now I want to know what happen. How did this accident happen?"

"I'm not sure. They're saying that someone ran a red light and hit her on the driver's side of her car. Immediately she went into unconsciousness. That was around 10:00pm last night. She's been holding on since then." Tammy looks at her watch… "It's 3:30pm…now. She held on long enough to see me, that's a miracle. I loved her as a little girl, even though I wasn't the mother I should have been to her, and you loved her as a teenager. I tried so hard to make it work between us. At times it seemed like it was working. But now I know she was so hurt that she couldn't let anyone in."

"I'm sure she understands that she was loved," Piper says.

"What are you going to do about your husband?"

"You know, we have been married for twenty seven years. I was always so afraid of living alone. I never felt that I could make it on my own. But, I decided that I'm going to divorce him." Tammy hugs her. "He won't be able to do this to someone else's child."

"That's good, Piper." Harry walks back with the baby. "Who is this little guy?" Piper asked.

"Oh, he's Hannah's baby brother." Piper stands up, "May I hold him?"

"Sure," Tammy said. Harry hands Ethan over to her. She plays with his fingers and rubs his little head. "Is he a Down's baby?" she asked. "Yes, he is," Harry said. Piper hands him back to Harry.

We will be christening him this upcoming Sunday. You're welcome to come if you want to. "No Tammy. I wouldn't feel right. But thank you for the offer," Piper says. Tammy gets up. Piper tells her that she needs to take care of the technicalities of Hannah's death. As Piper walks away she looks back at her. "Tammy would it be okay if I called you sometimes?" Tammy smiles amidst her tears and nods, "That would be great Piper."

On their way home, still shocked, she couldn't believe that this was happening. "How are you right now," Harry asked. "Baby, I'm sad, but I really didn't know Hannah. Yes—she was my blood child. But I didn't know her."

That Sunday, Harry and Tammy have baby Ethan christened at his grandfathers church.

She leaves the baby with Harry and drives out to Venice beach. As she looked fixedly out into the ocean waves, she becomes still to sort through her thoughts. Very closely she listens to the mind of her soul. A bunch of thoughts rumbling together that were confusing. There were her thoughts of wanting to be a better person, her evil thoughts, and

God's thoughts. Everything that has happened in her life left her wanting to find that place in God. The real meaning of life. *Why did He create me? What purpose does he have for my life? Why had he allowed so much hurt and pain, beyond my control? Why after all this time did he allow Hannah, troubled as she was, to surface into my life?*

With her knees up to her chest, and her hands over her face, she begins crying, trying to gather enough nerve to pray, then slowly she speaks. "I stand before you naked, open and vulnerable," her heart rate increases as she begins sweating. She's having an agonizing time trying to control her emotions…she blurs out… "The one that's all seeing and all knowing"…"God," she whispers.

"The one that holds life in the palm of his hands. Please, I ask you…help me to let go of my deepest pain. So that I'm at peace with what comes my way in this life. I don't even understand my own hurts, but you do. Free me to forgive!" Hannah pops into her mind, the short moments of times when they both laughed and talked together. She begins to think about her life today opposed to what it was like a few years ago, and she was thankful for the change.

A calming effect, with slower breathing begins to happen. She thinks about how she had reached her goals through determination, much emotional pain and tears. Her experiences taught her that she could do anything she set her mind to. She stands up and walks the beach for hours. Observing and thinking about the things that God created; the sun, the ocean, the sand, and people. Her need for total forgiveness for her past, today, and for the future. Her emotions needed healing. Not swaying back and forth between being up one day and down the next. Faith is what she wanted. Faith to believe that God would help her to forgive completely, once and for all, that she could *genuinely* trust God with every part of her life.

The following Tuesday was Hannah's funeral. Several of her friends attended and gave their condolences to Piper and Tammy. Harry, Tammy's grandparents, Evelyn and her children attended. After the service, she walks over to Piper's car. Piper tells her that it was official she had moved out of hers and John's home and had bought a condo with an ocean view in Santa Monica.

"How are you holding up?" Piper asked.

"Well, I'm doing well as expected. A lot has happened recently that has caused me to re-evaluate my life. I'm quitting my day job as a prep cook and working my business only part time so that I can spend more time with Ethan. He will be going to a nearby preschool program for children, with disabilities within a year. And I would like to be there at home for him, in case he needs me."

Piper embraces her one last time. "I meant what I said at the hospital. Please, let's keep in touch," Piper said. "We will," Tammy said. The hearse leaves for the funeral procession, with Piper following behind it. Tammy gets in her car and leaves. Harry rubs her arm, "Are you okay?"

"Yeah, It's going to be okay," she rubs his hand.

"You didn't want to attend the burial? he asked.

"No Harry, I've made peace with her, and want to remember only the brief good times with Hannah. I don't want to see her lowered into the ground," she's quiet for a few moments.

"You know Harry...God enabled me to make it right with Hannah before she died. And you and I have been clean for over two years. Look at how our lives are totally different now, from three years ago. We have a beautiful son and marriage, a home to be thankful for, we're both still able to work, and we have food to eat. What more could we ask for?" she turns and faces him with tears in her eyes. "The one thing I've learned, from all of this is, the choice to forgive is always there. If you sincerely choose to embrace it, no matter how hard it may seem." He smiles at her, while rubbing her hand... "You're right baby...it is!"

About The Author

AUTHOR J. CARRINGTON is president of *www.believeinmemedia.com*, a social advocacy website. For disadvantaged women and girls that lack life skills training and women in drug abuse recovery. She is also, a film and video production student who is passionately concerned with personal growth and development. Self-knowledge and self-improvement drives her imagination.

She cares deeply about the poor and their hurts, wanting to help others make the journey. Often inspiring others to grow as individuals and to fulfill their potential in life. She is a Christian and strongly believes in marriage before intimacy. Some of her articles, include; *"Getting Your Life Back: Older Women In Sobriety, Drug Abuse Recovery: Getting Past Deep Hurts, Stand Up, Instead of Giving In—Celibacy, Choices or Consequences, Literacy—How Can You Help?, Living A Recovery Life: Fresh Start, New Skills, and Sober Living—God's Hand Upon Your Life."* Be on the lookout for her pilot television shows and other books coming soon.